'I've got a j...
dark about ...

Jake said. 'Going ...

Sherry could alm... ...
truth. Staring at him, she gathered courage. 'There is
something I need to talk to you about,' she admitted.
Her heart began pounding. 'But I'm not sure now's
the time.'

'That bad, huh?'

'Or that good,' she whispered, dry mouthed.

Jake held Sherry's gaze. Then she heard herself say in
a low voice, 'We'll talk about it at the wedding.'

'We'll get it all straight then,' Jake agreed, getting out
of the car.

Sherry nodded thoughtfully as Jake slowly closed the
door.

It seemed inevitable, somehow, that the truth about
their child would come out at a wedding. A wedding
on Valentine's Day. On their daughter's birthday.

How ironic.

But somehow it felt right.

Dear Reader,

It's February and so we couldn't resist giving you a story with a tie-in to Valentine's Day; look for Natalie Bishop's *Valentine's Child*. It's a secret baby story with a difference!

Still on the subject of babies, this month our THAT'S MY BABY! title is by relative newcomer Martha Hix. She gives us a heroine who 'inherits' her baby sister and a smooth lawyer who'll look after both of them. Then, the other child orientated novel this month is a real tearjerker; the young son of the hero has had a heart transplant and he's already been abandoned by his mother so his dad's *very* protective...too protective...?

Substitute Bride by Trisha Alexander is a classic story of twins and substitution, but is the hero marrying the right or the wrong twin? Time will tell. Laurie Paige gives us a dramatic, romantic tale of passion, love and blackmail in *The Ready-Made Family*, and finally there's a story of a woman who's always known she loves Travis McCallister, but who's always had her advances rebuffed...until now.

Enjoy them all and come back to us next month for more great books.

The Editors

Valentine's Child
NATALIE BISHOP

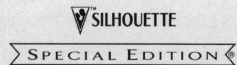

™ SILHOUETTE

SPECIAL EDITION ®

*All the characters in this book have no existence outside the imagination
of the author, and have no relation whatsoever to anyone bearing the same
name or names. They are not even distantly inspired by any individual
known or unknown to the author, and all the incidents are pure invention.*

*First published in Great Britain 1998
Silhouette Books, Eton House, 18-24 Paradise Road,
Richmond, Surrey TW9 1SR*

© Nancy Bush 1997

ISBN 0 373 24086 4

23-9802

*Printed and bound in Great Britain
by Mackays of Chatham PLC, Chatham*

NATALIE BISHOP

lives in Lake Oswego, Oregon, with her husband, Ken, and daughter, Kelly. Natalie began writing in 1981 along with her sister, Lisa Jackson, another Silhouette® author. Though they write separate books, Natalie and Lisa work out most of their plots together. They live within shouting distance of each other and between them have published over thirty Silhouette novels. When Natalie isn't writing, she enjoys spending time at her mountain cabin at Black Butte Ranch, where she catches up on her reading.

Other novels by Natalie Bishop

Silhouette Special Edition®

Saturday's Child
Lover or Deceiver
Stolen Thunder
Trial by Fire
String of Pearls
Diamond in the Sky
Silver Thaw
Just a Kiss Away
Summertime Blues
Imaginary Lover
The Princess and the Pauper
Dear Diary
Downright Dangerous
Romancing Rachel
A Love Like Romeo and Juliet
The Princess of Coldwater Flats

CANADA

Cascade Range

Puget Sound

Lake Washington

Olympic
Mountains

Seattle

WASHINGTON

IDAHO

● Oceantides

PACIFIC OCEAN

OREGON

All underlined places are fictitious.

Chapter One

Rain sheeted over the windshield, so thick it could have been honey. Oblivious to its intensity, Sherry Sterling opened her car door and was immediately met with a deluge that turned her brown hair three shades darker and relentlessly poured into her eyes. Blinking rapidly, Sherry jumped onto the rain-pounded street, one foot sinking into a low spot in the asphalt, instantly soaking her to the ankle.

"Welcome home," she muttered, shielding her eyes against the downpour.

Straight ahead the street sign for Oceantides' First City Bank glowed like a white rectangular eye. To her right, a pink neon crab and scripted letters that cried Crawfish Delish! beckoned to a café's warm interior. Sherry debated. She had a lot to do. Lots of decisions to make. Lots of people to see.

Screwing up her courage, she marched across the

street to another sign and another eating establishment, this one a tad less sharp and new but still appealing, more like a beloved but scuffed shoe. Bernie's Pizza. The hangout of her youth.

She'd sworn she would never return. Sworn she would never set foot in this dreaded place again as long as she lived. Oceantides, Washington. Population: 2,002. If there was a more hellish place on earth, Sherry couldn't think of it. This was where she'd suffered through an adolescence that had cut her so deeply that even now, years—eons—later, she still couldn't hear the town's name without feeling a burning pain that made goose bumps rise on her flesh.

Bernie's sign grew clearer as she drew near—a wash of red and white against a sky so dark and close it felt like the lid of a black cauldron descending upon her. Drawing a breath, she reminded herself that this was just her hometown, a coastal tourist trap filled with colorful locals and a few mean-spirited people about whom she had less-than-pleasant thoughts.

She slopped through puddles of rain. Red beams of light flashed onto the pavement—a scarlet blur that warned in intermittent blinks that the swinging traffic lights overhead were on the fritz. Not that anyone cared. She could have been on the moon, for all the signs of humanity moving about tonight.

Her fingers closed around the metal bar on Bernie's glass doors. Ghostly fingers walked up her spine. *Déjà vu.*

She shivered.

Inside, the warmth hit her like a hammer. The jukebox played at a decibel level she could no longer handle without pain. Sherry glanced around furtively, half expecting some old nemesis to leap up, point at her and scream out her transgressions.

Sherry Sterling. Sherry, Sherry. The easiest girl in town.

"Sherry?"

She gasped, one hand to her throat, too stunned to do more than stare at the balding man who'd spoken from behind Bernie's front counter.

"Is it you?" he asked in amazement, a smile hovering at the corners of his mouth.

Brushing back a strand of saturated hair, Sherry gazed at his face, waiting for her heart rate to return to normal. Her first impression was how old he was; her second—and this came with a jolt—was that he was one of her classmates from Oceantides High.

"Ryan?" she asked tentatively.

"It *is* you! God Almighty!" Flipping up a section of counter, he came toward her, arms outstretched. His apron was covered with flour and marinara sauce. He stopped short, right in front of her, apparently recalling, as she did, that everything had changed.

But his openness worked like a cure. Sherry stepped into his arms and hugged him hard. Her throat tightened. Ryan Delmato, Bernie's oldest son, had been one of the few people who'd stuck up for her when everyone else at Oceantides High had welcomed her demise.

"I'm covered with sauce and flour." He hugged her back, just as warmly.

"I'm dripping with rain." She gently disengaged herself and glanced ruefully at the tiny puddles germinating around her feet.

"Wow. I can't get over it! How long's it been?"

"A few years."

An understatement if there ever was one. It had been

over thirteen years since graduation and even then, Sherry hadn't been around for the ceremonies. She'd already left.

"Well, sit down, sit down." He gestured to one of the tan Naugahyde chairs: Bernie's version of serious Italian decor.

"Let me get out of my coat. It's hot enough in here to take a steam bath." Shrugging out of her overcoat, Sherry inhaled deeply, her pulse beating light and fast. She'd worked at Bernie's Pizza that memorable, disastrous year when she'd fallen in love with J.J. Beckett, captain of the football team, the most popular guy in school, all-around Mr. Wonderful.

Bastard.

"So, what are you doing here? I heard you'd moved to California. Heading for stardom."

"The rumor mill really did work overtime," Sherry murmured, surprised even though she shouldn't be. The collective minds of Oceantides High, Class of '83, weren't exactly on the brilliant end of the scale. "I went to Seattle."

"No kidding? All this time? What've you been doing there?"

"Working." Ryan waited expectantly and Sherry added, "I'm half owner of Dee's Seattle Deli."

"Wow."

"It's not all that glamorous. It's really just a job."

As soon as the words were out she regretted them. She'd spent so much time belittling herself, it had never occurred to her that in some people's eyes her ownership might seem the pinnacle of success.

"Sounds pretty great to me," Ryan declared without an ounce of envy. "I'm still here at the pizza place, making a nuisance of myself."

"How's your dad?"

"Oh, Bern's the same. Just a little grayer, y'know?" Ryan grinned and Sherry saw the boy she'd gone to school with. "He still asks about you. 'That Sterling girl. She sure was a looker.' You'll have to stop in and say hello before you leave." He paused. "How long ya here for?"

"Just passing through." Sherry swallowed and smiled, certain that if she showed any other emotion, she would break down and make a fool of herself.

"Wouldn't it be great to see some of the old gang again? I mean, jeez, it's been so long!"

"Yeah, great."

Ryan was oblivious to her sarcasm. And why not? He'd always been jovial and extroverted and completely innocent. He'd been incensed by the cruel things they'd said about her, a champion to the end, even when she'd wanted him to just shut up and let the whole thing die.

But she'd appreciated his championing nonetheless.

Well, that was what she was here for now, right? To put all this nonsense to bed. To face and forget about the mistakes she'd made, and then to try to forgive the people who'd hurt her when she'd been a miserable, mixed-up kid.

"So, are ya married?" Ryan asked, glancing down at her hands.

"Not at the moment." *Not ever.*

"Well, you remember Kathy Pruitt? I made her my lovely bride right after graduation."

"I remember Kathy."

A little on the plump side. A lot on the insecure side. A follower.

"We got two kids. Ryan, Jr.'s ten and Cecilia's nine."

"Congratulations."

"Ya want some pizza?"

He bustled back behind the counter where a girl in her teens was kneading pizza dough. She stared at Sherry through liquid, dark brown eyes with that incredibly dull, suspicious stare that lived in the gaze of too many American teens.

"Pepperoni's on special. I can make you an individual."

"That'd be great."

Sherry laid her coat over the back of a chair and perched at a nearby table, watching as Ryan and the girl worked on her order. The phone wasn't ringing; no one wanted to go out in the rain. Little wonder. Water still beaded and ran off her coat onto the floor.

"It's a monsoon out there," she said loudly.

"Huh?" Ryan glanced toward the now-steamy glass front doors. A gust of wind half blew them inward. "Oh, yeah! What a disaster. You sure picked a good time to come."

"My timing never was great."

"Huh?" He cocked an ear her way.

"Never mind."

Sherry settled back and sighed, ruefully aware that her heart still beat light and fast. Why did it matter so much? Why?

She knew why. That was the trouble. She'd known why nearly fourteen years ago when she'd decided to keep her pregnancy a secret.

A group of kids ran into the pizza parlor, screaming with laughter and shaking water from their hair. The girls hung on the boys and the boys pushed each other around, teasing and testing and generally showing off.

It could have been Sherry's senior year. It could have

been her and Roxanne and Summer and Ryan and Matt and J.J. One of the boys flipped a quarter from his pocket, caught it and headed for the jukebox.

Sherry held her breath. Gooseflesh rose on her skin. Memories danced inside her head.

He placed the quarter in the slot, leaned over the names of the songs, punched a few buttons. The words to ''Sherry Baby'' crowded her mind—an oldie that J.J. insisted on playing for her. She steeled herself, taut as a bowstring. Heavy-metal music suddenly screeched and blared through the room and Sherry relaxed.

Ryan brought her pizza. Sherry chewed several bites and gave him the thumbs-up. He grinned, delighted. She felt like a fraud, for it was all she could do to swallow— although it wasn't the fault of the food.

She stayed as long as she could before her conscience got the better of her. Finally, she paid and thanked Ryan, then waded through the rain-shrouded street back to her car. The white compact car started without a cough and Sherry eased toward North Beach Road— where the wealthy people lived.

The Becketts owned the house at the end of the lane, a Victorian seaside home with a wrought-iron-railed widow's walk and elaborate gingerbread surrounding every pillar and window. As a child, Sherry had dreamed of living in a house just like theirs. It was beautiful. A fairy tale. So perfect, it belonged in Candyland or a Disney movie.

And it was huge. Gargantuan! With ivy climbing around a wind-battered oak whose upper branches sported a tree house, a miniature copy of the mansion itself.

The Beckett kids had wanted for nothing. Sherry could remember sticking her face between the wrought-iron spikes of the surrounding fence, peeking at their wonderland, wishing with all her might that she'd been "to the manor born" instead of the skinny-legged daughter of one of Oceantides' poorest and most pathetically dysfunctional families.

Her father had beaten her and her mother. Not often. Only when he drank, which was on rare occasions. But it had created a pall over their home, a cloud of fear that Sherry could never completely forget. His horrified remorse afterward only made the whole thing a hundred times worse. It made her believe there would be an end. It made her believe that he would finally pull his life together and they could live as a whole, happy family. Maybe not as rich in wealth as the Becketts, but equally rich in love and happiness.

By the time Sherry understood that nothing would change, Sherry's mother had died. Not physically. She was still there, sitting in the living room or moving with the beaten weariness of the hopeless through the kitchen, where every moment was an eternity, every movement an expenditure of energy she couldn't afford, every teardrop an evaporation of her soul until there were no more teardrops left.

Sherry was virtually on her own at fourteen. No one regulated her. No one could afford the emotional commitment.

So…she searched for love elsewhere.

Her friends were her lifeline—at least, until she turned seventeen and her skinny legs lengthened and curved and her breasts developed and her cute, freckled face smoothed out and changed. Suddenly her eyes were violet, her lashes thick and sooty, her lips full and smiling with promise.

So long, friends. Hello, boyfriends.

The shame of it was that Sherry had welcomed the change. Reveled in it! Who wanted to be the plain girl? Not Sherry Sterling. No way! She wanted to be the siren, the girl everyone wanted to be, the most popular girl in school.

And she was bound and determined to win that trophy, no matter what it cost.

What a vain, silly, self-destructive goal. But for the girl who had nothing, it was a chance to have almost everything.

And everything included J.J. Beckett.

Sherry pulled into the Beckett drive and up to the gates. Her hands clenched around the steering wheel, headlights feebly arrowing through the pounding rain. The windshield fogged, and she switched on the defrost, glad the rush of air covered the surflike pounding in her ears.

She had to climb out to push the button of the intercom. Cold raindrops trickled down the back of her neck. Her shoes were soaked, ruined, and she stared down at them dismally, wishing she didn't have to go through with this.

But she did.

Punching the black button, she called, "Hello?" into the speaker.

Background fuzz. No answer.

She waited, then called again.

"Who's there?" a female voice demanded, so sharp and clear that Sherry gasped in shocked recognition.

His mother's voice. The Dragon Lady. As cold as ocean waves and just as treacherous.

Sherry had run afoul of her without even trying.

Swallowing, she announced, "Hello, Mrs. Beckett. It's Sherry Sterling."

She'd said it and her voice sounded strong and clear. *Thank you, God.*

"Who?"

Dragon Lady knew damn well who it was. For the first time since she'd decided to make this pilgrimage, Sherry smiled. Nervous as she was, she was no longer the frightened little girl Patrice Beckett had scorned with such fury. "Sherry Sterling," she said distinctly.

There was no answer.

"I'd like to talk to J.J. I need to get his address or phone number."

"J.J.'s not here."

Did I say he was? Sherry controlled her temper with an effort. But it was good to be mad. Great, in fact. She'd cowered as a teenager but she was a teenager no longer. She was a woman who, for better or worse, had made some tough choices over the years and had lived with them. They hadn't all been the best choices. Many times they'd been the only choices. But she'd made them all on her own.

"Would you be kind enough to give me his address? I'd really appreciate it."

"Excuse me."

Sherry waited and as the time spun out she realized she'd been cut off for good. Cut off as permanently as she had been nearly fourteen years ago.

Pressing the button, she said distinctly, "I won't go away. I'm staying in Oceantides until I finish what I came for. I'm going to come every day and press this button until you either help me, or give me a good reason why you won't. You can call the police. In fact, I'm sure you will. But it will only hurt you in the end because you know J.J.'s going to want to hear what I have to say."

Back in the car, Sherry inhaled several angry breaths before she started the engine. In a spurt of indignation she backed out of the driveway, spraying wet-black gravel in all directions. Her right rear tire slipped off the road into a muddy bog. Yanking the wheel, Sherry punched the accelerator but the car only succeeded in spinning in a circle until she was sideways in the road.

"Damn..."

Sherry tried to baby the car forward but the right rear tire spun deeper into the mud.

"Wouldn't you know," she muttered, sure this was some kind of punishment for arguing with the ruler of Beckett Manor.

Suddenly headlights flickered eerily. A car was coming—and coming fast! Panicked, Sherry tried to twist the steering wheel. If this car didn't slow down, it would plow right into her driver's side as soon as it made the last turn! Stomping on her accelerator again, Sherry prayed for help. Her back tires whined and spun.

"Oh, God!"

The approaching vehicle whipped around the corner. Its headlights bore down on her like huge, glaring eyes. Sherry jerked back in the seat, as if that would save her from impact. A black Jeep. Racing toward her. Huge tires spewing water. Crying out, Sherry covered her face with her arms.

The driver slammed on the brakes. The Jeep shimmied and slid sideways, hydroplaning toward her car in a slow-motion nightmare. Sherry braced herself. Inches from her car, the Jeep suddenly shuddered to a stop, as if the driver had suddenly found a magic brake.

Sherry let out her breath. She fumbled for the door handle. Hallelujah! No impact. No injuries. But her pulse was galloping at breakneck speed again.

The driver leaped out of his Jeep at the same moment she scrambled out of her compact. "You okay?" she asked.

He strode toward her, hard, fast, his shoulders thrust forward.

"Oh, God." She would know that walk anywhere. *J.J.!*

"What the hell are you doing?" he demanded furiously. "Meditating? You want a view of the beach, go somewhere else. This is private property."

"No kidding."

"I nearly smashed into you! You're damn lucky I've got new tires or we'd both be examining the wreckage!"

He looked the same. Incredibly the same. From the thick black strands of hair now slapped lank with water against his forehead, to the dense, spiky lashes now starred with rain, to the rock-hard jaw, wide, muscular shoulders, lean hips, and long legs.

J.J. Beckett. All-around athlete. Her knight in shining armor.

Except he'd used her and thrown her away.

And suddenly Sherry couldn't tell him. The words wouldn't even form in her brain, let alone reach her lips. This angry man glaring down at her as if he wanted to rip her limb from limb, much the way he'd glared at her years before, didn't deserve the truth.

"I'm sorry," Sherry murmured, turning away. "I made a mistake."

That threw him. He was ready for battle and she'd capitulated without an angry word. Running a hand through his hair, he only succeeded in pushing the rain-slicked locks away for a second before they flopped forward once more. He peered at her through narrowed eyes, his mouth tight with fury.

"Wait," he muttered as Sherry climbed into her car and slammed her door closed.

Rain blurred the windshield. Sherry trembled again. A shadow loomed outside and suddenly J.J. was right beside her, peering in the window. Panic overtook her. She fought it; she had no reason to fear him now. But she couldn't help herself.

The beams of his headlights were aimed through her windshield, glancing off her eyes, blinding her. She shaded her face, happy to hide from J.J.'s probing gaze.

"Hey." He rapped on her window.

She toyed with the idea of simply tearing away, spinning through the mud and hopefully avoiding both him and his Jeep in her bid for escape. But running hadn't been the answer in the past; it wasn't the answer now.

Cracking the window a sliver, she kept her face averted. Courage apparently wasn't her strong suit, she thought ruefully, avoiding looking at him straight on.

"Are you lost? There isn't anything else down this road except this property." He gestured toward the house.

"The Becketts'."

"You know the family?" he asked, surprised. Now he was really staring at her.

"I've heard of them." Sherry twisted the ignition but one of his hands, wet and strong, clamped over her window.

"Wait a minute."

"I'm in a hurry," she retorted, pressing her toe to the accelerator.

His breath swept in, almost in a gasp. "My God," he whispered in amazement. "Sherry!"

She cringed. "Hard to believe, isn't it?" she muttered. Thankfully the compact crept forward, the tires gripping easily now that she wasn't stomping on the gas. Still, she had to work to avoid his bumper. But J.J. hung right on, walking alongside, gazing at her until, unable to stop herself, Sherry stared at him full-face.

His eyes were gray, clear as a star-studded night, full of undisguised shock. "What are you doing here?" he demanded.

"Haunting the neighborhood."

It just slipped out. After years of habit. Sarcasm, her favorite protective device.

And it was as if she'd suddenly awakened him from a hypnotic trance, for his face changed as he, too, remembered their last, acrimonious parting.

"You came to see me." His voice was hard. "Why?"

"I came to see a lot of people. Don't let it go to your head."

"You haven't changed."

"Fortunately, that's not true. Let go of the window, J.J."

"No one's called me J.J. since high school."

"Really? What do they call you? Or should I even ask?"

He didn't miss the jab, and she remembered with a tiny dart of pain, that he'd always been quick—one of the few intelligent jocks Oceantides had ever turned out. His mouth quirked, almost with amusement, and she suddenly remembered the taste of his lips and the whiteness of his teeth.

Her heart jolted painfully. Why? Why did she remember these things?

"Jake," he said quietly.

"Well, Jake, I gotta go. It's been…interesting."

"How long are you going to be in town?"

"As short a time as possible."

He stared at her, long and hard. Sherry's breath caught. She was mesmerized. As mesmerized as she'd been that first time he'd stared at her when she was scarcely sixteen, when he'd singled her out from the rest of the giddy sophomore girls.

"Maybe that's a good thing," he told her in a tight voice.

And then he slipped away from the window and strode through the rain to his waiting Jeep.

Chapter Two

The motel room was drab and smelled of mildew, but it was relatively clean, possessed an ocean view, and several of the units looked to be under renovation. Sherry flung her rain-drenched coat over the back of a desk chair, ran her fingers through her damp mane, then flipped out the lights and stood in front of the sliding glass door, staring at the dark, moving waves as they spread across the shore. There was a beach of sorts below the cliff, tucked tightly between angry bluffs of black rocks. A rickety wooden staircase hugged the headland for anyone who dared to climb down to that spit of wet sand. On a night like tonight it would be tantamount to suicide. Sherry stood where she was and longed for a glass of hot spiced wine.

J.J. Beckett. Excuse me—*Jake*—Beckett. Her inner eye remembered his glistening, wet hair, tense jawline, broad shoulders and jeans-wrapped hips. She shook her head in disbelief. Why was she so focused on his body parts? Why? *After all this time!*

Groaning, she exhaled heavily, an ironic smile playing on her lips. She hadn't even noticed his physical attributes that much in high school. Even when they'd been stripped naked and making love in the Beckett tree house, Sherry couldn't remember thinking of him as so incredibly male. She'd been in love, and as such, she'd wanted to make love. A part of her had even done it for him, because she had wanted to please him and lovemaking had seemed such a natural end to her feelings of adoration, need and happiness.

Lust? No, she hadn't felt it then. She hadn't known what it was. Still didn't, actually, although her mind seemed stuck in a pretty carnal track right now! How could it be that after all this time what struck her the hardest were all those male parts working seductively together?

J.J. Beckett. She'd had her chance to tell him tonight. Her shining moment. But in the heat of emotion she'd simply run. Run away. Just like she did before.

What had he said? *You haven't changed.* Well, that was a big lie. She'd changed mightily, and for the better. Gone was the Sherry Sterling of yesteryear. Gone was the painful yearning for things out of her reach, the anxious hours of waiting—waiting for that special something to happen to her.

Closing her eyes, Sherry tipped her head to one side and remembered....

Sophomore year. The lunchroom was a shrieking, humming machine of humanity where shouting was the only form of communication. Sherry sat on a plastic chair, munching an apple, wishing her breasts would grow. Sixteen and still gawky, she eyed her friends with faintly veiled envy, noticing their rounded curves and coquettish giggles, and wanting for all the world to be one of the popular, cute girls instead of a slightly serious, boyishly-slim wannabe whom no one looked at or cared about.

Popularity was everything. With it, you were *somebody*. Without it, you were less than nothing. A negative number. Below zero.

With a swift sigh, she eyed her friends across the lunch table. Jennifer had breasts, so some of the guys checked her out and said hello. Unfortunately she was too shy to do anything about it. Her eyes would bug out and she would stammer and generally make herself look like an idiot. Julie was just the opposite. Loud and almost obnoxious, her laugh was like a donkey braying, and although she was loyal and guileless, she drove Sherry crazy.

But Jennifer and Julie had been her friends for years, all through elementary school and junior high. Good friends. Friends you could count on.

Sherry bit fiercely into her apple. The trouble was *she* wasn't so good a friend. All she wanted was to be part of the cool crowd. Jennifer and Julie's conversation ebbed and rose like a tide, the subjects inconsequential. None of it interested Sherry anymore. Now that she was a sophomore their chatter seemed inane and boring. She wanted something more! Something *better!*

As soon as the thought crossed her mind Sherry squelched it, hating herself a little. What was wrong with her? Why was she so mean?

"Hurry up," Jennifer mumbled around the last bites of a maple bar. "I've got to get to my locker before *he* shows up."

Sherry groaned inwardly. "He" was J.J. Beckett, the cutest—and richest—guy in the sophomore class. But he knew it. Boy, did he know it. Sherry had seen the way he strutted down the hall, girls trailing after him like a bride's train. It was enough to make an intelligent female puke.

To that end, she made retching noises. Jennifer's eyes narrowed. She knew Sherry's feelings about J.J. and did not approve.

But why shouldn't Sherry feel this way? From the first day of kindergarten, J.J. Beckett had been Mr. Perfect, too cool to notice the shy girl in the third row who hid the bruises on her arm from the teacher by wearing long sleeves, even on hot days. Day after day, from the classroom window, Sherry watched J.J.'s perfect mother pick him up from school and drive away in the Becketts' sleek black BMW toward that house on the hill that everybody else talked about; that beautiful, fairy-tale house above the cove.

She knew the house; knew exactly which one it was because it was her dream house. She could imagine the parties and tea cakes and velvet that waited within those magic walls. But shy Sherry Sterling, whose clothes were a size too small and frayed along the cuffs and hems, wasn't one of the chosen twenty-seven asked to J.J.'s kindergarten birthday party. Only the best and brightest had received the gilt-edged invitations. Snotty Caroline Newsmith brought hers to school and flipped it in front of Sherry's nose.

"You aren't going, are you?" Caroline had taunted. Five years old and already well versed in the art of snobbery, Caroline was a have while Sherry was clearly a have-not.

Sherry hadn't answered. She'd just looked down at her colored drawing of a sunny beach with a blue sky.

"He's got his own beach, J.J. does. They've got a boat, too." Caroline had leaned over Sherry's shoulder, staring wide-eyed at the picture. "And a tree house. Our parents are friends. I'm going to marry him someday."

Sherry's continued silence had caused Caroline to lose interest and she moved on to another loser who hadn't made the J.J. Beckett friends-of-choice club. Surreptitiously, Sherry crumpled her drawing in one fist and shoved it into the pocket of her sweater.

From the window she had watched the Becketts' BMW arrive to pick up J.J. that day, only this time nearly the entire class had tripped gaily toward the car, swarming it. J.J.'s mother stepped out and arranged the kids in rows on the sidewalk. Other mothers—the chosen drivers—came in their own cars, and after the kids piled inside, the vehicles serpentined away from the school, following the gleaming black leader, all on their way to paradise.

Sherry had gone home on the bus, only to walk in on her father swaying drunkenly in the living room, and her mother, half cowering, her cheek covered protectively with one palm.

There had been other Beckett parties over the years. Sherry Sterling was never invited. Neither were Jennifer and Julie, social nobodies as unimportant as she was. The three friends found each other and bonded—a case of need and desperation none ever openly admitted to but all felt.

And now, it was such a visceral betrayal that Jennifer had a crush on J.J. Beckett!

"How do you know he's going to show up?" Julie demanded.

Jennifer lifted a dismissive shoulder. "He walks by my locker on his way to biology every day."

Julie snorted. "Like he'd even notice you."

"He says hi to me!" Jennifer stuck out her chin and her breasts lifted to attention, too. Sherry suddenly wondered if she stuffed her bra.

"Down, girl," Sherry muttered. Julie stifled a giggle and Jennifer glared at her, wounded to the core.

"What's the matter with you?" Jennifer looked about to cry. "You always say something mean about J.J."

"So, what should I say that's good?" Sherry demanded.

"He's a great athlete," Jennifer retorted. "He's on the varsity football team."

"Big yawn..." Sherry patted her hand over her mouth in boredom.

"He's really cute." Jennifer was undeterred. In fact, she was on a roll. "He's got these thick eyelashes and, like, almost a dimple in his cheek. You can see it sometimes when he smiles."

"He hardly ever smiles," Sherry countered.

This appeared to be just another plus. "He's serious. If he doesn't get a football scholarship, he'll get an academic one. He's really smart."

"And he's got the coolest muscles," Julie chimed in.

Sherry narrowed her eyes at her. The Benedict Arnold. She was supposed to agree with *her*.

"J.J. Beckett's a stuck-up jerk," Sherry declared.

"He's nice to me," Jennifer answered defensively.

"Fine. He's nice to you." Sherry scooped up her book bag and headed for the halls. She had to get away from them. From their silly desires and stupid fantasies.

"I can't wait to get out of Oceantides," she murmured aloud, a litany she recited at least twice daily.

Twisting the combination on her locker, Sherry glanced over her shoulder and groaned. J.J. Beckett, the object of her wrath himself, was heading her way. He wore a blue-and-gold letterman's jacket—varsity football his freshman and sophomore year, thank you very much—and was surrounded by adoring girls from all grades.

"Hey, J.J.," one of them suddenly sang out. "What are you doing after the game tonight?"

"Sleeping," he answered in that studied voice Sherry found particularly annoying. Didn't the guy possess one ounce of spontaneity? Everything was so careful, so orchestrated.

"With anyone I know?" the girl responded on a laugh. "Or is there a vacancy I can fill?"

Wild, braying laughter accompanied this come-on. The whole entourage whooped and snickered like a pack of witless hyenas.

"Brother," Sherry muttered under her breath.

J.J. and friends stopped directly opposite her, as if she were their one-and-only audience member and the show was meant for her alone.

"I feel like I could sleep for a year," he answered, ignoring the girls' sexual banter. "Me and my dad are going to Pullman tomorrow to see a Cougars game."

"My dad and I," Sherry corrected softly.

Her voice seemed to suddenly clang like chiming bells. Either that, or it was a trick of fate, but whatever the cause, her words fell into an unexpected lull and hung there, a red flag of challenge to Oceantides' favorite son.

"What's *your* problem?" one of the groupies demanded.

"The brainiac speaks," another sniffed.

"What a bitch," still another said on a half laugh of derision.

A pair of blue jeans over slim thighs topped by a tan-leather and blue-and-gold-wool jacket moved into her line of vision. J.J. Beckett, his jacket unzipped to reveal a black shirt, stood directly in front of her. His chest rose and fell several times, ten inches from her nose.

God. Her heart somersaulted painfully.

"My dad and I are going to Pullman tomorrow to the Cougars game," he corrected himself. His low-timbred voice raised a rash of goose bumps along her arms.

Sherry found she couldn't look up and meet his eyes. Her pulse raced along, light and fast, a traitor, too. Ignoring him, she pulled several unneeded books from her locker. But he just stood there, eyeing her hard, his breath deep and even, a faint scent of leather and musk reaching her nostrils. Sherry's nerves screamed for release. Glancing up, she saw those clear gray eyes she hadn't forgotten since her terrible elementary-school days, although she hadn't looked at him this closely in years.

"Why do you try so hard to put me down?" he asked.

"What?" Sherry stared.

"It's always that way with you. A sneak attack, something slipped in sideways."

She was stunned. "Me?"

"I can't walk by you without a remark."

She was incensed. Of course it wasn't true! J.J. Beckett didn't even know she existed!

"I don't know what you're talking about," she sputtered, slamming her locker. The entourage had moved back, waiting for him, the girls regarding her smugly as if they knew she was about to get slam-dunked by their hero.

"You're just mad at me all the time. Like I've done something to you. Did I? Something I don't remember?"

"I don't care what you do!" Panicked, Sherry fumbled with her book bag. The stitching on one handle was dangerously close to ripping out altogether. She plucked at the thread, intending to tighten it, but it came undone as if by unseen hands, and the bag fell to the floor.

J.J. automatically reached forward to help, bending down at the same moment she did, his arm brushing hers. At the contact, Sherry jerked compulsively, nearly overbalancing, and just as automatically his hand grabbed for her arm, holding her steady.

The heat of his fingers nearly overpowered Sherry. That and the recognition of his innate strength. Frozen, she could do nothing but balance precariously on the balls of her feet. He held her steady, his face registering only normal concern.

"Whoa, there. Sorry I bumped you."

"It's okay."

"Looks like that bag's destroyed." He smiled.

White teeth and sexy lips. The guy didn't smile very often but when he did, it was a stellar show! Sherry suddenly snapped back to reality, hating him for being so perfect. "Well, it was on its last legs," she muttered, pulling her arm free and snatching the bag by its other handle. She and J.J. rose in unison, each awkwardly trying to figure out how to get out of this strange little moment gracefully.

"I'll try to speak better, okay?" he told her as a goodbye, heading toward his hovering group of admirers without another look back. Sherry hugged her lumpy book bag in her arms and turned down the opposite hallway, glad that Jennifer and Julie hadn't been around to witness her downfall.

Throughout geometry class she revisited their conversation, her spirits sinking lower and lower as she realized how awful she'd been. Not just to him, but socially. Good Lord, what an idiot! She'd only succeeded in proving *she* was the loser, destined for nothingness.

Sherry finished sophomore year with a vague feeling of things left undone, and over the summer she distanced herself from Julie and Jennifer until neither girl called her anymore. By the time school started in the fall she was virtually friendless, but tensions ran so high at home—her parents lived a silent war of wills—that Sherry only felt relief.

Junior year, a miracle happened. Almost overnight, she metamorphosed from a skinny, unremarkable ugly duckling to the proverbial beautiful swan. Her legs lengthened and took on definition, her tiny freckles smoothed out, her skin growing so sleek and fine it was hard to believe she possessed pores. Her breasts grew to an acceptable size. Not nearly as huge as Jennifer's, but rounded and lush enough to provoke more than a few looks of male admiration. Her lips seemed to thicken into sensual, pink crescents, and her eyes gleamed like amethysts with only the faintest application of makeup. Lastly, her brown hair deepened into a rich mahogany. Shoulder-length, it swung like a shiny curtain, thick and soft and inviting.

From the Girl Most Easily Forgotten, Sherry became Oceantides High's newest sensation.

There was only one problem. Although she could see

the physical changes, and could feel the heightened awareness of her from her classmates—especially the males—within herself, where it mattered most, she was still Sherry Sterling, the girl not good enough to be asked to J.J. Beckett's birthday parties, the girl whose razor-sharp tongue was her only defense.

Then two things happened within a week of each other. The first was a golden opportunity. Early into her junior year, on the verge of her seventeenth birthday, while she sorted through her uneasy emotions, Ryan Delmato told her his dad was looking for someone to work at Bernie's Pizza Parlor, the family business.

"My dad wants somebody who'll be there every day," Ryan explained, his dark gaze serious, although Sherry watched it skate quickly over her face, down to her breasts, and back again. The old Sherry would have been embarrassed, but the new Sherry was faintly amused.

"Well, I don't have any extracurricular activities," Sherry told him. "And I'd really like a job."

"That's what somebody said." Ryan nodded enthusiastically. "Head down to Bernie's after school. Tell my dad you talked to me. He'll hire you. If it's what you want."

"Thank you," Sherry said, meaning it. Bernie's was a cool place to work. Everyone wanted a job there, but Bernie only hired a few teenagers each year—select ones who filled his own special requirements of poise, friendliness and efficiency. His system worked, for he invariably hired the best employees and therefore ran a successful establishment.

"No problem." Ryan grinned and the tips of his ears turned red. Sherry smiled back. Ryan Delmato was one of J.J. Beckett's closest friends and definitely a member of the popular crowd. He didn't live in a house "on the water" like the Becketts and Newsmiths, but he was one of those guys everyone liked and so the snobs accepted him.

Ryan hadn't really had a girlfriend yet; he'd palled around mostly with J.J. and his other football buddies' leftovers, but no one had reported any major kissing between him and any girl. He seemed to prefer the role of J.J.'s sidekick, and he was J.J.'s greatest promoter and marketing agent.

"Did'ja see that pass? Right into his hands. Into his hands! Beckett smokes 'em again!" Ryan had yelled at the last football game. He stood in front of the crowd, arms lifted as if he were about to join the cheerleaders in a "Hail to J.J. Beckett! Reigning King of Oceantides High!" and induced the crowd to scream J.J.'s name over and over again until they were hoarse.

Sherry had felt plain sick.

But that was last week, and now Ryan grinned at her in excitement and Sherry wondered what would happen if she made Ryan Delmato her boyfriend....

"Thanks, Ryan," she said, blinding him with her smile.

"You bet." Slightly dazed, he wandered away, glancing back at her once. Sherry waved, thrilled with a power she heretofore had not known she possessed.

Ryan's father, Bernie Delmato, was a pussycat. He shook her hand, then embraced her as part of the Bernie's Pizza team, flourishing an apron emblazoned with Bernie's in red and green letters before placing it in her hands. His joy and exuberance caught at Sherry's heart. This was a father to love. She suddenly envied Ryan so thoroughly she wanted to cry.

"What is it, sweetie?" Bernie asked, concern pushing aside his laughter for the moment. "Something wrong?"

"No..." Sherry clutched the apron tightly between clenched hands. "Thank you. Thank you very much."

She started work the next afternoon. At first she worked the till, marveling at Bernie's expert toss of the dough so that it spun into a round circle, the perfect size for the pan. He winked at her, showed another teen-ager, Wendy, how it was done, watched her rip fifteen holes in the dough as it landed on her untrained hands, then slapped his thighs and howled with laughter. He was like Santa Claus all year long.

Sherry ached to love him as a father should be loved, and their relationship throughout her last two years of high school was as close to that kind of father-daughter feeling as she had ever had. When she found out she was in trouble she'd thought of going to Bernie; he would have helped her. But events took place that su-perseded her chance for Bernie's surrogate-parent sup-port, and she'd walked away from him just as she'd walked away from the rest of her life in Oceantides.

The other more important event that took place that fateful week was an encounter with J.J. that changed everything between them, even though nearly another year would pass before she actually admitted that she loved him.

She ran into J.J. Beckett after a football game and saved his life.

She herself had not gone to the game; she hated watching J.J. lead his team to victory and then embrace the accolade and adoration from his band of groupies. She'd stayed home, listened to music, half written a paper on teen nutrition and then, because she'd heard her father stumble in drunk, had sneaked out the back door and taken a long walk toward the beach.

Mariner Lane was a small street at the edge of town that ran perpendicular to the beach and was flanked on each side by summertime businesses like bike-rental places, kite shops, and ice-cream huts, and ended in a wide cul-de-sac parking lot. Mariner Lane was also not too far from North Beach Road—the rich people's haven. It was there Sherry ended up walking, heading toward the concrete stairs that led down to the beach. At this time of year the whole area was closed up and lonely, perfect for her mood. She just wanted to be alone.

But a blue BMW was parked against a piece of driftwood that doubled as a bumper barrier. J.J.'s car. Sherry recognized it instantly and huddled into her coat. It was chilly. Downright cold. Half expecting to find him making out with some girl in the BMW's back seat, she hid in the shadows of the shuttered-up snow-cone hut.

And then she saw a dark figure staggering up the beach toward her. Sherry gazed in amazement. The figure had come straight from the water. A skin diver? Good Lord. No one in their right mind would go swimming in water cold enough to kill them!

She gasped as he came into view. J.J.! She almost stepped forward to help him up the stairs to the parking spot but her own reserved nature made her hesitate.

He was shaking from head to toe—hypothermia. His pants and shirt were sodden with icy water. His keys rattled between blue fingers. He couldn't get them in the lock. He leaned against the car, spent and frozen. She knew he would collapse.

She stepped forward and went to him, standing several feet away. She said something, something cool and aloof and undoubtedly sarcastic. She couldn't remember exactly what, now.

And then she'd taken the keys from his hand, helped him into the car, driven him to his home, stripped off his clothes and led him into the shower.

Oh, God!

That was it. The beginning of the end. Even now, the memory was so sharp it cut and, with an effort, Sherry thrust it away. Shivering, she took a step back from the window. Her fingers dug into her cheeks. She'd helped him and he'd thanked her for saving his life.

But that wasn't all. Oh, no, there had been so much more....

Snatching up her small suitcase, Sherry snapped open the locks and began unfolding her clothes. She couldn't think about the past anymore tonight. Recalling every word and gesture was exquisite torture, and although she was here to resolve the hurt, there were still areas she refused to touch. She couldn't. It was just too painful.

Tomorrow, she thought shakily. I'll face the rest of it tomorrow.

Chapter Three

"Is that you, J.J.?" Patrice Beckett called from her sitting room, her voice dry from years of bitterness. It rubbed against Jake's flesh like sandpaper, a near-physical sensation.

He stood just inside the front door, in the circular entryway beneath the crystal teardrop chandelier. Before him was the sweeping staircase his mother had sued a wood craftsman over, demanding each post be relathed, each step be shortened, each board be reset until the man had quit the job and his occupation and retired to a small fishing town on Puget Sound, beaten and old.

The wood—a polished, glossy, deep reddish-brown mahogany that looked as rich as caramelized frosting—shone softly in the spreading light. Everything smelled sweet, like cinnamon and apple, and Jake's gaze flicked to the crystal bowl of potpourri on the hall sideboard.

Everything smelled sweet for the Becketts and looked even sweeter. Patrice made certain of it.

"J.J....?"

He almost corrected her. He corrected everyone else these days who made the mistake. But telling Patrice Beckett to call him Jake instead of J.J. was an exercise in futility, so he bit back the automatic retort and strode down the hallway to the room at the end from which a yellow light melted outward.

He found her just where he'd expected her to be: stiff-backed in a leather recliner, half-moon pewter glasses perched at the end of her aristocratic nose, a *New York Times* crossword in her lap. She was a widow, and it seemed she had been for nearly as long as Jake could remember, although truthfully his father had lived until Jake was in college. Rex Beckett just hadn't been around, that was all. Inherited wealth had made him self-indulgent and family life wasn't for him.

Rex's father, Elijah Beckett, had made a pile of cash buying up beachfront property in the forties and fifties, selling it off little by little, then buying it back at bargain prices because most of the subsequent purchasers found themselves in dire need of ready cash sooner or later. Young Rex never lifted a finger to help out, as near as Jake could tell. Jake didn't know exactly how his father had spent his youth, but it hadn't been as a model for the Protestant work ethic. And that attitude had spilled into adulthood because as a husband and father, Rex had spent his days depositing money in the bank, making love to young women with long legs, then kissing Patrice's expensive cheek with dry lips before retiring to his own bedroom.

Rex's self-indulgent life-style had produced a few minor scandals. It was rumored that Rex had fathered more than one out-of-wedlock child. Jake used to lie awake and wonder about his other brothers and sisters. Apart from Heather, his elder sister by twelve years, those other siblings were never admitted to, or acknowledged. It bothered Jake deeply, but neither Patrice nor Rex would speak on the subject.

As for Heather, Rex paid as little attention to her as he did Jake. Heather was not Patrice's child and although Patrice had agreed that Heather be raised under the Beckett roof, pseudomother and daughter never quite got along. Heather was a by-product of one of Rex's amorous liaisons before Patrice had actually gotten him to the altar. Heather's biological mother had dropped the child on Rex's doorstep and run away, and although Patrice did her duty by Heather, the child was a bastard and therefore something to be "dealt with."

Still, the acknowledged Beckett children wanted for nothing. Heather was given the same lavish childhood—if not the affection—that Patrice heaped on Jake. However, when Heather married young and moved to Alaska to live a simple life, Patrice was infinitely happier. Unfortunately, with little else to do, Patrice then turned her intense attention on *her* only child, and although Jake struggled for his independence, it was a losing battle. His mother scrutinized everything he did, every move he made, every award he won. He could not recall a time when she hadn't tried to monopolize his life and his attention. Jake learned to outfox her at a very early age, but she won the most important battle.

During his sophomore year of college, dreaming of occupations that would take him far from Oceantides, Jake was summoned home one rainy weekend right before his father's death to learn a strange truth: Rex's will left everything to Heather. Neither he nor his mother would get a dime. Jake should have been indignant, but he was more hurt than anything else. Although he and his father hadn't been close, there were a few shared memories, and they were bonded by their love of football.

It was at the reading of the will that Jake learned the real truth, however. If Jake would stay and run the family business, Heather would get a sizable chunk of fortune but the bulk of the estate would go to Jake and Patrice. If Jake refused, both he and his mother would receive nothing.

He knew, then, what had happened. Patrice had set this up. She'd convinced Rex that Jake would never accept his duty as head of the family interests unless he was coerced—blackmailed—into it! If Jake didn't take over, his own mother would be penniless.

A terrible gamble. An incredible risk. Jake could remember staring at Patrice in cold disbelief.

He'd refused, of course. Ranted and raved and fled back to school. But then Heather had called him. What Patrice had done was sick, rotten and totally unnecessary, she explained, but she, Heather, really didn't want the problems of the Beckett business, either. Couldn't Jake forgive his mother and realize just how lonely and desperate she was? Sure, her methods were diabolical, but the truth was: Jake *should* run the business. It was his heritage, his duty. "She's as screwy as she can be," Heather stated flatly, "but she only wants what's best for you."

What's best for you…

Jake was sick to the back teeth of that, but with Heather siding with Patrice, he had no real choice. It was his dubious distinction to inherit charge of the family real-estate holdings, and so he finally agreed.

Patrice reveled in her victory, but quietly, as if she knew Jake might change his mind and chuck the whole thing at a moment's notice. She did make a stab at pretending remorse, but her intense pleasure at hearing a full accounting of every boring, nebulous transaction that took place during the workday revealed the real truth: she was a control freak through and through. Her machinations were merely the means to have everything she wanted: Jake, the business and ultimate power.

He managed to graduate from college before she really pushed the job on him, but she steered him through a degree in business administration after a knee injury knocked him out of football in his junior year. Looking back, he could remember her concerned face as he was taken into surgery, but superimposed on that picture was another one: Patrice faintly smiling as Coach Miller bemoaned the fact that he'd lost his star running back, at least for this season.

She'd been glad he was finished with football. Glad she had control again. Rex had died the previous spring and she wanted Jake to take over as soon as possible. Not that she couldn't do the job herself. She was tough, smart and every bit as cagey as any wheeler-dealer he'd had the misfortune to run across. She did take over, in fact, while he finished up school, but there was another aspect to Patrice that was almost laughable. She was a strict traditionalist and in her mind, women didn't overtly run the family business. It didn't look right. She'd been, after all, a Huntingford before she married the far less prestigious Mr. Rex Beckett with his oodles of money and distressingly nouveau riche ways, and Huntingford women behaved in certain undisputed ways.

It never seemed to matter to Patrice that Huntingfords

might have connections to all the important political families of Boston since America was a colony, but nobody gave a damn who or what you were in Oceantides, Washington. She was going to have her son run the company, come hell or high water. Jake was doomed.

Huntingfords…tradition…appearances…

What's best for you…

Now Jake stared at his mother and wondered for the billionth time why she'd ever left her prestigious East Coast roots. She must have lived in misery with a man as untamed and unrepentant as Rex Beckett, yet the word was that she'd loved him once.

They'd met at Brown University where Rex had taken some graduate courses. Jake's Great-aunt Trudy, who loved a good yarn with her tea and rum cakes, had implied on many an occasion that Patrice Huntingford had "lost her head and virginity" over that "good-looking cowboy" and that it was a "love match—nothing more, nothing less." This truly was an overly romantic scenario, since Jake's father had been no more a cowboy than he was. No, it was much more likely that Patrice had smelled the sweet, flourishing scent of Beckett money and had gone after him like a rocket since the Huntingfords were well-spoken, well respected and well documented, but not well-heeled. Their lineage needed a little shot in the arm with the money needle.

As for love and desire, Jake couldn't believe that anyone as cool and controlled as his mother had ever succumbed to even the briefest moment of passion.

Never did he assume his parents had "done it" more than once.

If Jake wasn't such a carbon copy of his father, with the exception of Patrice's uncompromising jaw, he would have given the idea of adoption more credence. As it was, his heritage was stamped all over him—and as the only Beckett male, his future was sealed.

So, here he was, facing his mother, his own expression as impassive as hers as she put down her crossword puzzle, pulled her glasses from her nose and let her steely blue eyes rake her son from head to toe.

He noticed, then, her trembling hand and watched as she folded one palm over the other to hide their shaking. She was under some inordinate amount of stress.

"Is everything all right?" she asked, stealing the words from his own lips.

"Yeah, I was just going to ask you the same thing. You look kind of—"

He cut himself off on a sharp breath. *Sherry,* he realized. Sherry had visited his mother. That was why Sherry had been on North Beach Road!

With an effort, he hid the swell of emotion that suddenly rocked him. She'd talked to Patrice. On the intercom, he realized, his gaze darting to the switch on the desk. Patrice's eyes followed his and her jaw tightened. A long moment passed between them while Jake speculated on what that conversation must have been like. Oh, to have been a fly on the wall! Patrice positively loathed Sherry Sterling even to this day, and although Jake had put that portion of his past firmly behind him, his mother somehow never could.

Ridiculous. A vision of Sherry as he'd last seen her—startled eyes and pale white skin—floated through his mind. He swallowed, sensing his heart rate accelerate.

"You saw her," Patrice accused icily.

Jake nodded carefully. "Nearly ran into her."

"Did you talk to her?"

Her voice was quick and anxious. Jake sighed, confused as ever by his mother's naked aversion to Sherry Sterling. "Not really."

"What did you say to her?"

"I said..." He paused, drawing out each syllable, a parry to his mother's thrust that irritated her to the roots of her silver hair. "I said, 'Hey, Sherry, how're you doing? It's been a long time. Wanna come in and have a cup of coffee? I know my mother would love to see you.'"

"Stop being facetious."

"Oh, come on. Have a sense of humor."

"I want the truth, J.J. What did you say?" Patrice insisted.

"I said, 'What are you doing here?' and she said..." *Haunting the neighborhood.*

He cleared his throat, struck by that for reasons he couldn't name. She'd haunted him for a long time, he realized. Maybe if she'd stuck around Oceantides it would have been different, but after that wild fall and the subsequent events of their senior year, she'd run as fast and as far as she could. He'd hurt her. And although he'd never admitted it to anyone—scarcely even to himself—she'd hurt him, too.

"She said what?" Patrice prodded, her blue eyes flashing with growing alarm.

"She said she was going to be in town as short a time as possible."

"What is she doing here?"

"Visiting, I guess." He glanced away. He didn't want to think about Sherry. It was surprising how long pain lasted. He hadn't believed it was possible to feel anything for her except faint regret, but there was a sting inside him now—a sharp little seed that had the power to grow and swell and suddenly burst out and punch you in the solar plexus when you weren't looking.

"Well, I certainly hope she makes it short. She was nothing but trouble as a teenager and, though I know it sounds unkind, I don't believe people change that much as adults."

"Oh, I don't know." Jake shrugged, feeling perverse. "I've changed."

"You're still the same."

She sounded so positive he almost laughed out loud. How the hell did she know? She hadn't paid the least bit of attention to Jake Beckett, the person, *ever*. He was only a product to be molded; an extended part of herself to be used for the benefit of the Beckett clan as a whole, which to date consisted only of herself, him and sometimes Heather.

And Caroline, when they found the time to get married, he reminded himself.

As if discerning his thoughts, Patrice added casually, "Caroline called earlier. She said she could skip her last seminars and be back in Oceantides tonight."

"I thought this conference lasted through tomorrow." Jake lifted an eyebrow. His mother—for all her manipulations—could be so transparent sometimes.

"It does, but those seminars aren't worth attending, or so Caroline says. She gave me a number for you to call." Patrice made a big show of trying to remember where she'd placed the scrap of paper with Caroline's hotel number, but Jake wasn't fooled. Patrice wanted their marriage so badly she couldn't help herself from playing all these coy games. Most of the time he was amused. After all, in the end she would have her way and, in this case, he was willing to play his part. He and Caroline were good for each other. They always had been.

But once in a while, like tonight, a lick of fury ran through him, stirring sleeping embers.

I could have had another life, he thought. I could have had something special.

Sherry jumped into his inner vision again—beautiful, smart and sarcastic.

And passionate.

With an effort he took a deep breath and reminded himself that juvenile love affairs should be remembered with nostalgia, nothing more.

"I'll call her," he promised, moving away.

"J.J.?"

He turned back, making eye contact. Patrice's gaze searched his desperately. Silence stretched between them until he was compelled to glance away first, wondering what she was asking.

He strode from the room and up the winding stairway to the suite of rooms at the back of the house that were his. He had his own place but Patrice kept his old rooms available and ready for him. Not that he ever stayed here. But sometimes he stood by the window and stared toward the beach, far below the headland. Sometimes he stared toward the tree house.

He was drifting. Had been for years. Letting himself bob and sway on life's waters as he used to bodysurf in the waves outside his windows.

Now, he gazed down hard at the ocean's feathery white-capped waves, black until they frothed against each other like frosting. Once, he'd dreamed of something else, something better. His jaw twitched and he remembered....

* * *

She was just one of the girls in his class. Skinny. Studious. Nondescript except he couldn't ever remember hating her for being either a tattletale or a shrieking idiot all through grade school. He'd hated every other girl—useless creatures who liked to laugh and whisper and slide looks at you. Jake had spent his youth certain that girls were some kind of punishment guys just had to endure for strange, mystical reasons that began with the dawn of the human race.

She was a freshman before he took a second look. By then hormones were raging, and he spent half his time desperately trying to ignore girls, and the other half devoted to sports. Sports saved him, in fact, because they kept his mind focused and his body exhausted.

But even sports couldn't control his every waking moment, and it was to his everlasting joy and despair that girls found him attractive. He had his pick, really, and maybe because of that he chose no one.

He remembered her in science class. Shoulder-length hair, clean and shining and straight. He watched the way light glinted off those brown strands shot with gold. Daydreaming was a dangerous occupation, however, and not just because Mr. Tindel glared at him when he lost track of the discussion. No, examining Sherry Sterling's lush hair brought on other thoughts that played havoc with his body—an embarrassment he could really have done without.

She wasn't part of the popular crowd, but the popular crowd was full of well scrubbed, bright faces and shallow dispositions that could easily disintegrate into downright meanness. The only girl in that group worth knowing was Caroline who seemed somehow impervious to the churning nastiness around her.

He hung out with Caroline and the other groupies who seemed to constantly be circling around like manic satellites, but he watched Sherry Sterling. He liked the way her eyebrows drew together when she was reading. He liked the curve of her cheekbone and the fullness of her lips. In fact, those lips drew him as much as her gold-streaked hair. She rarely wore lipstick. Maybe never. But she was a Chap Stick freak and watching her slide the waxed tip over her lips was almost X-rated in Jake's mind. He remembered groaning aloud once in class and his best buddy, Ryan Delmato, had asked him what was wrong. He'd blamed it on exhaustion and pretended to collapse on his desk.

After that he fought even glancing Sherry's way.

He thought he would get over his physical attraction. Everybody else went through women like candy, and he certainly dated a few and made out with even more. But Sherry Sterling went from being just okay, with nice hair and lips, to outstanding with long, toned legs and breasts that clothes seemed to want to hug.

Jake looked around at the other guys in his class and wondered why no one else saw it. Okay, she was still a little gawky, slower to develop than some. But he could almost watch her daily and predict what was going to happen. Beauty and unconscious sensuality were heading her way like a freight train.

The coming transformation was enough to leave him weak at the knees.

Yet she was still Sherry Sterling whose family was a source of head shaking and lip pursing to the adults. She *had* to be loose, he'd heard more than one old biddy pronounce. Father a drunk. Mother a weak and weary woman. No money. No family honor.

It was a wonder Sherry had gotten as far as she had.

For the remainder of his freshman year she circled his fantasies. Once, he seized an opportunity to talk to her. She was with her two friends, Jennifer and Julie, but Sherry seemed disassociated from them. There was a faraway look in her eyes, a haunted yearning for something that touched an answering chord inside Jake. He approached her as she was leaving school, her two friends chattering in her wake. They shut up as if someone had slammed a door in front of them as soon as Jake approached Sherry.

"Hard to believe school's almost out, isn't it?" he said, mouth dry. He heard his voice as if he were an outsider and cringed. What a dork! As a pickup line it left much to be desired.

She slid him a glance. Her eyes were bluish violet beneath long, sooty lashes—and they shimmered with hostility. Jake was taken aback.

"Hard to believe," she agreed coolly.

"I just meant it's gone kind of fast. Freshman year."

"Uh-huh."

He'd been frozen out by girls before. Margot Agner had treated him like he had the plague when he dumped her after they'd made out in eighth grade at Caroline's fourteenth birthday party. But Margot's kind of freeze was different; she turned up her nose when she saw him, then cried gallons of tears to her friends and made sure he knew it. She'd been kind of fun to hang out with but he'd sensed a desperation beneath her cool-girl exterior and warning bells had sounded.

At a tender age he'd learned about girls' manipulations and sometimes-clinging ways, but Sherry Sterling didn't fit the pattern. And so she intrigued him.

School let out for the summer and Jake spent his time surfing or bored to tears in his father's real-estate office, learning the ropes. Thoughts of Sherry faded as those summer nights turned warmer. Tourists arrived, an influx of nubile girls with bodies just starting to curve. He lost his virginity the night before school started with a girl who possessed huge blue eyes and even huger breasts.

Tina Trumbull. A transferee from California who'd practically thrown him down in the sand and made love to him. Jake had gone through the motions, slightly detached, and then had suffered acute embarrassment and annoyance at himself. He tried to explain to her that he wasn't interested in some kind of serious relationship, but Tina wouldn't listen. She followed him around school, waited outside the gates of his house, broke into his BMW, called him incessantly.

It was psychological hell, and Jake didn't know what to do.

Enter: Patrice. The ultimate Mother Bear.

"Who is that girl?" she demanded, while Tina strolled along North Beach Road. "Did you give her a ride? You've barely got your license. You shouldn't pick up strange girls."

"She's not a strange girl." Jake refused to talk about it with Patrice.

No problem. His mother called up the school and talked to the teachers, counselors and principal. Then she phoned the Trumbulls and they packed up and moved back to California.

Jake thought that would be the end of it, but his first conquest called him long distance from California three nights out of seven and started saying things like she would commit suicide if he didn't love her. Patrice grabbed the phone and warned Tina that she would institute legal action if she didn't stop harassing her son.

Embarrassment! Humiliation! That one night of love-making became the talk of the school because Patrice made no secret of the fact that her son was wanted by the feminine gender. It was some kind of badge of honor for her, like having him be captain of the football team or pitcher on the baseball team.

But worse was the fact that Jake was glad Patrice had stepped in. It sure as hell made things easier. Tina finally stopped calling. He'd wondered about her over the years and found, to his astonishment, that his mother knew all about her. She'd made it her business. To date, Tina had married twice, borne a child by each husband, and was currently fighting an alcohol problem.

Obsession. He swore to himself he would be more careful in the future. And when one night he discovered one of the most outrageous, on-the-edge senior girls in his bedroom, he nearly freaked. It was all he could do to maintain his cool and pretend the reason he wasn't interested in a little recreational sex was because Mom and Dad were right downstairs.

When Jake complained about the girls, his friend Ryan spoke plainly. "You've got it all, buddy. Money, looks and athletics. My dad always said it'd be a problem someday."

"Yeah, some problem," Matt snorted. "Hurt me some more." And he and Ryan both howled with laughter and envy.

Jake gave up confiding in them, but the situation nearly scared him off girls entirely. He spent most of his time hanging out with Caroline and her wholesome friends. He grew to appreciate Caroline in a way he hadn't before, and he became aware that her fondness for him was blossoming into romance and better yet, sexual desire. But his previous experience had made him cautious. Fooling around with Caroline would be prime disaster.

Wasn't there any girl who just wanted a good time, no strings attached?

He was pondering that very issue in biology class one afternoon and when the bell rang he was so turned on he could scarcely think. His flock of admirers waited outside the door but they just made him feel tired and frustrated. Any one of them could be another Tina Trumbull.

He wanted something else, something fresh and exciting. Something to think about while he lay on his bed at night. Something to look forward to every morning and let his thoughts touch on throughout the day.

His group walked with him down the hall, chattering like magpies and grabbing at his arm and letterman's jacket, generally being a royal pain in the butt. Briefly he flirted with the idea of taking one of them to bed, but no, that was disaster in the making. He couldn't just blow them off, however; it wasn't in his nature. So, he put up with their attention.

And then he saw Sherry Sterling by her locker.

He sighed. Every time he noticed her he'd been subjected to a frigidity that could have ended global warming for all time. She clearly hated him. And she'd come out of her shy cocoon to zing him with some sharp remarks that had left him feeling confused and angry and certain he was missing something. This time was no different. She made some remark about the way he spoke.

What the hell was her problem, anyway? He turned to stare at her in surprise. This was the first time she'd dared to challenge him overtly. His admirers glared at her and made rude remarks, but she kept packing up her bags with unhurried regality and suddenly he wanted to crack that icy facade once and for all.

Before he had time to think, he was in front of her, crowding her space, and although a hundred comments flashed through his mind he said only, "My dad and I are going to Pullman tomorrow to the Cougars game."

In fascination he watched the flush creep up her slim neck and burn her face. She wouldn't look at him, however, so he stayed where he was, waiting, secretly glad this moment of confrontation had arrived. He'd been longing for it, he realized then. Biding his time. Hoping for an opportunity.

The other girls faded from his sight as if they'd magically disappeared. He saw no one but Sherry. Her head was dipped down, her eyes focused with studied concentration on the pile of books she'd stuffed into her bag. Eventually she half turned, lifting those clear, vulnerable eyes to meet his gaze.

He couldn't remember the rest of the conversation. He'd accused her of always making snide remarks, or something, but all he saw and felt was her—those eyes, that pert, slightly freckled nose, that lustrous skin.

For an instant they connected. He felt it viscerally, breathlessly. It startled him but he managed to keep it hidden. At least he hoped he did, but then she slammed her locker and tried to leave but the stitching on her bag gave way and books flew everywhere.

Automatically he bent to help her, his arm brushing hers. It felt like the proverbial electric current and he barely had time to marvel at this when she jerked away, nearly overbalancing herself. He reached out and grabbed her arm.

It seemed so perfect. He wanted her like none other and now he was holding her and, well, his own youthful cockiness rose to his rescue. He was, after all, J.J. Beckett, and heretofore women were as available as the air he breathed. Smiling, he simply waited for her to recognize that they had something here—chemistry or magic or just plain old sexual energy. He forgot all his reservations about getting too involved with a girl. He *would* sleep with her.

But Sherry Sterling didn't respond like he'd imagined. Her eyes narrowed and she slowly and deliberately pulled her arm free. For an awkward moment he expected her to say something, but she merely hung on to her bag and waited for him to leave.

"I'll try to speak better," he told her. She didn't respond, so he was forced to return to his hovering group. Confounded, he refused to look back, although it killed him to walk down the hall without her.

Months passed, the end of sophomore year came, then summer, then football season once again. Junior year and he was with Caroline. He'd gotten over that weird thing with Sherry Sterling, or so he told himself, and although his antennae seemed to twitch whenever she was around, he made a pact with himself to stop thinking such dorky, romantic thoughts about her. He'd been a kid last year. Stupid and eager and somehow attracted to this girl who wasn't even in his league. Besides, all he'd wanted was sex, wasn't it? No strings attached. Sherry Sterling possessed a sexy body and time had only added to its desirability.

Enclosed in this self-protective fog, Jake wandered around clueless for weeks, certain he knew how he felt. But slowly he realized that he wasn't the only one who'd noticed Sherry Sterling's various attributes. Other guys slid her surreptitious looks, only now she slid them looks right back!

What had once been Jake's secret passion was suddenly everyone's newest craze: Sherry Sterling, Babe Extraordinaire. He heard her name on his friends' lips. They spoke of her in terms of body parts: eyes, legs, breasts, butt. They repeated clever things she'd said to them—not the cold remarks she'd tossed *his* way, but nice words and compliments that made his friends' eyes glaze over when they were recounted and enjoyed anew.

Even Ryan was particularly smitten. He babbled on and on about her. About how he hoped she would take a job at Bernie's Pizza. About how he was working on it.

Jake could scarcely stand it. Time and time again he felt a passionate rage lick through him when some guy mentioned Sherry. Ryan was bad enough, but other guys weren't as nice about it. Once Jake nearly picked a fight with Tim Delaney, the team's wide receiver, for making a crude remark about what he would do for Sherry Sterling when he got her into bed. Bets were placed on when that would be.

Jake ground his teeth and reminded himself that he didn't give a hot damn about any of it.

Homecoming came and Jake threw a dozen passes into Tim's waiting hands. They were an awesome team on the field, making mincemeat of the other team and showing up the lazy seniors who were big on bragging but small on talent. Off the field Jake and Tim couldn't stand each other, however, and that was a battle that had begun long before Sherry Sterling.

Still, for that night they slapped palms like old friends and grinned deliriously at their success. It was great to be on top. To be the best of the best. To be J.J. Beckett, all-star quarterback.

He went to the homecoming dance warm with satisfaction. People paid court to him, and he ate it up like any other teenager who was the center of attention. But somewhere during the evening he realized he felt vaguely dissatisfied. Checking around inside himself, he couldn't come up with an answer to his problem. Here he was with blond, popular Caroline Newsmith on his arm, his buddies, Ryan Delmato and Matt Hudson, hanging nearby, and Tim Delaney, his worst rival, a friend for tonight at least, as they basked in their shared triumph.

It should have been perfect.

"Hey," Caroline whispered, reading his mood. "You were great tonight."

"Yeah?" He tried to pay attention. She smelled good, her hair shining gold beneath the colored lights. Inhaling deeply, he wondered with a certain amount of alarm why she didn't stir his blood. Maybe it was a good thing. Sexual involvement with Caroline would be a major problem. She just wasn't that kind of girl.

But why not? Why not feel just a little healthy lust?

"I swear I'm hoarse from cheering," Caroline continued, resting her head on his shoulder. "Did you hear us? Annie and I were screaming at the top of our lungs and some older people told us to quiet down. We didn't, of course." She giggled. This was the height of true rebellion for Caroline.

Jake dragged her closer until the contours of her body melded to his. Inside, his own rebellion seemed to be heating up, burning like molten steel. He hadn't slept with a girl since Tina, and he was beginning to feel angry and frustrated.

He thought, *I want a bad girl....*

Caroline squirmed at the pressure, but she tried not to let him know. Instantly he eased up, mad at himself.

Just as instantly she relaxed against him again, peering up at him sideways, searching his expression.

"You want to leave?" he asked abruptly. "This is so boring."

"I'd kind of like to stay." Her brows knit in confusion. She was totally at sea about his feelings and that bugged Jake, too.

"Well, I'm going. I can drop you off, or somebody'll take you home."

"I can catch a ride with Annie," she responded frostily, and although Jake should have felt remorse, he was too anxious to feel much of anything but relief.

He drove for hours, the car window down so that the bite of fall air cleared his head, the radio up so that music throbbed and deafened. He circled Oceantides in erratic loops, passing by all the hangouts, consumed with an urgency that was almost violent. For the first time in his life he wanted to drink and fight and indulge in meaningless sex and damn the consequences. He yearned for relief from this nameless demon that rode him.

What the hell was the matter with him?

With a screech of tires he pulled into a viewing spot at the end of Mariner Lane, at the edge of the beach. Tearing off his letterman's jacket, shoes and socks, he tromped down to the ocean and let the water numb his feet and ankles. Flinging himself into the surf nearly stopped his heart; the water was glacial. Dragging in a choked breath, he didn't back down. It was as if he were on some nameless, self-destructive mission, like lemmings throwing themselves into the sea.

He bobbed aimlessly, sometimes floating like a dead man, eyes open to a black, cold sky; sometimes swim-

ming against the tide until his arms felt like lead weights
and his breath rasped in his throat.

He was so cold by the time he fought his way back
to the beach he could scarcely stand. His own foolish-
ness finally penetrated his dull brain, and he marveled
that he could have tempted fate this far. Was he trying
to kill himself? No. Was he stupid enough to put his
life at risk because he felt frustrated and disconnected
and unhappy? Yes, apparently.

At the car he couldn't manage getting the key into
the lock. His fingers were yellow-white with cold and
his whole body shivered uncontrollably as if it were in
its last death throes. He couldn't move his lips even to
swear; his jaw was frozen half-open. Unable to perform
this one tiny task that would save him from freezing,
he wondered if he would actually die of exposure outside his BMW, his keys in his hands.

At first he didn't feel her presence; he was way too
immersed in more physical problems. But suddenly she
was there, her coat flapping against her legs, her hair
lifted by the wind and moving seductively against her
shoulders like sea foam. He stared at her like the village
idiot, unable to move, speak or think.

"You went swimming," she observed. "Probably
not the choice I would have made on a night like tonight."

His teeth chattered in response. The keys rattled in
his palsied hand.

Sherry hesitated for the length of one heartbeat, her
brows drawn together in alarm and understanding. Ex-
tracting the keys, she made short work of the lock but
when Jake couldn't climb inside, she put her arm
around his waist and half hoisted him onto the seat.

"What in God's name were you doing out there?"

she demanded, puffing from exertion. Her luminous eyes caught a glancing beam of moonlight. Jake felt faint and light-headed and wondered if he was going to pass out.

"Do you need someone to drive you?" she demanded.

He shook his head. Fine, bright lights seemed to dazzle his eyes.

"Are you certain?"

Jake fought his shivering but hypothermia had grabbed him in a death grip. He was going under and part of him didn't care.

He didn't feel the slap; numbness overrode everything. But he was suddenly blinking and awake, and Sherry's open palm explained it all. He thought she might hit him again, but when he looked her way, she ordered, "Stay awake, J.J., do you understand?"

Oh, he understood. He was in big trouble. He nodded.

"You've got to stay awake."

"Okay," he mumbled, but it was just a whoosh of sound from his lungs that didn't form words.

"Move over," she commanded, pushing him until he fell over the gearshift and against the passenger door. He felt so brittle he thought he might break into a million pieces. Climbing behind the wheel, she stated calmly, "I don't have my license, but I figure this is something of an emergency."

With that she twisted the ignition and with a cautious expertise that Jake appreciated much later when he was finally warm and safe again, she drove him home. She made noise about taking him to the nearest hospital, but he adamantly refused and so she drove him up the hill to what she referred to as Beckett Manor.

The house was dark; his parents were in bed before

ten every night. Sherry helped him from the car, through the gates and back door into the kitchen.

He fumbled with his clothes. There was no hope for it. Sherry hovered by the door, wanting to bolt, but he heard her mutter something under her breath that sounded suspiciously like a string of obscenities, and then she was helping him while he stood by, passive as a sleeping baby.

She undid his belt and dropped his wet jeans to the floor. His boxers were plastered to his legs. She pulled his shirt and undershirt over his head in one swoop, then said calmly, "You need a shower or bath or something."

He shuffled down the hall, and Sherry followed slowly behind, unwilling, he supposed, to abandon her patient until she was completely assured he would live. He was glad she was there. He needed someone, and he realized vaguely that he'd needed someone all night.

There was a guest room and bathroom—more like a maid's quarters really—beneath his own wing of rooms. He led the way, Sherry behind him. The shower had been redone in a curve of translucent glass brick and Sherry briskly turned the taps. A rush of hot, moist air filled the room.

A moment later, she said, "I'm going to leave it on the barely warm side or you won't be able to stand it."

Jake was hardly in a position to argue even if he'd wanted to. Still numb, he hobbled into the shower with his boxers on. Through the glass he could see her wavy form move toward the door. "Wait!" he croaked out.

She stopped. Silently. Jake's gaze stayed on the distorted colors that were Sherry as the heat from the shower hurt his frozen feet and limbs. It seemed as if the water were boiling hot until his flesh began to warm and he realized the shower was barely lukewarm. Slowly he turned up the hot tap, but it seemed like hours before he felt his blood heat. The whole time, his gaze stayed glued to Sherry who hung by the door as if waiting for someone to open it from the other side and free her. Jake chafed at the delay. What if she left too soon? He didn't want her to leave. He wanted her here, with him; and with growing insight, he realized that she was what he'd been waiting for all night.

Eventually he stepped from the shower. She still hovered by the door, looking oddly scared now, although earlier she'd been in such maximum control. Grabbing a towel, he wrapped it around his waist and wished he could peel the wet boxers off without spooking her into running like a deer.

That was what she looked like—a scared fawn. Gone was the steel-voiced woman who acted with such cool determination. This was a new, vulnerable Sherry, and he could tell by the way her lips pursed that she didn't like it one bit.

"Thanks," he said, swiping wet hair from his face. He was glad his voice was back.

She nodded. "You probably would have frozen to death if I hadn't come along."

"No kidding. I must have been out of my mind."

"It looked that way."

He snorted in agreement. Now that the initial crisis was over he felt like a moron. God, what did she think? He practically owed her his life.

"What possessed you to go swimming in the ocean tonight? I mean, what's the water temperature? Forty degrees? Are you crazy?"

"Yeah…" He half laughed. "I guess I am."

"Do you have some kind of death wish?"

"Not usually."

"Was this some kind of macho dare?" she asked, her starch returning.

"No, I was just thinking that I wanted to get away from everything."

"Rather drastic measures."

"Hey, it wasn't a suicide attempt, if that's what you're thinking. I just wanted everything—to stop."

The words came from somewhere inside himself. What had been eating at him all day, all week, maybe all year, suddenly seemed so clear.

"Thanks for saving me," he said quietly.

"Oh…no." She shrugged that off, embarrassed. "I'm just glad you're okay."

"Don't tell anybody, all right?" He half smiled. "They wouldn't understand."

"Who would I tell?"

"Your friends."

"I don't have those kinds of friends," she said without rancor.

"Neither do I," he said, because it was the truth. He didn't have the kinds of friends he could really trust. But he didn't see how Sherry might take it. However, J.J. didn't realize how condescending he might sound until Sherry's face flushed pink and her eyes glittered.

"Oh, excuse me. J.J. Beckett doesn't have any friends. I didn't realize."

"I didn't say that."

"Yeah?" she arched one disbelieving eyebrow.

"I said I don't have those kinds of friends. That's what you said, and I agreed with you. That's all."

"What about Ryan Delmato? Matt Hudson?"

"Look, I just said—"

"Don't feel sorry for me, okay? I can handle myself.

I don't need you telling me you understand my problems, or that you can feel what I feel. You don't have a clue!''

"Hey." He lifted his hands in surrender. "Stop being so defensive. I guess I made a mistake. Sorry. I didn't mean it that way."

Silence pooled between them. He was truly baffled by her prickliness. Okay, so she hadn't been born with a silver spoon stuck firmly between her teeth like he had. Big deal. Some people were just born with inner class and she was one of them. He could appreciate that. Too bad she couldn't.

"I've gotta go," she said abruptly.

"Wait."

This time he put his hand on her wrist. That was a mistake because he could feel her recoil from his touch. But it was a mistake he was glad he'd made because he wanted to touch her, and he was also glad in a perverse sort of way that his touch affected her.

"What are you doing?" she demanded suspiciously as he leaned toward her.

"I don't know," he admitted honestly. He was just reacting. Reacting to a long, hard night and a brush with death that had left him light-headed.

She was rigid as steel but warm. She'd tried to freeze him out so many times he'd half believed she was made of ice. But her skin was smooth, supple and hot beneath his hand and because he wasn't thinking quite clearly, he pulled her into his arms and kissed her full on the mouth.

If she'd truly believed he was going to kiss her she would have pulled away; she told him that later when they could laugh about it. But at that moment she was so stunned that he'd actually dragged her into his arms that her lips were parted on a gasp of disbelief. The feel of her half-open mouth was an invitation. Jake thrust his tongue inside its heat and groaned with desire.

And she bit down with all she was worth.

"Goddammit!" he howled, shoving her away from him. He could taste blood.

"You bastard," she whispered. "Touch me again and I'll kill you."

And then she was gone. Jake was left to nurse his injury and thank his lucky stars that she hadn't tried to bite off his tongue in earnest. In reality, it was a minor wound.

Later, lying in bed reviewing the scene, he was embarrassed at his strange and inappropriate boldness. For a moment he'd believed she was his, that she wanted him. For a moment there'd been no question. For a moment...

With a groan he shoved his head under the pillow and vowed to forget her, but even as he made the pledge, he knew it possessed no teeth.

He was going to do his damnedest to have Sherry Sterling. She was the one and only thing he'd wanted in a long, long time.

Now, Jake blinked awake like a sleepwalker. The waves still roiled toward shore outside his windows and the piece of paper with Caroline's hotel number still lay in his hand. Only he'd crumpled it into a minuscule ball.

Emotion sang through him, down every nerve fiber. So long ago yet so powerful. It could have been yesterday. First loves were impossible to forget, but he wondered if others still felt them as keenly as he sometimes did. It bothered him a bit. What if this was some irreparable flaw in his character that would haunt him forever?

A moment later he chuckled. Then he threw back his head and laughed. Good grief, he was getting maudlin! So Sherry Sterling had materialized in Oceantides. So what? It wasn't like she had the power to turn his life inside out again. That was a symptom of his teen years, and he'd been cured of the illness long ago.

No, as far as he was concerned, there was nothing Sherry Sterling could do or say that would make any difference to him now. There were no ties between them, apart from a few bittersweet memories.

With a renewed sense of control he picked up the phone to call Caroline.

Chapter Four

The espresso shop two blocks from the beach also sold magazines and newspapers, and it smelled like a combination of briny air, rich coffee and newsprint. Sherry cradled a raspberry mocha between cold hands, a treat to herself that she seldom otherwise drank. But these were desperate times. She needed sustenance and strength and a whole lot of courage, and if a sweet, hot drink would help, so be it.

The clientele of Beachtime Coffee was as varied as Oceantides' residents. A couple in the corner wore matching royal blue sweaters tied around their necks, preppy-style, their heads bent close over an article in the newspaper. An elderly man sat rigidly in a chair, eyes focused on the clock although Sherry had come to understand he wasn't watching the time; he was merely faced that way, focused on inner thoughts entirely his own. Two teenagers with long, ragged hair, baggy pants, T-shirts and skater shoes were digging coins out of their pockets in a combined effort to purchase coffee, leaving their skateboards propped against the wall outside the door.

Sherry did a mental inventory of her own appearance: loose ponytail, blue jeans, black body-hugging ribbed turtleneck sweater, black belt with a silver buckle winking at her waist. She doodled on a pad with a red felt pen and found to her dismay that she'd written "J.J." several times. Well, he was on her mind, wasn't he? He was the reason she was here, wasn't he? It was only natural.

She'd blown their meeting the night before. Blown it. He'd taken her by surprise, and she'd reacted like a teenager. Maybe that was to be expected since the last time she'd seen him they'd been teenagers.

Not that she was so incredibly mature now. She still had trouble reviewing the events of the night she'd found him shivering by his car, for crying out loud! She didn't want to recall that first kiss, when he'd wrapped her in his shower-dampened arms and pressed his mouth urgently against hers.

Her pulse jerked in recollection, a wave of emotion rushing over her. Damn it all. Swiping furiously at a loose strand of hair she wondered when—*when!*—would she be immune to those memories. Ridiculous! She should have quit with him right then, right after biting his tongue; but no, that hadn't been the end but the beginning. She'd come away from that night with a new awareness of J.J. Beckett. No longer could she cover her feelings with sarcasm; she was too affected, too aware.

And the number of times after the rescue that she'd felt the weight of J.J.'s gaze on her said he felt the same way, although they both tried to act like nothing had happened.

At school and at Bernie's doing her homework, life settled into a pattern. Somewhere after midnight every night, she would fall into bed to dream about J.J. She lived for those moments when she caught a glimpse of him, reviewed every nuance of every rare smile he sent her way, every intense look. She liked school because it was where he was—and it was away from home. She liked working because J.J. dropped in at Bernie's on a regular basis, and Bernie himself made Sherry feel special.

Even now she could still visualize Bernie, hands covered with flour, shooing the other teenage employees home around ten o'clock. "Get outta here. Get some rest. Study hard," he would yell at them, but Sherry stayed later, unwilling to leave. This concerned Bernie at first, and he shook his finger at her and demanded she do her homework if she was just "gonna hang around and make trouble." But later he seemed to understand that home to Sherry was not a home at all.

Bernie, himself, never seemed to tire. He had stories galore about growing up in a family of fifteen and what it was like raising five children of his own. That he loved them fiercely was self-evident, although Ryan seemed to always be in trouble for not treating one of his friends or family members the exact way Bernie wanted him to.

"Don't you want to talk to your mama?" Bernie demanded one afternoon. "All day long she waits for you to come home and then you go off with your friends."

"I come to work here!" Ryan replied, exasperated.

"And then where do you go?"

"Home!"

"No, you don't. You run around with that Jay Beckett in his fancy blue car and never talk to your mama."

Sherry felt empathy for Ryan. Ryan did spend a lot of time with J.J. but he was the first to say it was time he got home. Bernie was a bit unfair in his assessment of Ryan's family duties, but at some level Sherry realized Bernie was just protecting Ryan from hanging out with the rich crowd from North Beach Road. He worried that his son would get hurt.

She was the one who should have listened to his advice.

As Sherry pored over her homework in a booth on the other side of the restaurant, she couldn't help but be witness to Bernie and Ryan's arguments on the subject.

"It's J.J., not Jay," Ryan would mutter, a last stab at rebellion.

"I don't care if it's Gottrocks. It's not a good idea, you hanging with that crowd and neglecting your mama."

"I'm not!"

Bernie would then turn to Sherry with a "You see?" expression before shooting Ryan a dark look and slamming through the door to the back storage room and office, and Ryan would turn to Sherry with a "Can you believe this?" look, and she would laugh and want to hug them both.

"I just love your dad," she declared one night, smiling fondly.

"Yeah..." Ryan gazed at her. Underneath his outgoing personality was an inherent shyness, particularly with girls. She knew he had a crush on her, and she'd been debating what to do about it. J.J. filled her thoughts and her original plan to make Ryan her first boyfriend had lost its appeal.

The truth was, she liked him too much to play with his emotions. And she was head over heels for J.J.

Unfortunately her heartfelt remark about Bernie only seemed to increase Ryan's admiration for her. She had to do something, and do it fast.

In what would turn out to be her own particular behavior pattern, she ran.

"I've gotta go," she muttered, collecting her books and heading for the door.

"It's still early."

"I know, but I've got tons of homework."

"Do you want to do something, sometime...?"

Too late. The words were out, hanging between them. Sherry felt awful. Once again, a girl had fallen for J.J. and Ryan was just his sidekick. She wished with all her heart that she felt differently.

"I can't," she murmured, hating herself a little.

"Oh, okay."

He didn't even ask why—which made her feel even worse. Hesitating, she reached out a hand and touched the sleeve of his jacket. "Thanks, Ryan."

"For what?" he asked, perplexed.

Shaking her head, Sherry hurried out. A car throbbing with stereo music suddenly zipped into the parking spot in front of her, scaring her so badly that she jumped back and gasped.

J.J. Beckett. Emotions swarmed through her as he levered his lean body from the car. His scent reached her through the soft autumn air and the squeak of leather from his letterman's jacket sent a frisson down her spine. She loved him so much, sometimes it left her breathless; yet, apart from that one intense night, they'd done nothing but share a few stolen glances.

She was lovesick and stupid and vulnerable. She couldn't stand herself!

"Hi, Sherry," he said in his husky voice. The memory of his shower-dampened arms surrounding her swept over her, enveloping her. She pushed it away with an almost-physical effort.

"Hi." She scurried into the night. Her parents' house was five blocks west and three blocks north—a bungalow built fifty years earlier, ramshackle now and sadly in need of repair, but it was close enough to walk to.

"Where're you going?" he called after her.

"Home."

"Want a ride?" he asked, his keys rocking musically between his fingers.

She turned and stared, ignoring the raven thickness of his hair, his long, jeans-clad legs and his attentive look. Focusing somewhere near his neck, she shook her head. "Naw, it's close by. Thanks anyway."

"You can drive again...."

She refused to acknowledge their connection, refused to meet his gaze, refused to *know* him. A long moment stretched out. Her heart beat heavily. She wanted to say something clever and sarcastic, but there was a blockage in her throat and her ears were deafened by her own heartbeat. Besides, she was crazy to feel this way. She'd bitten him, for God's sake. He wasn't likely to forget.

At that moment Bernie's door flew open. Ryan peeked his head out, shattering the moment. "Hey, Sherry, let me walk you home," he called, oblivious to J.J.

Sherry opened her mouth to protest, but suddenly

found herself saying instead, "That'd be great," her smile a blinding light. Its effect on J.J. and Ryan was unmistakable, and Sherry groaned inwardly, aware she was toying with emotions she shouldn't. She knew better! Ryan deserved better.

But she wanted J.J.

"I'll walk with you guys," J.J. said, pocketing his keys, and the three of them made their way to Sherry's house.

Sherry's moment of feminine glory disintegrated. Growing dread took its place. What would they think when they saw her house? And what if her father was home, drunk and surly? She suddenly couldn't bear the thought.

"Thanks a lot, guys, but it's right over there." She waved vaguely. "I can make it the rest of the way by myself. See you later."

She half ran to the end of the block and the darkened house around the corner. Ryan made an aborted attempt to follow after her but J.J. stood back and watched. She raced up the front steps, gasping for breath, her books slipping from her arms. Twisting the knob, she was relieved to find the door unlocked, but held her breath until she saw her father fast asleep in the armchair in front of the television.

In the sanctuary of her bedroom she turned on a light, undressed quickly and climbed into bed, dragging her books with her. But although she furtively studied, frightened of wakening her father with the merest sound, her vision was clouded with images of J.J. Beckett climbing from his blue car, stretching his legs, and gazing at her with such studied vision that she read the same page of her history book over and over again.

Now, a lifetime later, she could remember each and

every feeling as if it had been yesterday—not fourteen years ago. Twiddling her red pen, she scratched out J.J.'s initials by drawing scarlet hearts over the damaging evidence. Valentine hearts.

Valentine's Day...

Pain was suddenly huge inside her, filling her lungs, squeezing out all the air. Her throat grew hot and arid. She felt weak all over. Drained. Empty.

Picking up her raspberry mocha, she glanced around, certain Beachtime Coffee's other customers would somehow divine her thoughts. Her lips quivered and she covered up with a quick swallow of mocha. Wishing for a miracle—the chance to live her life over again—she whispered, "Oh, J.J.," in a suffocated voice. She had to tell him the truth—and soon.

"Could I pay a hundred dollars now," the voice on the end of the line entreated, trembling, "and maybe the rest later on? I just don't have it right now, and I don't know what to do."

Jake stared out his office window. Jill Delaney had been perennially late with her rent since the moment she took over one of his least expensive apartment units. Already she was two months past due and getting deeper into debt each day that passed. She was Tim Delaney's ex-wife, a sweet girl whose love for her husband couldn't save their crumbling marriage. Tim just wasn't made of the kind of stuff husbands should be. Three children and one half-baked reconciliation later, she was struggling to make ends meet, but Tim still wasn't holding up his end of the bargain, and Jill had become dependent on Jake's charity to survive.

What the hell was he supposed to do?

"I can't turn you out, Jill," he admitted with characteristic honesty, "but we're both in a tough position."

"I know." Relief sang through her voice. She could hear he was about to relent—again.

"Pay what you can now," he said brusquely. "We'll work it out."

"Thank you," she whispered, fighting back tears.

Jake gently hung up the phone. Jill was not his responsibility. His responsibility was to the family business. Now, if Patrice were running the business she would evict Jill flat out, but since Patrice had abdicated to the only Beckett male, well…he would just have to handle things his way, and she could stew. That is, if she ever even found out. Since taking over the business wholeheartedly, Jake had made a point of forcing his mother to stay out of his way. She still fought him, but Jake had learned the power of "No"—"No, I'm not interested in your help…. No, I've got everything under control…. No, it's time for you to relinquish control…. *No, thank you…*"

She might hate it, but there wasn't a hell of a lot she could do about it. Poor Patrice.

Outside his window lay a second-story view of Oceantides' main street—a crooked two-lane avenue where lazy traffic crept between the shops, and intermittent rain spattered the cars and pavement. Late January with weather alternating between stormy and furious, and calm and benign. Yesterday was hell, today was okay. Life goes on….

Watching a couple of kids, hands clasped together, surge between the traffic and scamper down the street, Jake was struck by an urgent desire to run. *Run!* Run away forever! The feeling was so strong Jake gripped the arms of his chair, heart thudding. His chest ached.

Then the wave passed and he sank backward, nearly breathless.

He shook his head in wonder, afraid to examine this sudden panic attack. He wasn't normally prone to paranoia and stress.

With a niggling feeling that he was somehow being a coward, unable to face his true self, he shrugged the moment's anxiety away. Nothing to worry about. A symptom of too much reflection and not enough action. Not his style.

Across the street and nearly out of his range of vision, he could just spy the sign for Bernie's Pizza glowing dully under gray skies. Jake snorted in derision. Was Sherry there? The two went together in his mind: Bernie's Pizza and Sherry Sterling. Although Ryan Delmato was still a friend, Jake had scarcely set foot inside Bernie's since Sherry's disappearance right before high-school graduation. At first the idea had been painful, and then it had just seemed wrong somehow—a symbol of all that wasted, high-school emotional trauma.

God, it was good to grow up!

The telephone intercom buzzed. "Caroline's here," his part-time receptionist sang out.

"Send her in," he replied in his mock-important voice. Although the Beckett holdings were vast, the actual day-to-day operations were minimal and using an intercom amused him when he could just as well shout through the partially open door.

But, hey, the trappings of wealth and success were supposed to be important, weren't they?

When Caroline came into the room, Jake found himself holding his breath. There was about his fiancée a quality that always put him a little on guard, even though he truly cared about her. Sometimes she was cool to the point of icy—a personality trait that bothered her a great deal, but one she couldn't seem to change. Sometimes she was overly friendly and clingy, as if she were trying to subvert her own inherent reserve by pure force. Jake had told her to "relax" so many times, he'd given up. She was what she was. Take it or leave it.

Sometimes he wondered....

Today she wore an emerald-green shirt and black slacks, her blond hair tied back in a black velvet ribbon, her face nearly obscured by a huge potted fern from which she peeked around, smiling.

"I told you that you need a little life in here," she said. "Look at this office! It's so *sterile*."

Jake shrugged in agreement, just as he always did when she fussed over things that meant zero to him. This office. This job.

This life...?

Setting the plant on his desk, she leaned over and deposited a quick peck on his cheek. He caught a whiff of perfume, heavy, expensive and nameless, before she backed away. Caroline couldn't handle hugs and sloppy affection, but then, Jake realized wryly, neither could he. They were both dispassionate to a fault, which was why, he supposed, he'd felt his skin crawl at the thought of getting married on Valentine's Day—a suggestion that had come up recently from a surprising source.

"So, what's new this early morning?" Caroline asked, perching on a corner of his desk. Her breasts lay directly in his line of vision. Jake gazed at them through half-closed lids, wondering vaguely why his body didn't react. There was a time when he'd been consumed by sex in any way, shape or form. His teen years had been full of unrequited lust and a few conquests. Then at college, a few more. Then finally back to Caroline and a new, more mature relationship that had eventually moved to the bedroom.

But he'd never again felt those raging, thrilling shots of pure desire he'd experienced with Sherry Sterling.

Just teen hormones, you moron.

"Jill Delaney called and I gave her an extension on her rent," he said.

Caroline clucked her tongue. Her brows lifted. Blue eyes regarded him with empathy. "She's using you."

"I know."

"You're not falling for her, are you?" she teased.

Jake shook his head, irritated with her for no good reason. "What the hell is it with Tim, anyway? He's got three kids to think about, and he doesn't care about them one whit. They're his responsibility, but he expects Jill to carry the entire burden!"

"And you," Caroline reminded.

"He doesn't know I give her a break on the rent."

"Ha. Guys like Tim expect it. He's always been a loser." Caroline smoothed back a strand of hair. "No sense of responsibility."

"You got that right," Jake muttered, irritated anew that he was agreeing with her. "Tim's something else. If he and Jill hadn't broken up, he'd probably have a dozen kids by now and not care for any of them."

"You're just mad because he's self-indulgent and you're careful and concerned." Caroline touched her finger to the tip of his nose, smiling like a proud mother. Jake's annoyance with her intensified but he kept it to himself.

Besides, she was infuriatingly correct. Tim's behavior reminded Jake of Rex, although Jake's father had at least attempted to make financial reparation for his actions—or so Jake had been told. But the whole idea of indiscriminate fatherhood hit some tender part of his soul that had been hurt when he was young and had never quite recovered.

"As I recall, you sowed a few wild oats in high school yourself that could have ended in disaster," Caroline reminded him.

"I made some mistakes, but if I'd fathered a child, believe me, I would have taken care of it."

"Hmm."

She sounded suspiciously disbelieving.

"Tina Trumbull was not pregnant when she went back to California," Jake growled, covering old, old ground.

"I wasn't thinking of Tina."

"Then who were you thinking of?"

"There were other girls."

"Oh, right."

"There were." She studied her nails.

"Give me a break. I was there. I ought to know."

"I could name one."

Jake's gut tightened. He knew where this was going and now he was really bugged. Refusing to fall into the trap, he stayed silent. Caroline, however, seemed intent on making this an issue. Her gaze was level and accusatory. "You know who I mean."

"I didn't keep a scorecard," Jake declared through his teeth. "And I never got anybody pregnant."

"Okay, okay." Caroline suddenly capitulated, lifting her hands in surrender. Maybe she was as tired of the subject as he was. "Let's drop it."

Perversely, Jake now found himself wanting to jab the needle a little bit more. He was in that kind of mood. "You're not talking about *Sherry,* are you?" Caroline didn't immediately answer, but the skin on her face drew tightly over her fine bones.

"I don't want to talk about her."

"Then why did you bring it up?" he demanded.

She glanced at him, then gazed out the window, the corners of her mouth turning down. Jake's annoyance melted. What was he doing? What were they doing to each other? "That was just—" He broke off, unable to find the words.

"Just what?" Caroline pressed softly.

"Nothing. An infatuation that lasted a few months, that's all."

"Do you ever think about her?"

He shook his head. Guilt gnawed a bit. He *did* think about her sometimes. He'd certainly thought about her last night after their run-in. Memories had danced inside his head so hotly that he felt almost hungover this morning, as if he'd indulged in some wild, bacchanalian orgy.

"You talked to my mother, didn't you?" Jake accused gently. "She told you Sherry was in town."

Caroline nodded. "It just kind of took me aback."

Jake shrugged. "It's all over and done with. Sherry left just before graduation. She left *me*. It hurt, but for Pete's sake, Caroline, I was eighteen! That was so long ago, I barely remember."

"*I* remember," she said softly, and there was a wealth of feeling in those few words.

He gazed at her thoughtfully, uncomfortably. "Things matter too much when you're young. It wouldn't be the same now."

She half laughed. "Well, I hope things matter now!"

"You know what I mean."

Caroline was reflective. "You had a hard time getting over her, Jake."

"Yeah, I did. We had this huge fight, and she was gone. I couldn't believe it." Jake straightened his shoulders, frowning. "You know all about it."

"It's just that sometimes I think if it had just faded away, it would have been better. For me. And you," she added haltingly. "Why do you think she came to see you?"

"She said she didn't come to see me."

"Patrice said she did."

Jake's pulse jumped, but he hid his reaction, realizing Caroline was feeling too insecure to understand. "Patrice can't stand Sherry. She never could. God knows why. Maybe because Sherry didn't live 'on the water.'"

"Don't be so hard on your mother," Caroline defended quickly, hearing the implied rebuke. Her feelings paralleled Patrice's too closely for her to take any criticism in that direction.

"Don't be so kind. Patrice can take care of herself!"

Caroline fiddled with her fingernails before curling them into her palms. "Would I be out of line if I asked you not to see her again?"

"Who? Sherry?"

"I know it's silly." She lifted one shoulder helplessly.

"It is silly," Jake agreed.

"I know, but, will you humor me?"

Jake watched her closely, aware of undercurrents he'd never heretofore suspected beneath Caroline's placid exterior. "I don't even want to see her, but if I run across her, I'll probably talk to her."

"Just don't go out of your way, okay?"

"Caroline!" Jake laughed at her fears, both touched and irritated at the same time.

"Promise," she demanded, blue eyes gazing anxiously into his.

"What is this?"

"Call it leftover paranoia from that last year of high school. I was so in love with you, and all you thought about was Sherry Sterling!"

Her passion surprised him. She was incredibly intense, and it was so out of character that Jake could only stare. With a feeling of unreality, he lifted his hands in surrender. What did it matter, anyway? Sherry Sterling was a chapter from his past.

Ten-fifteen and Beachtime Coffee spilled over with people. Sherry felt positively guilty about hoarding one of the few tables all to herself, but she was powerless to move. Apathy had settled over her at the chore she'd been given. Why couldn't J.J. Beckett just be a bittersweet memory? That was where he belonged, between the pages of a faded photo album, occupying a tender, but minuscule, corner of her heart. He was her first love. That was all she wanted him to be!

Unfortunately, he was so much more.

Sherry drew a deep breath, inhaling the scents of coffee and cinnamon, hearing the amiable chatter around her. Closing her eyes she was hit by a memory: the first time she and J.J. had made love in the Beckett tree house.

It was the beginning of senior year. She'd worked at Bernie's during the summer and slowly, little by little, she'd drawn closer to J.J. whose reasons for dropping by after work grew thinner and thinner until he made no pretense at all that he was stopping in to see her.

This put Sherry into orbit. It was unbelievable. The word on the street was that J.J. Beckett and Sherry Sterling were an item—*and it was true!*

First day of school. The other girls glared at her in envy and disbelief. She could read it in their faces: What's *she* got that's so great? Sherry basked in the glory of it. She didn't dare tell them that apart from a few moments alone, when he'd either driven or walked her home—she'd had to get over her fear of him seeing her ramshackle house double-quick or lose out on being with him altogether—they hadn't shared much of anything except that one kiss.

That all changed after the first football game. It was a hot night and Sherry waited near the sweating cheerleaders for the game to end and for J.J. to be all hers. She still detested football. It was a brutal sport in a league with boxing, as far as she was concerned. But she kept those thoughts firmly to herself and after a fabulous game where J.J. threw seven completed passes to his receiver, Tim Delaney, she was ushered away from the screaming fans by Mr. Quarterback himself for a secluded drive up the beach and a make-out session that left her breathless.

"Just don't bite me again," he whispered after their first bout of frantic kissing.

Sherry struggled with the gearshift knob, which stubbornly inhibited how close they could get to each other. "I'll try to restrain myself," she murmured, thrilled by his low-throated chuckle.

"I've got to get a bench seat," was his response before his mouth was crushed against hers again and he twisted around so the gearshift was his problem.

Heaven. Pure heaven. That was what it was. Their trips to an isolated spot on the beach became more frequent. At first she tried to play it cool, of course. She wanted him to think she didn't care that much. It was safer that way. But in truth, her old attraction was revved up, full throttle. With every kind gesture and happy grin he rained on her, she lost herself a little more. Like an undertow sucking her beneath its dangerous swirl, she felt herself pulled down under the power of J.J. Beckett's personality. She told herself that he was fast; his reputation had been earned honestly. She still remembered how he'd kissed her the night he'd nearly frozen to death from hypothermia. That one kiss—the one she reviewed in her head almost nightly—had told her everything. She *knew* his advances weren't to be trusted.

But Sherry's heart was involved now, and her careful conscience was ignored. She and J.J. began engaging in some heavy petting and although she told herself not to be stupid, she *wanted* him.

Then one day in the girls' bathroom she overheard some disturbing news about J.J.'s feelings for her— news she didn't want to believe.

She was inside a stall, just getting ready to leave, when she heard Annie, a friend of Caroline's, talking with several other girls, among them one Sherry liked, Summer Stanton. It was a riveting conversation and Sherry couldn't help eavesdropping.

"You know what he wants from her," Annie was saying, heaving a huge sigh. "I mean, I love J.J. to death but he certainly moves through the women, y'know? This Sherry's doomed. She's too easy."

"You really think so?" one of the listeners asked eagerly. Everyone loved to think some other girl was a slut. It made them feel superior.

Sherry swallowed hard and waited.

"Well, she doesn't have a curfew. She's hanging around all the time. Her dad's a drunk and the mom's a basket case. She's clinging to J.J. for dear life, if you know what I mean. Personally, I feel sorry for her. He's going to use her and break her heart."

"Maybe he really likes her."

"Oh, he *does* like her," Annie agreed earnestly. "He likes her a lot. But it won't last. That's just J.J.'s way. As soon as they're won—" she snapped her fingers "—he's on to the next conquest. And he tries to remain friends with them, which is the worst 'cause it just gives them false hope. Take a lesson—never give your heart to J.J. Beckett. Remember Tina?"

Sherry leaned closer to the stall door, straining to hear. She knew all the J.J. Beckett stories but now that she was involved with him she wanted to hear them again, in case there was something she'd missed. Tina was another notch in J.J.'s belt—a notch that Sherry didn't plan to be.

Annie's voice lowered confidentially. "Tina tried to trap him. Actually told him she was pregnant!"

"Tramp!" one of the girls breathed.

"I know, I know. But J.J.'s mom took care of everything. Paid her off and shipped her back to California. I think she had an abortion."

"So, she *was* pregnant, then? It wasn't just a rumor?" This was from Summer whom Sherry knew to be cautious about unsubstantiated rumors. Thank God someone was!

"Well...it stands to reason, doesn't it?" Annie hedged. "Tina didn't leave school for nothing." The other girls murmured their agreement, and Annie added, "God, she stalked him like a psycho!"

"Why would she have an abortion, then?" Summer

asked. "Sounds like she'd want some connection to him. She'd probably keep the baby."

"That's just what I heard," Annie sniffed, annoyed. "Maybe she wasn't pregnant, but I think she was!"

There was a shuffling of feet and backpacks, and they left in a herd. After several minutes Sherry carefully let herself out of the stall. To her shock Summer was still there, lost in moody introspection as she stared at her own red-haired, freckled reflection. Sherry's eyes widened and met Summer's in the mirror.

"Oh, eavesdropping," Summer remarked without rancor. "I don't believe much of what Annie says. You shouldn't, either."

Embarrassed, Sherry shrugged. After a moment she added, "I don't really want to be the next notch, though."

"Yeah. You gotta be careful." Summer was pragmatic. Always. Sherry learned that fact quickly over the following months for, although she didn't know it at the time, she and Summer, along with Roxanne, were destined to become good friends—the first truly good friends Sherry had ever known.

But for the moment Sherry was cautious. "What would you do, if you were me?" she asked.

"About J.J.?"

Sherry nodded.

"Do you really like him a lot?"

"I don't know." *Yes.*

"Then you've gotta play hard to get. One thing I know about J.J. Beckett, one thing *everybody* knows about him—he doesn't want an easy conquest."

"So, what am I supposed to do? Right now we're just sorta hanging out together. He calls me up and we do something with a bunch of his friends."

"Never alone?" Summer arched one russet eyebrow. "Sometimes…"

Sherry didn't want to talk about that. It wasn't anybody's business but hers—and J.J.'s. Yet, she had questions. Questions about how far to go. Were other kids doing *it?* she wondered constantly. Should she?

Ever since their first kiss, Sherry had dreamed of something more. Passion, desire, aching need—just thinking about it made her blush. When she was kissing him she felt as if they were melded together. The only two people on earth. All that mattered.

Somewhere in the last few months they'd begun to trust each other. Gradually. She was J.J. Beckett's girl now, or so people liked to say—and she liked them to say it. And it wasn't all just making out, either. J.J. was opening up. After that first fateful kiss, when Sherry stopped zinging him with sarcastic remarks, J.J. had warmed up in a way she wouldn't have thought possible.

In time she believed he would tell her he loved her.

"You gotta be cool," was Summer's advice. "Careful. Hide your feelings a little."

"Hide them?"

"Oh, yeah. The more you show, the more he knows he's got you."

Sherry absorbed that news silently, knowing she would never be able to follow through. The impenetrable wall around her feelings had crumbled, disintegrated completely. She was so in love there was no hope of erecting a new wall now. When he looked at her, really looked at her, she could read his thoughts and knew he was thinking of their private moments together. No, she couldn't act like she didn't care.

"You've got it bad, don't ya?" Summer shook her

head. "Well, okay, then you need a ton of advice, and I mean a ton. Do you think he loves you?"

"What?" This was bold, intimate talk. Sherry hardly knew Summer.

"Don't be shy. Do you think he loves you?"

"I—I don't know."

"Tell me about a typical 'date' with Mr. All-American."

"Well, there really haven't been that many dates. He kinda comes over to the counter at Bernie's and talks to me. Then he hangs around and fiddles with the napkin dispenser and Parmesan cheese...and..."

Did this sound as stupid as she thought it did? Lord, she was an idiot!

"True love," Summer observed sardonically.

"We did go with Ryan and Kathy Pruitt to a movie one night," Sherry said defensively.

She didn't add that Ryan and Kathy had made out like crazy in the back seat to and from the movie, and Kathy had shot Sherry sharp, distrustful looks all evening. It had nearly ruined Sherry's time with J.J. She'd been forced to merely hold his hand in the front seat, too uncomfortable to even share a kiss with the two of them going at it. As soon as she and J.J. were alone, he made her promise they would never go out with them again. It was a promise Sherry could easily keep.

But since that time, things had heated up between them at an alarming rate—and Sherry had done nothing to stop it.

A dangerous, dangerous game. It was incredible how fast things changed. From their first few times together, when Sherry's pulse ran a few beats fast, to holding hands or feeling his arm thrown carelessly over her shoulders, to soft, stolen kisses, to a brush of his hand across her hair, ostensibly to pull it away from her face except that his hand lingered, sensuously stroking, before he seemed to recall himself—from those first times, things had progressed at lightning speed. Each time his gentle hands had explored a bit further, tenderly touching while "No" ran through her mind, left unsaid, until she decided that this, too, was okay.

So, where did it end?

"Have you made love?" Summer asked curiously.

"No!"

"Just asking."

"I don't think I should," Sherry said with a hard swallow.

"Not if you want to keep him," Summer agreed. "But sometimes it's hard to say no and mean it. It seems like it would be cut and dried, but it never is."

"You sound like you know what you're talking about."

Summer wrinkled her nose. "My advice is this: just don't get alone with him. He's a really attractive guy and things happen. Make him commit first—but that won't happen, 'cause J.J. Beckett doesn't commit to any girl. Go out with someone else. Keep a lock on your heart. Make him work to win you, and if he doesn't even try, you haven't lost anything because he didn't care in the first place."

"Whoa." Sherry's head reeled from Summer's clinical assessment.

"I've been through a few break-ups, okay?" Summer finally admitted. "They're not fun. This is your first guy, right? Pardon me if I sound blunt, but J.J. Beckett's a bad choice for a boyfriend. Especially a first one. He's too cute, too popular, and basically too used to having everything come easy."

"I'm not easy."

Summer gave her a look Sherry wasn't sure she liked. "Everyone knows you never have to go home. It's like it doesn't matter what you are—with that much freedom, you're every guy's dream."

"I'm *not* easy!" Sherry repeated.

Summer nodded, as if she'd heard it all before. Then she suddenly broke into a grin. "Guys are stupid, aren't they? They make all these judgments on us and think they can get away with anything. It's total crap!"

"Total crap," Sherry agreed. She smiled back. Summer was someone who spoke her language. She hadn't known there were girls at Oceantides High who could. "So...?" she asked.

Summer didn't hesitate. "Go out with another guy. Meet someone new. Toy with some jerk's emotions like they toy with ours. It's rotten, I know—" she spread her hands innocently "—but it's the only way I know to come out on top."

"I don't think I could be that mean."

"Just wait for it. Some guy'll come along who's got his own ideas about what you need and how he'll give it to you. That's the guy who deserves to be slam-dunked. But not at first. Let J.J. see that he's interested in you, then do it."

"Maybe that works for you—"

"It works for everybody. I'm telling you, if you shower J.J. with attention he'll lose interest like that." She snapped her fingers. "You gotta be smart."

Sherry went away from that conversation with two ideas beating at her brain: one, Summer was a friend worth pursuing, and two, holding on to J.J. would be next to impossible without some sort of manipulative stratagem. Although a part of her rejected the idea

straight out—it went completely against the grain!—
another part recognized the wisdom of her words. It was
as if some distant, primeval feminine piece of herself
that had known eons ago to use wiles and deception in
order to keep the upper hand in a male-dominated
world, suddenly sat up and grew ears. Yes, she needed
to play this game. Yes, she needed another attentive
male to play his particular role.

But who? How?

The answer dropped his lunch tray on her table with
a clatter. "Oops," he said, grinning like a stooge. Tim
Delaney wasn't bad looking, was a great athlete and
hailed from the wealthier side of Oceantides' tracks, but
he was a zero in the charm department and Sherry suspected there was a Vacant sign glowing somewhere inside his head. Still…

It was child's play—frightening, really—how little
she had to do to win Tim's attention: a small compli-
ment here, an attentive look there, an expression of admiration when Tim waxed on about how great he was
on the football field. Sherry found it so easy, in fact,
that she tried out her tactics on other members of the
male gender and soon she was surrounded by admirers
who stumbled over themselves for the merest sign of
her approval.

In the space of a few weeks her popularity quotient
rocketed to the heavens. Now, not only did the guys
talk about how great looking she was, they crowed
about how much she liked *them* and how Sherry
Sterling was halfway to being *their* girlfriend.

And J.J. Beckett glowered in silence while the
Oceantides High girls turned stony and bitter. Except
Summer and Summer's friend, Roxanne. They alone
understood what was going on because they thought in

larger terms. And they liked Sherry and were willing to open the door to friendship—the best by-product of all.

It was a magical fall, made better by J.J.'s change of attitude. Gone was the cocky boy who charmed with the ease of long practice. In his place was a young man unsure of himself, whose discomfiture around Sherry, and contained fury directed at her admirers, made him seem all the more desirable and finally, attainable, to her. It was sometime during those heady weeks that she realized she would make love to him. It was like an epiphany. He wanted her—he really wanted her—and she wanted him right back. How silly that they'd had to play this game to realize it, but better to play the game than never to understand the prize to be won.

Football season waxed on. J.J. spent all his extra time—which wasn't much—around Sherry. But she caught him driving by her house and although he'd quit stopping in to talk to her at Bernie's, on weekends he hung around outside in the pizza parlor's parking lot, talking with a bunch of his friends and hers.

Roxanne and Summer adopted Sherry and would separate themselves from the pack to come and update her. It was as if they were double agents delivering top-secret coded messages.

"Notice the way he looks out of the corner of his eye at you. He's watching, all right," Roxanne would mumble, her head bent over Bernie's menu as if she didn't already know every item by heart.

Summer sniffed. "Yeah, and he's not that good at it. He wants you to think he's talking to Kathy and Caroline, but they're just there for show."

"You think so?" Sherry asked, hoping it was true, needing to hear it again and again.

"Have I been wrong yet? God, I love it that you've got J.J. Beckett!"

"I don't have him," Sherry reminded Summer quickly.

"Oh, yeah? He's never been like this with anybody."

"We barely see one another anymore!"

"That's because the plan is working."

Roxanne snorted. "Besides, you can just tell he's into you by the way he acts."

"She's right. We've got a lot of body language going on." Summer shot a glance outside Bernie's glass doors to where the group was standing around. J.J. half turned to look, then pretended oblivion.

Roxanne and Summer both eyed Sherry with "I told you so" grins on their faces. Sherry smiled, pleased. They were right. It was working! Except before the plan she and J.J. had been closer. Now they'd taken ten steps backward. When would they make that giant leap forward?

"The guy is had," Summer assured her one night while Ryan, J.J. and Matt hung around joking with each other, shooting looks the girls' way.

"You really think so?" Sherry's gaze followed J.J.'s broad shoulders.

"Trust me. Have I been wrong yet?"

"No..."

But doubts remained, hanging just outside of reach. Even when J.J. plugged a quarter into Bernie's jukebox and The Four Seasons belted out, "Sherry, Sherry baby..." Sherry still couldn't believe he loved her like she loved him. She'd blown off Tim Delaney long ago and pretty much ignored all the rest of the guys' attentions, but J.J. had kept his distance and things weren't the same as they'd been at the beginning of school.

October melted into November and soon it was the end of football season. The senior boys' last game neared and Sherry and J.J. were still at the same stalemate. Oh, they started going out together again, but there was no more hand-holding, no more soft kisses and touches, no more passionate touching.

Because she wasn't naturally manipulative, Sherry suffered serious second thoughts about this plan to attract other male attention in an effort to make J.J. see how desirable she was. All she wanted was to be with J.J., and she was tired of pretending that she wanted to play the field. It was a dumb game with even dumber consequences.

She was through with it.

The day of the last regular-season game she debated what to do. There were posters and an assembly and cheerleaders jumping around. Everyone was in a frenzy because this one game would determine whether the team would make it to the play-offs.

Big whoop.

Sherry still believed football was a moronic sport made for Neanderthals. Except she couldn't quite shake the image of J.J. in his uniform—formfitting black pants, blue and gold jersey stretched over muscles and pads. Arm cocked back for a spinning pass. Even she wasn't immune to that!

And since she wanted to be with J.J. if that meant going to the game and rah-rah-rahing with the rest of the silly fans, so be it. She was tired of walking by and giving him a quick smile of interest only to flirt with some other guy. It wasn't her style. And as time passed, she determined it wasn't even necessary.

So she went to the game and cheered the team on and was slightly ashamed of herself for falling into the fever of it. Every completed pass between J.J. and Tim Delaney brought a scream of excitement from her throat. She was hoarse by the end of the game and was swept along with the crowd when they made a long line to welcome their conquering heroes.

J.J. was nearly crushed to death by bear hugs from his own linemen. They lifted him up and down and pounded on their chests and howled like wolves, heads thrown back in victory. J.J. just grinned, even when they doused his head with Gatorade and water.

Briefly, his eyes met Sherry's. Briefly, a flicker of understanding passed between them. A spark of acknowledgement. A promise. Confused but excited, Sherry waited on the track that surrounded the football field for all the congratulatory nonsense to end and for J.J. to come to her.

It was inevitable, she told herself later, once everything was said and done. Like two planets on a collision course, there was, in the end, nothing to do but let the explosion happen. It was their fate; written in the stars. So she waited for him and he eventually came.

His entourage came with him, a steady stream of fans and groupies and parents and teachers and administrators all wanting to tell J.J. how great he was. But J.J. quickly eluded them and suddenly they were alone. He must have read her mind because they talked very little. She climbed into the passenger seat of his car, let him drive to a secluded lane that abutted Beckett property, made no protest as he held her hand and led her through the back gate and along a private path that approached the Beckett tree house from the rear. Silently, she followed him up the ladder to a clean, cozy room complete with a huge canvas hammock stretched from a post on one side to a metal ring screwed into the opposite wall, next to a real, paned window. Thick, wool plaid blankets were stacked in a pile, and he grabbed one and spread it over the hammock.

Sherry's heart beat fast. She watched him light an oil hurricane lamp tucked onto a corner shelf and turn the wick low.

Shadows played on his face. He was all angles and serious intensity. He loomed over her, his palm caressing her face. She closed her eyes and a sigh escaped her lips. Finally, finally, the moment was here. The moment was right.

When he kissed her, there was passion heating beneath his searching lips and Sherry answered in kind. Looking back, she marveled at how quickly they'd fallen into a tangled heap on the softly swaying hammock. There'd been no laughter, just urgency. Urgent hands. Urgent mouths. Urgent bodies.

Their lovemaking had been quick and glorious, her brief moment of pain lost beneath the wonder of it all. She could still see the burnished light moving on his shoulders, the muscles working so smoothly they appeared to be oiled, the curve of his hip, the power of his thighs. She could feel his hardness, his hands exploring her anxiously, his body pumping rhythmically. His groans of ecstasy were burned into her memory. And the taste of him—goodness! His slightly salty flesh and sweet tongue were a delight she'd never again experienced.

Now, goose bumps broke out on her flesh at the memory. Lips trembling, she took another gulp of raspberry mocha, heat staining her cheeks. No wonder she never reflected. Not only was it painful, it was *embarrassing!* How long had it been since she'd really thought about J.J. like this? Had she ever?

Shaking her head in wonder, Sherry blinked rapidly, stunned to realize that she hadn't let herself think about J.J. Beckett, the maestro of lovemaking, since she'd run away from Oceantides. In all these years she'd never examined the reasons she and he had collided and crashed with the force of two freight trains. She'd focused on her pain, her anger, and her responsibility, but *not once* had she really thought through those passionate moments in J.J.'s strong arms.

"Holey moley," she muttered now, aware of her rapidly beating heart and uneven breathing. The man still had way too much power over her. And he didn't even know it!

If she were smart, she would remember that her introduction to lovemaking had merely been a setup by the master of feminine conquests. J.J. had clearly hung that hammock for one reason and one reason only. And if she were smarter yet, she would remember that she couldn't have been his first guest there. She knew the names of his other women, for Pete's sake. She'd known even then. But had she thought about that while J.J. pressed her willing flesh beneath his weight?

No. On that magical night her conscience slumbered and love blinded her. Blinded her and turned her deaf, as well. But not mute. Oh, no...she couldn't be that lucky! No. Instead, Sherry Sterling spent those hours whispering over and over again how much she loved him, aware that he wasn't repeating the pledge but unwilling to believe it was because he only wanted to score like he had all evening on the football field.

Rah, rah, rah.

Pinching the bridge of her nose, Sherry fought back a tide of resentment. Sure, it was his fault, but it was hers, too. He was a bastard but she'd been about as

NATALIE BISHOP   97

dumb as she could be. Summer had warned her; she'd
warned herself. But no, no, no. Her own swelled head
had gotten in her way! For a few weeks she'd actually
believed J.J. Beckett loved her. Mr. Man-About-Town
himself was in love with Sherry Sterling!

And then what happened—after that night of wonder,
love and passion? Then what happened? Why, J.J.
Beckett cooled right off, that was what he did. He said
adios and good riddance. And Sherry Sterling, silly little
fool that she was, begged him to take her back.

Humiliation. Lord, she could scarcely look on those
wretched days following their lovemaking any more
than she could remember the physical act itself.
Wounded, sick at heart, full of self-loathing and naked
pain, she spun headlong into Tim Delaney's waiting
arms.

And J.J. punched Tim out. After school. The night of
the first play-off game. Tim punched back and they
were both ejected from the team, effectively ending
Oceantides High's chances of winning. The result was
a slaughter while rain poured down on the depressed
Oceantides fans who watched their broken team strug-
gle miserably and futiley against damning odds.

Everyone blamed Sherry. She blamed herself. Except
some part of her rejoiced. J.J. must love her, mustn't
he? she reasoned. He'd broken Tim's nose for her. He'd
gotten himself thrown off the team for her. That meant
something, didn't it? Well, didn't it?

Yeah. It meant that J.J. wouldn't speak to her and it
was only Tim who still wanted to see her. Not J.J. Never
J.J. And although Sherry ignored Tim and did her best
to show J.J. that she still loved him—to the point of
employing Summer and Roxanne to try and plead her
case, to the point of trying to plead her case with Ryan

and Matt herself—she only succeeded in driving him further away. She drove him to Caroline. To his own kind. To other people who lived "on the water" and away from riffraff like Sherry Sterling.

And that was the way the rest of the year went— except for Valentine's Day, which she wasn't going to think about because it didn't matter anymore and it was too depressing anyway—until one night in late May when the rhododendrons were in bloom in a rainbow of pink and bloodred and lavender. The air was warm and smelled of romance and J.J., for reasons she never fully understood, was waiting for her when she got off work at Bernie's.

They stared at each other nakedly and something broke wide open. When he dragged her into his arms and kissed her through her tears it was Sherry whose heart and body betrayed her desire to rekindle their passion.

There was only one place on each of their minds: the tree house.

In the heat of their lovemaking, bathed by the warm light of the oil lamp, wrapped in each other's embrace, Sherry forgot all her warnings to herself and let her heart speak.

"I love you," she moaned. "Don't leave me again."

"Sherry…" he muttered, kissing her fervently. "What are you doing to me?"

"Don't say anything. Please, don't say anything.…"

They made love as if they were starving for each other—his body pressed urgently to hers, her own writhing with need, loneliness and love. His mouth was hot with possession and her limbs melted beneath him.

She should have demanded an answering vow of love and commitment. She should have been more careful.

She should not have mistaken the ragged desire in his voice for something more.

Now, years later, Sherry drew a shuddering breath and pushed her empty cup aside. She covered her face with her hands, then raked her fingers through her hair, tugging on the ends to feel the pain, as if she needed to be reminded. Her mouth twisted in irony. How strange that it was she who'd ended up leaving him.

Because of that last night together.

The night their daughter Mandy was conceived.

Chapter Five

"Would you like anything else?"

The waitress gazed at Sherry and smiled, her eyebrows lifting in silent query.

"No, thanks. I'm fine."

Wondering if that was Beachtime Coffee's polite way of saying "Hit the road, we need the table," Sherry made a show of picking up her purse and getting ready to leave. Then she realized there were more tables empty now, and with a weariness born of anxiety, she sank back down.

Mandy, Mandy, Mandy...

Here it was. The one issue she'd never resolved. Mandy. Her daughter. Hers and J.J.'s. The child she'd given up for adoption and who now wanted to know *both* her parents.

Feeling older than she should, Sherry reached into her purse and pulled out the photograph she'd received eight days earlier. The girl in the picture wore a green army jacket that hung to her knees, her hair was plaited in two dark brown braids, her blue eyes stared straight ahead, unforgiving and painfully familiar. She'd shifted her weight to one hip and at thirteen she was the epitome of disillusioned youth.

She reminded Sherry so much of J.J. Beckett her throat hurt. Especially now, when his attitude toward her was so angry and distant. Amanda Craig. *Mandy.* Their daughter. The cool little rebel who'd dropped into Sherry's life unexpectedly, having used a private investigator to search her out, and then had baldly demanded that she get to meet her father.

Apocalypse. The end of the world. Sherry's shock, joy and heart-stopping thrill at meeting her own child were smashed by Mandy's first cold words.

"So, you're her," she'd said in a peculiarly flat voice, as if she'd scrubbed all emotion from it—which she probably had. "You're prettier than I expected. Younger, too." When Sherry saw her standing beneath a flooding rain on her front porch, a black knit hat covering the top of her head, her braids dripping water, her mouth flat and unhappy, Sherry's first thought was, Whose miserable child is this? Her next: Holy God, she's *J.J.'s!*

"What…what…" Sherry stammered.

"Bet you hoped you'd never see me, huh?" A sardonic flick of a pair of unusually sensual lips. Blankly, Sherry recognized a trait of her own. *Her child, too!*

"Don't worry, I won't stay long. I just wanted to meet you face-to-face."

Distracted and shocked, Sherry had stared in disbelief, too poleaxed to do more than gape in wonder at the daughter she'd borne. Mandy was a far cry from the sweet little bundle of love Sherry had envisioned all these years, but she was still so incredibly beautiful. When Sherry's phone began to ring persistently, she didn't even hear it.

But Mandy did. "That's probably my mom and dad," she announced blithely. "Tom and Gina Craig. I'm Mandy, by the way. And you're Sherry, aren't you?" As Sherry's knees trembled wildly, Mandy added pragmatically, "Better get the phone. They don't know where I am."

And that was Sherry's introduction to her and J.J.'s love child.

Now, setting down the photograph and smoothing it with slightly unsteady fingers, Sherry reminded herself that she was here on a mission. Mandy had crashed into her life, and her well-meaning adoptive parents, the Craigs, seemed to be almost as undone about it as Sherry. Clearly they'd fought their daughter's demands to meet her birth mother; just as clearly, they'd lost the battle. Later, when they came to Sherry's apartment, they eyed her with distrust and fear and a bit of empathy because Mandy was a handful, to say the least.

But before their arrival Mandy had already made an indelible impression on her mother. She'd stepped into Sherry's life as if it were her right, which in a way, it was. But there was no cautiousness in Mandy, no need to tentatively pick her way through the minefield of emotions her sudden appearance had wrought on both the Craigs and Sherry. She simply didn't give a damn.

A bit of Patrice Beckett there, too, Sherry thought with faint humor.

"You had to give me up because you were too young and he wouldn't marry you," Mandy said matter-of-factly as she entered Sherry's apartment and dropped her duffel bag on the floor. "Isn't that right?"

"I...was too young," Sherry had answered in a voice so breathy she couldn't recognize it as her own. Her head swam. *He wouldn't marry you.* That was true, too.

"It's okay." Mandy looked around Sherry's apartment, assessing. Sherry knew it wasn't "okay," but what was there, really, to say? Besides, her underpinnings had been knocked from beneath her and she couldn't think.

"Do you have a picture of him?"

"Of...your father?" Sherry choked out.

"Yeah."

"I don't think so...."

Mandy's blue eyes stared. "Not one picture?"

Her youth almost broke Sherry's heart. Beneath all the trappings was a small girl who wanted to believe that Sherry and J.J.'s romance was a once-in-a-lifetime thing, something to be treasured and remembered and haunted by. Well, Sherry was certainly haunted, but not in the way Mandy hoped.

"I...have a yearbook," Sherry had offered, wondering frantically where she'd put it. She hadn't graduated with her class but she'd already paid the fees at the beginning of her senior year and her mother, in a rare moment of independence, had gone down to Oceantides High, picked it up and shipped it to Sherry.

Sherry had received the book with mixed emotions, running her fingers over the gilt-edged blue cover, afraid to turn the first page. She'd managed eventually to peruse it from cover to cover, but then she'd buried the book under boxes and boxes, stuffed away in some cobweb-gathering corner because she couldn't bear all those pictures of J.J. Beckett.

"Could I see?" Mandy asked when Sherry remained rooted to the spot.

For the next hour and a half Sherry dug around but to no avail. Her nerves were shot and with Mandy hovering around, waiting expectantly, her concentration was broken so badly she wanted to huddle into a corner and cry. The Craigs arrived and the situation intensified, growing more uncomfortable.

"I'll keep looking," Sherry told Mandy hoarsely. "How long will you be in Seattle?"

"Just 'til tomorrow," Tom Craig said quickly.

Gina Craig added, "We're sorry we didn't call and warn you. The investigator thought maybe we should, but Mandy... Well, she was anxious."

Sherry read that to mean Mandy had taken matters into her own hands before her adoptive parents could intervene. Sherry smiled wanly. She shook their hands and wished she knew what to say. But words escaped her.

After that they all stood outside Sherry's apartment for a while, no one knowing what to do. Small talk prevailed. Sherry explained that she was part owner of Dee's Seattle Deli and Mandy bluntly announced she would come visit her the next day before she left. The Craigs wrung their hands and didn't argue. Sherry could only nod, exhausted. She watched them drive away in their white rental car, then headed straight for the liquor cabinet, which consisted of several airplane-size bottles of vodka, mixed herself a tasty concoction of vodka and water and drained it so fast it brought tears to her eyes.

It didn't help.

The next day she appeared at work looking gray and ill. Dee, who was deep into creating one of her delicious soups of the day, looked up from deftly chopping onions and gasped in alarm. "My God, girl! What happened to you?"

"It's a long story." One Sherry had never told.

Dee, who was five foot seven and whose chest looked large enough to balance a tray, came over and hugged and kissed Sherry on the cheek. She then went back to her chopping while Sherry stood in the center of the tiny deli kitchen and cried, silent tears rolling unchecked down her cheeks to splash on the red tile floor.

She told Dee the story.

Dee, herself, was a single mom raising a fourteen-year-old son, Jonathan, and she was very verbal about what a pain in the neck Jonathan could be, although she loved the "little devil" dearly. Upon hearing that Sherry possessed a daughter the same age, she gazed at her friend in pure sympathy. "I know you're reeling," she said. "But you gotta roll with the punches. That's what parenting is, when they're this age."

"But I'm not really a parent."

"Honey, she came to you. You're a parent now. It's outta the closet and in your face. Don't think it isn't."

Sherry shuddered from head to toe. "I always dreamed of this. I've thought about her every day, ten times a day. I've wanted her so much. But now…"

"You're in shock. It's natural. And she's not a little girl in pink ribbons, is she?"

"No." Sherry half laughed, brushing her tears aside.

"So, what are you going to do?"

"I don't know! She's coming by the deli today, and I'm so torn. I want to see her. God, you don't know how much! But she scares me. I feel so—inadequate."

"Ah, honey."

Dee enfolded Sherry in her arms again, patting her on the back. With an effort Sherry pulled herself together and prepared for her next meeting with Mandy, but as soon as her daughter breezed through the door, panic seized her again. If possible, Mandy seemed more direct, and yes, more antagonistic, than she had been the day before.

"Did you find that picture?" Mandy demanded before she even reached the front counter.

On the other side of the barrier Sherry curled her fingers over the tile edge, hanging on for support. She shook her head. "I'm still looking."

"You don't have it, do you," she stated flatly.

"I just don't know where it is."

"Is that true?" Mandy's blue eyes searched Sherry's so thoroughly, Sherry felt her very soul was explored. "You didn't really want any reminders, did you?" she added with terrible adult understanding.

"It wasn't the best time of my life," Sherry admitted in a small voice.

Liar! It was the very best time!

"I want to meet him," Mandy announced, shattering what was left of Sherry's precarious world.

"So, you're Mandy," Dee interjected at that moment, placing a hand on one of Sherry's trembling arms. "Your mom told me about you. You live in California? Whereabouts?"

"Oakland."

"I have a sister who lives in Oakland. Do you like it?"

"Yeah," Mandy said, obviously bored.

"My son and I are going to San Francisco on vacation this year. Maybe in a month or two. I really love the area...." Dee rolled on but the conversation was terribly one-sided. It seemed to swirl over Sherry's head like dark, roiling clouds, full of doom. She was powerless to do anything but stand there and let it happen. Meet J.J.? My God! He didn't know. He *didn't know*.

Eventually Mandy's monosyllabic responses to Dee's well-intentioned probing halted the conversation altogether. Mandy gazed at Sherry, waiting. Sherry had neither the heart nor the courage to tell her that her father did not know she existed. It wasn't fair to Mandy, and it wasn't fair to J.J. But at the time, Sherry had been too young and too scared to do anything but bend to Patrice Beckett's wishes.

Except she hadn't let J.J.'s mother talk her into an abortion.

"I've got to talk to him first," Sherry heard herself say from a long, long distance away. She felt as if she were in a tunnel and Mandy stood at the far end. "I'll tell him you want to see him, and I'll let him contact you."

Mandy pitched a fit. She wasn't used to being thwarted. She wanted to know who her father was and where he lived, and she wanted Sherry to tell her right now! But there was no way to tell her, or Sherry might have been tempted. She let Mandy spend her adolescent rage and was almost glad that she still had this little bit of power and control left. She couldn't believe it when she'd finally persuaded Mandy to wait. Mandy was the best and worst of her and J.J.; that was clear. And Sherry needed all her wits to keep this emotional ember from exploding like a volcano.

So, here she was in Oceantides, her first meeting with J.J. a complete disaster. She'd run like a frightened bunny and had even let Patrice's frigid fury upset her a little. Just a little. The Beckett name and power didn't affect her nearly as much now as it had when she was a teenager.

But J.J. affected her. There was no denying that.

The Craigs sent Sherry a picture of Mandy within the week. With a thank-you prayer to the gods of good fortune, Sherry recognized how lucky she was that Mandy had been delivered to such caring, fair people. Although reluctant, at first, they were embracing this new relationship with their daughter's birth mother, and for that Sherry would be ever-thankful.

But J.J....?

Like the older man seated several tables ahead of her, Sherry caught herself staring at the clock. Eleven o'clock. The morning was nearly gone. It was time to get a move on. Time to face J.J. with the truth.

As Sherry rose from the table, the preppy couple stood at the same time. Sherry gasped in recognition. It was Roxanne and J.J's old buddy, Matt Hudson!

As if her shocked stare penetrated their own cocoon of self-interest, they both looked over at her as one. Roxanne's face broke into a delighted grin. "Sherry!"

Sherry lifted a hand. "Rox."

Matt merely gave her a funny smile, as if he didn't know what to feel or how to act.

"What are you doing here? Oh, my gosh, it's been so long! Are you just visiting or back to stay?"

"Visiting," Sherry assured her.

"Oh, wow." Roxanne pressed her hands to her cheeks, eyes bright with delight. "Oh, this is great. You know Summer lives in Los Angeles now. Married. Two kids. An English sheepdog. Can you believe it? And, and, you know Matt, of course. We're getting married on Valentine's Day! You've got to come!"

Valentine's Day. Mandy's birthday.

Sherry was speechless for a dozen reasons. Roxanne sank down beside Sherry and tossed her feet on an adjoining chair. Her dark hair had developed streaks of gray although she was barely over thirty, but it only made her gypsylike looks seem even more exotic.

"How *are* you?" she demanded seriously. "Man, when you left school before the end of senior year we were all so worried. And then no word! We were afraid that…"

Sherry swallowed. *Afraid that I might be pregnant?*

Roxanne, who had never been coy with her thoughts, proved to have changed little in the intervening years. "We were afraid your dad was somehow responsible." She paused. "You know. Because of his drinking."

Sherry didn't know whether to laugh or cry. So her sudden disappearance had been given a different cause. Was that better? She didn't know, especially since the truth of her indiscretion was soon to be public knowledge.

"Hey, Rox, we gotta get going," Matt murmured. He looked as uncomfortable as he undoubtedly felt.

Roxanne frowned. "I thought we were meeting here. He's the one who's late."

"He?" Sherry asked automatically.

"Jake. I mean, J.J. Beckett to you, I guess. He's supposed to show up so we can nail him on his duties as best man. The guy's a workaholic. No fun. Hard to believe, isn't it? He's turned into a real pain in the butt. I think it's Caroline's influence."

"Roxanne." Matt looked pained.

"You think so, too," she reminded him, scooting out another chair with one foot. He took it reluctantly. Sherry began to wish fervently that she hadn't run into them, no matter how glad she was to find a friend. Those memories of her and J.J. weren't dead for Matt, either, apparently, although Roxanne seemed to be having no problem with the past.

"They dated forever," Roxanne revealed. "He finally asked her to marry him and now the engagement's lasted eons. Just to kinda kick him in the butt I suggested they make it a double wedding. Hey, Valentine's Day's romantic, right? Caroline went for the idea and even though she's not my favorite person, she's tolerable." Roxanne sniffed. "I wouldn't say the same of Jake!"

"Jake's okay," Matt interjected.

"He got old before his time."

Old? His image was indelibly etched on Sherry's mind, and last night's encounter hadn't changed it. In fact, her impression was how little he'd changed. She could still feel his fingers on her arm.

"He ducked the whole issue. Too busy. Not the right time. Blah, blah, blah. I don't think he really loves her."

"Roxanne!" Matt rolled his eyes.

"Hey." She lifted her hands, then dropped them in her lap. Conversation over.

For Sherry, though, the knowledge that J.J. might appear at any moment galvanized her into action. She didn't want to confront him here, among reminders of the past. "I've got a bunch of stuff to do while I'm here, so I'd better get doing it."

"Where're you staying?" Sherry named the motel, and Roxanne said, "Call me." She scratched out her number on a paper napkin. "I want to catch up."

"I'll do it," Sherry promised.

"Don't lie to me." Her old friend grinned.

"I'll *do* it."

"Come to the wedding," Roxanne urged. "It's only a couple of weeks away."

"If I'm still in town," she demurred.

"Oh, Sherry, make a point. Please. I want you to come. Summer's going to be there!"

"I... I'll try."

Sherry's back was to the door while she slung her purse over her shoulder. A waft of cool air silently announced another visitor. Scared to look, she nevertheless darted a glance behind her but there was no need. *J.J.,* she thought with a sinking heart, her gaze clashing with his.

"Speak of the devil," Roxanne declared in mock anger. "You're late. And you almost missed an old friend. You remember Sherry Sterling, don't you, Jake?"

It had been a bitch of a morning after Caroline's departure. Tenants from his rental properties called one after the other, as if they'd somehow divined his generous treatment of Jill Delaney and wanted the same. Then the chef at the Beckett restaurant, Crawfish Delish, quit because of a fight he'd had with one of the busboys, a local tough who'd been hired by the manager in a weak moment and who'd let it be known that all chefs were gay and stupid. The manager fired him but not before Gerald, who was really little more than a glorified cook but who could make magic with seafood, stalked out of the restaurant and into his Renault and headed straight for the Tank House, a local watering hole. Gerald was always looking for an excuse to drink, and Jake had gone to the Tank House to try and reason with him. Gerald could not only drink, he could drink fast, and Jake ended up driving him home to the Windsurf, another Beckett apartment building, so he could sleep it off. Jake had then returned to Crawfish Delish and told the beleaguered assistant cook the bad news: lunch and dinner were his.

Thank God it wasn't high season.

Jake had then been tempted to take up residence on Gerald's stool at the Tank House. Half the time he felt like a baby-sitter; the other half, a psychologist. Neither occupation was where he'd ever hoped to be.

What's best for you...

And then he remembered that he had to meet Roxanne and Matt at Beachtime Coffee and talk wedding.

It had about ruined his day.

But now, here, face-to-face with Sherry, he realized the worst of the day had yet to happen. His promise to Caroline hung over his head, but it wasn't foremost on his mind. No, what he was feeling now was frustration and annoyance and a certain amount of flat-out anger. What the hell was she doing here, anyway? She'd run out of town nearly fourteen years ago, and he didn't feel one iota of pleasure that she'd returned.

Oh, sure, she still looked great. Better, in fact, in some ways. Truth to tell, his first impression was how full and soft her lips seemed, how thick her lashes, how deep the bluish-violet of her irises appeared and how those eyes swam with secrets. Her hair was lustrous, shoulder-length and shining with good health. Her skin as smooth as satin, pale and nearly poreless—just like in high school. Only the finest of lines gave away her age, and an overall maturity—and sadness?—that seemed to have infected her personality.

Still, passion simmered beneath her cool expression. He could feel it like a pulse. And she'd certainly been sharp and prickly with him last night. That was the Sherry he remembered. The one with the wicked tongue.

Except she'd lost that particular trait over the time they'd dated. He couldn't recall getting the rough side of her tongue at all, in fact, until that last fight they'd had the night before she'd left town. Amazing. He could remember every word and expression from that argument and still he didn't understand.

One year of his life he'd given to her. Oh, not as a gift, really; as part of his youth that he couldn't help himself from granting. He hadn't loved her, but he'd certainly felt passionate about her. She'd consumed him for that year. Had been a part of his days and nights. As important to him as air and water.

Yet, he couldn't let her know. He'd been smart enough to recognize those pitfalls without actually tripping into them. Giving her that much power would have been like ripping out his soul and handing it over to a force as mercurial and inconstant as the wind. Sherry Sterling had whispered words of love and need and he'd responded with silence and a certain amount of skepticism. Other girls had sworn their love, but love was sometimes a cover-up for a person's own hidden agenda. People fell in and out of love all the time. It was an overused four-letter word.

He'd never, never been in love.

So, why was his heart thundering like a racehorse? Why did he feel so intensely conscious of the heat of the room and the noises of laughter and conversation, the smell of Sherry's perfume, sweet as sugar—or was that just another odor of the coffeehouse?

He had the strangest desire to reach out and grab her by the hair and haul her to him, so that he could stare into the deepest recesses of her eyes and guess her secrets. *I want to know,* he thought desperately. *Why? Why? Why did you leave?*

Instead, he heard his own voice say coldly, "I remember Sherry. She's hard to forget."

The blush that raced across her pale cheeks surprised him. He hadn't expected her to be sensitive. She'd reached epic proportions as an ogre in his mind, he realized.

"It's good to see you, too, J.J.," she answered with an identical coolness, and he wondered if she'd used his initials deliberately, as a tiny weapon.

You're cynical as hell, he told himself angrily.

Roxanne leaped into the moment. "Oh, my gosh, maybe it isn't *Sterling* anymore! Sherry, I forgot to ask. Are you married? Holy cow, you probably hitched up with a doctor and have six children and two vacation homes and an English sheepdog yourself!"

Jake's stomach clenched. It took every ounce of control he possessed not to react, but he kept his gaze trained on her lovely face and witnessed the shadow of emotion that crossed her features. *No husband.* But something, he thought.

"Well?" Roxanne asked.

"Not married." Her voice was tight.

"How about children?"

She actually flinched and then Matt moaned, "Rox!" in utter embarrassment as he often did. Jake wondered how they would ever stay married; their personalities were exact opposites.

"What?" Roxanne demanded. "She could have children from a previous marriage, couldn't she?" She turned to Sherry. "Right?"

"No previous marriage, either," Sherry muttered, clutching her purse. She drew a shaky breath and said, "I'd better get going. I've got a lot to do."

With that she scurried for the door, glancing back,

her lips parting as if she had something more to say.
Jake realized she was looking at him, and he lifted his
brows, aware she was struggling.

"What?" he asked.

"I..."

Incredulously, he thought she was going to say, *I love
you.* He could practically reach down her throat and
grab out the words. Instead she closed her mouth and
regarded him with an expression of anguish and fury.

What the hell is going on? he wondered.

Sherry could do nothing but stare. Words wouldn't
pass her lips, no matter how hard she tried. She couldn't
tell him right here, right now. Maybe she couldn't tell
him at all!

Damn him, she thought half-hysterically. He looked
as virile and beautiful as she remembered from the
past—and as tough and unforgiving, she knew from last
night's encounter. In that split second when his gray
eyes met hers, Sherry recognized the turmoil in her
breast for what it was: love. A love that would not die
no matter how impossible and terrible it made her life.
A love that defied reason and common sense. A love
she wished she could kill, for it had brought her nothing
but heartache and misery.

She pulled her gaze from his. He was too powerful.
Too male. She could smell his musky cologne and when
he moved, his black leather jacket hugged his frame
appealingly. She couldn't think. Her chest felt too tight
inside her skin.

How about children? Roxanne had asked.

Just one... Just J.J.'s...

"Sherry, for Pete's sake, you can't leave yet." Roxanne waved at her to sit back down. "We don't know

anything about you. No children, no husband... Is there a 'significant other'?''

''Rox!'' Matt clearly was forever embarrassed by his future wife, but there was an element of love in the way he looked at her, too. Enough love to let him see the humor of her ways, Sherry realized. What would it be like to have that kind of relationship? That kind of trust?

''I'm single and intend to remain that way,'' Sherry told her. ''I'm glad for you and Matt. I'll try to make the wedding, but really, I've got to go.''

J.J. seemed impervious to the conversation. His brows were drawn together, his jaw tense. Sherry wondered what he was thinking. He'd always been so incredibly insightful except in one area—her.

''I saw Ryan Delmato last night,'' she added as she pushed open the door.

''At Bernie's?'' Roxanne asked, interested.

Sherry nodded.

''Looks the same, doesn't it? Remember when we used to all hang out there? Hard to believe so much time has passed. Grab a seat, Jake,'' she finished, waving him to another unoccupied wooden chair.

''I can't stay. I just dropped by because I knew you were waiting for me.'' The timbre of his voice did strange things to Sherry's equilibrium. She couldn't believe herself! So many years and yet she still reacted like a lovesick adolescent! It was unreal and she was furious with herself.

''Are you nuts? You've *got* to stay. This is my wedding, for Pete's sake!''

''I'll get things straight with Jake,'' Matt interrupted. ''Later,'' he said to his friend.

Sherry practically bolted from the coffee shop, unwilling to have J.J. so close on her heels. This was not the time. She wasn't ready.

On the street, rain fell in an unrelenting January drizzle, swept sideways by sudden rushes of wind off the ocean. Sherry hesitated a moment, angry with herself. The hell it wasn't the time! What was she waiting for? A voice from heaven dictating her path? Here was a golden opportunity—away from Patrice Beckett, no less—and once again, all she could do was run.

Closing her eyes, she willed up courage from some deep well inside her soul. She'd come to tell him about Mandy. She had no choice. For her daughter—and for herself, she realized dimly—she needed this secret revealed. But a cowardly part of her kept saying, Don't rush. It's only the first day. You've got time. Give yourself an opportunity to adjust. You've had a lot of shocks. Be kind to yourself.

Suddenly he was just behind her right shoulder. Sherry faced the parking lot, afraid to look at him. Belatedly, she realized she was standing right next to his black Jeep. He had to think she was waiting for him.

"So, why did you stop by the house last night?" he asked, his breath tickling the nape of her neck.

He'd thought that one over, she realized. She remembered that about him, too; his intensely analytical mind. He dissected everything, searching for its true meaning. She'd been afraid he would discern the secret of her pregnancy before she got away from him. Patrice had.

She shrugged. "Just reacquainting myself with old friends."

"Try again," he muttered.

She was afraid to move. He was so close. Close enough to lean back and touch. "How like you to distrust me," she answered with forced bitterness. "I guess it's true what they say—some things never change."

"I never distrusted you."

"Oh, yes, you did."

"You mean, after you slept with Tim Delaney?"

"I didn't sleep with him, and you know it!"

"I only know what you told me. And damn near everything out of your mouth was a lie."

He said it without heat. Matter-of-factly. As if it were proved truth and she should agree with him completely.

Sherry was flabbergasted. Steeling herself, she twisted half-around, meeting those deep gray eyes and hostile face with a fury she hadn't known she possessed. They studied each other like the angry foes they were.

"How many years has it been, J.J.?" she demanded. "Over a decade. Closing in on fifteen. And the first thing that we have to talk about is whether I slept with Tim Delaney when I was a senior in *high school?*"

He had the grace to look slightly ashamed, but it didn't alter the belligerent slant of his jaw, or his battle-tense stance.

"I didn't lie," she told him flatly.

"You lied about Caroline."

A barb of truth hit home. She hadn't actually lied about Caroline Newsmith, but she'd definitely done her part to let others know Caroline wasn't the sweet thing everyone thought. "I didn't like her much," Sherry admitted. "She didn't like me, either. We were always in a cold war over you."

That stopped him. His lips parted, as if he were about to refute her, but how could he? She and Caroline had been J.J. Beckett's chosen women. Only Caroline had been the blond angel and Sherry the dark-haired seductress. Or at least that was how Caroline told the story, and in the end, Caroline's was the only tale to tell.

"Well, it doesn't matter now," he said, attempting to end the conversation. But now, perversely, Sherry wanted to keep going.

"Oh, I don't know. There're a lot of unresolved things in our past, don't you think?"

"Just high-school stuff."

Sherry managed a taut smile. Her high-school experience had set the stage for the last unhappy fourteen years. She'd been acting by rote, just going through the motions. The events of her youth had stripped the rest of her life of color and meaning.

Just high-school stuff, indeed.

"I'm sure you heard Caroline and I are engaged," he said, thrusting his hands into the pockets of his jacket. "It took us long enough."

"Roxanne told me." She could feel a lead weight in her stomach.

He nodded.

"But you didn't want to get married Valentine's Day."

"Valentine's Day," he repeated, staring over her head to some distant point she couldn't see. Her heart pounded heavily. She knew he was thinking of that last Valentine's Day in their senior year, when she'd flirted so dismally with Tim, hoping to hold on to the last remnant of J.J.'s affection. She'd loved him so desperately but he hadn't cared for her the same way. And everything had backfired.

"You're really a slut," Annie had whispered out of the side of her mouth, mean and hard, as Sherry walked out of school one disastrous afternoon. "Everyone knows you're doing it with Tim just to get J.J. back.

Well, J.J. hates you. He had you and now Tim has, too!''

''It's not true.'' Sherry's voice had been a weak breath.

Annie's stare had raked Sherry's pale, miserable face. ''Everyone knows.''

Sarcasm was Sherry's armor but that time it had failed her. She'd had no defense. Stumbling down the front steps of the school, she'd fought back gasps of anguish. When Tim had called her that night to ask her to dinner the following week on Valentine's Day, she'd huddled beneath her covers and cried herself to sleep.

What happened? she'd asked herself over and over again in the weeks following their night in the tree house. She'd given herself to J.J. because she loved him and almost as soon as the deed was done, his ardor had cooled. Was he really that shallow and uncaring? She wouldn't believe it. But regardless, she knew she'd made a terrible mistake. She had no desire or intention of making the same one with Tim. She still loved J.J. so much.

So she'd limped through until Valentine's Day, accepting Tim's invitation. But as soon as she and Tim arrived at one of Oceantides' nicer restaurants, lo and behold, J.J. and Caroline were two tables over. Because she had to, Sherry brightened, acting as if she were having the time of her life, but her performance was lost on J.J. He paid no attention. All he could see was Caroline.

Or so Sherry had thought.

Later that night, sunk in misery, she'd finally found the courage to call up J.J. To her surprise he was home. She'd expected him to still be out with Caroline, his other half, but he'd already returned and was cautiously willing to talk to her. She asked if they could see each other and he drove to her home, picked her up and they went to Bernie's Pizza Parlor and ate a late-night heart-shaped pizza together.

It wasn't exactly a reunion but it was a coming-together that gave Sherry hope. He hadn't liked seeing her with Tim; he didn't say the words but his feelings were clear.

When he dropped her home that night she turned her face toward his, heart thumping hard, praying that he would kiss her. But he didn't so much as look her way. She could still remember his harsh profile and clenched hands around the wheel. Whatever he might feel, he refused to succumb, and Sherry left more depressed than ever. If she should have learned anything from that night, it was that J.J. Beckett didn't care about her.

But her miserable, loyal heart refused to see it.

Now, with his stern visage directly in front of her and so much of the past hanging between them, she said the words she should have uttered long ago. "I was poor white trash to you, so you believed every ugly rumor about me. I loved you, and you used me. If I'd been Caroline Newsmith, you might have loved me back, but who could love someone as socially worthless as Sherry Sterling? Certainly not a Beckett."

J.J.'s eyes were riveted on her mouth, as if he couldn't believe the words issuing from her lips. When he glanced up again, his eyes simmered with unnamed emotions. "It was a lot more complicated than that," he stated flatly.

"At least you don't deny it," Sherry said, surprised. "I'm not sure how to feel about that."

"I knew we weren't right for each other for a lot of reasons I couldn't have explained back then. I don't think I can explain it now, either. I know I don't want to,'' he added as an afterthought.

"You sound just like a Beckett," Sherry said. "How sad."

His gaze found her mouth again and his own lips curved, caught somewhere between a grimace and a smile. "I am a Beckett." He drew a long breath, closing his eyes for a moment as if he were gathering strength. It was a curiously vulnerable gesture, and Sherry, reacting on pure emotion, actually reached forward to touch him, as if contact would assure her that he would handle the information about Mandy like a mature adult and father.

But he expelled his breath harshly, shooting words from his mouth like bullets. Mean words. Sherry dropped her hand before he could open his eyes and view her with contempt. "So, is this why you came?" he demanded. "To say all these little hurtful things and hope it helps? Because it won't. It's too late for a postmortem on a high-school love affair. It just makes it seem all the more meaningless."

"And I thought I was the cynical one!" Sherry gasped, amazed.

"You aren't cynical. That was just part of your game."

"Game?"

"That whole thing you played out our senior year." He shook his head. "Sarcasm, and a quick fling, then flirting with the whole damn team, then back after me.... Then, right before graduation—gone." He snapped his fingers.

"I had my reasons."

"Did you think I'd charge after you like some lovesick knight in shining armor?"

"No! That wasn't why I left!"

"Oh, yeah? Three weeks 'til the end of school and you just decided to chuck it all in."

"I...couldn't stay," she objected.

"Why?"

"Because of you."

"Because of me," he repeated flatly.

"Because I loved you, and you didn't feel the same way."

"High-school love isn't the same as real love," he argued.

"Oh? Who says?" Sherry demanded.

"You left school because you loved me? Is that what you're trying to say?"

"I left because you *didn't* love me. And I needed you to love me." She bit into her bottom lip. "I needed to know that what we shared had meant something to you."

"It meant something to me."

"That's not what I mean!" Frustration nearly ate her up alive. Did he have to be so incredibly dense? "I mean, I wanted—*needed*—to think I was more than just another notch in your belt. And you couldn't give me that."

"This is just like that last fight we had," he said suddenly, frowning.

It was, Sherry realized at almost the same moment. Their last fight had been just the same—an attempt to clear the air that failed dismally. "Of course it is. It's the same issue. I practically begged you to tell me you loved me, and you couldn't do it."

"And that's why you left?" he asked, trying to hide his disbelief.

She sounded small and pathetic. A part of her could

understand J.J.'s inability to understand. But another part was wounded anew. Her battled soul, so scarred and worn she'd thought it couldn't be hurt again, ached with remembered pain. And once again she was furious with herself for caring so much.

"Actually, I'm here for a reason. I have something to say to you, and I've waited way too long to say it."

"We haven't seen each other for fourteen years. If this is some kind of delayed therapy, go for it." J.J. was expansive, sweeping his arm out so that Sherry suddenly saw where they were standing—on a dreary, rain-drenched sidewalk in front of a coffee shop where people walked by every half-minute or so and stared in curiosity.

This wasn't going to work. "Could we go somewhere and talk?" she asked. "Somewhere private."

A huge drop of rain landed in his hair, then slid down his cheek. All the while Sherry watched the glittering water-diamond, J.J. watched her. "I don't think so," he said, after a drawn-out moment. "I don't have a lot of time. If it's psychological healing you're looking for, go find it somewhere else. I'm just not that interested in raking up the past."

Before she could do more than gape in amazement, he'd unlocked his Jeep, climbed inside and sketched a fatal, final goodbye.

In total disbelief Sherry silently swore several pungent curse words. Momentarily defeated and furious, she headed to her motel room, intent on fleeing town and getting back to Dee and the safety of her other life. But then she thought of Mandy and knew she would never earn her daughter's respect by being a coward.

Gritting her teeth, Sherry sat down at the desk and began to compose a lengthy letter.

Chapter Six

"Honey, you stay in Oceantides until you get this thing straightened out." Dee's voice rang strong and warm over the telephone wire. "I've got that trip comin' this summer, and I'm going to be gone for three weeks. So, you take all the time you need, 'cause it's payback time come August."

"Thanks," Sherry murmured, clutching the envelope in her hand.

"If I could help, I would. Just take your time, and relax."

"Has Mandy called?"

"Mmm-hmm. She's kinda anxious, poor thing. But don't worry. Kids that age think there's a quick fix for everything, so they don't know how to wait."

"She doesn't have a clue," Sherry murmured.

"Of course, she doesn't. She's thirteen! And don't go blaming yourself. What is, is. You did the best you could. I told her you were explaining things to her daddy, and you'd let her know as soon as everything was arranged.'' Dee hesitated. ''Have you seen him?''

''Oh, yeah.''

''Told him?''

Sherry sniffed, more in annoyance at herself than anything else. ''It was terrible. I hedged. I couldn't bring myself to just blurt it out, and now I'm not sure how to approach him. I've...I've written a letter,'' she admitted.

''Mmm... Bad idea,'' Dee muttered.

''I know.''

''Be brave, honey. You can do it.''

''Captain Courageous, I'm not,'' Sherry disagreed. ''Every time I look at him I just feel *hysterical.* I thought if I wrote everything down, it would come out better.''

''Well, it's a mess, but I think the direct approach, face-to-face, would be best. I'd hate to do it myself, but I think I would.''

''You're stronger than I am.''

''Oh, bull!'' Dee chortled with laughter. ''I'd be feeling the same way you do—probably a hundred times more scared. But when it comes to duty, both of us always do what's best, don't we?''

''I guess.''

''You read over that letter and see if you really want to give it to him. Then make your decision. You'll know.''

Sherry hung up slowly, knowing Dee was right, wishing fervently that she wasn't. In the back of her mind she'd always felt that the day would come when she would confront J.J., but in her everyday life she'd never been able to envision it. It was just too damn hard!

Smoothing her hair with one hand, she glanced down at the letter clutched tightly between her fingers. With sudden fury, she ripped open the envelope, scanned its contents, then groaned in frustration. It was terrible! Rambling and apologetic and downright embarrassing, now that she looked at it. Nope—telling J.J. he was father to a thirteen-year-old girl in neat cursive handwriting wasn't what she wanted. She had to do it in person. Period. Deliberately she tore the missive into half-a-dozen pieces, dusting them into the wastebasket next to the motel room's nightstand.

With a sigh she swept her purse from the bed, then caught a glance at her reflection in the mirror above the dresser. All she saw were a pair of anxious, violet eyes gazing back at her.

There had been moments in Jake Beckett's life when he'd glimpsed the future. Oh, it wasn't anything magical or mystical. Hardly. He'd never felt any connection to the unnamed forces around him apart from an occasional jolt of déjà vu. No, what he sometimes felt was a surety that at some given point his life would turn out a specific way. The threads of his life were woven into a fabric; a fabric that would not unravel unless he forcefully cut it apart—something he would never do.

He'd known from the outset that he was meant to be with Caroline. It was fate. She was a part of him. Another side. A facet. She didn't demand, she waited—a paragon of patience. She was his other half.

And it didn't matter that he neither loved nor wanted her. Waiting for the right woman, his perfect match, was a romantic notion he'd given up in high school. Marriage wasn't like that, anyway. It was living with someone day by day—a friend and companion. It was keeping everything in perspective.

He'd resolved himself to his marriage to Caroline years ago—almost from the moment Sherry Sterling had left Oceantides High. Sherry had messed with his mind all through senior year. He'd been forced to share her with Tim Delaney, for God's sake! To this day, he didn't understand it.

Looking back, he was pretty certain she'd cared about him. She'd actually given herself to him—a memory he still couldn't quite shake. But he'd fought his feelings, pretended he didn't care. It was too intense and he was too young and scared. In retaliation, she'd looked Tim's way and that had been Jake's undoing. He'd smashed the grinning bastard in the face, starting a fight that had gotten them both thrown off the football team during play-offs.

His father had never forgiven him for that, and jerk that he was then, Jake had tried to blame Sherry. Her friends pleaded with him to talk to her, to meet with her, but he'd been too arrogant, proud and just plain stupid. Then she'd called him up Valentine's Day and he'd buckled. He couldn't stand it, but all he could remember now was how she'd looked at him, warm and tender and available, and moron that he was, he'd refused to accept the invitation, wrapped up in his own false nobility that had nearly suffocated him.

He'd kicked himself over that. He'd wanted her like he'd never wanted another woman, before or since. And then there was one last chance. One last night of lovemaking with May rain pouring all around the tree house while Sherry whispered words of love and commitment. He'd soaked it up like some life-renewing elixir.

Then she was gone.

How to play

and claim as many as
FIVE FREE GIFTS:

1. With a coin, carefully scratch away the gold boxes opposite. Then check the Super Bingo Claim Chart to see how many FREE GIFTS you can claim.

2. Send back this card and you'll receive specially selected Silhouette Special Edition® novels. These books are yours to keep absolutely FREE.

3. There's no catch. You're under no obligation to buy anything. We charge you nothing for your first shipment. And you don't have to make a minimum number of purchases - not even one!

4. The fact is, thousands of readers enjoy receiving books by mail from the Reader Service™. They like the convenience of home delivery and they like getting the best new romance novels at least a month before they are available in the shops. And of course postage and packing is completely FREE!

5. We hope that after receiving your free books you'll want to remain a subscriber. But the choice is yours - to continue or cancel, anytime at all! So why not accept our no risk invitation. You'll be glad you did!

YOURS FREE WHEN YOU MATCH 5 NUMBERS!

You'll look like a million dollars when you wear this lovely necklace! Its cobra-link chain is a generous 18" long, and the beautiful puffed heart pendant will add the finishing touch to any outfit!

Play
★SUPER★BINGO!...

Scratch away the gold boxes above to reveal your five lucky numbers and see how many match your bingo card. Then simply check the claim chart below to see how many FREE gifts we have for you!

SUPER BINGO CLAIM CHART

Match 5 numbers	**WORTH 4 FREE BOOKS** **PLUS A PUFFED HEART NECKLACE**
Match 4 numbers	**WORTH 4 FREE BOOKS**
Match 3 numbers	**WORTH 3 FREE BOOKS**
Match 2 numbers	**WORTH 2 FREE BOOKS**

YES! I have scratched off the gold boxes above. Please send me all the gifts for which I qualify. I understand that I am under no obligation to purchase any books, as explained on the opposite page. I am over 18 years of age.

E8BI

MS/MRS/MISS/MR _____

BLOCK CAPITALS PLEASE

ADDRESS _____

_____

POSTCODE _____

The Reader Service™
FREEPOST CN 81
Croydon
Surrey
CR9 3WZ

NO
STAMP
NEEDED

Sure, he'd been a jerk. He'd played with her emotions because he didn't know how to handle his own. He'd been consumed with puppy love and scared spitless over his feelings, so he'd never actually said the words back, although he'd sure felt them.

Love... Man, it had hurt. But, thank God for small favors, he'd kept his feelings to himself and escaped without making a total fool out of himself. It would have been an even more hellish summer after graduation if he'd given his heart and she'd stomped all over it. The way things stood, he'd told himself nightly, it was a smart thing to keep his emotions locked inside. She might have massacred his heart, but at least he'd held on to some dignity and self-respect.

But sometimes he still thought back....

J.J. screeched his Jeep to a halt in front of his parents' home. Climbing out, he turned his face to a wild breeze that slapped wetly against his face. Good. He needed a slap to his senses. He'd looked at Sherry Sterling standing in Beachtime Coffee and felt like he'd been kicked in the groin. Damn it all! What was wrong with him?

Unlocking the gate he jogged to the front door, thought better of it, then circled to the rear of the house and entered through the back door. But that reminded him of Sherry, too. The time she'd saved him from hypothermia.

Glancing at the clock he realized it wasn't even noon yet. Wishing he'd succumbed to his first inclination and was now holding up a stool at the Tank House, he threw open the refrigerator door and swore violently when he realized there wasn't a beer to be had.

''J.J.?'' Patrice's voice scraped along his nerves.

Closing the door he saw her standing at the edge of

the room, one hand holding open the swing door. Without a word he turned on his heel.

"Where are you going?" she demanded.

To get drunk, he thought to himself while his voice stated automatically, "Don't call me J.J...."

Their first night of lovemaking was etched in his memory. The hammock, the scent of fall leaves, the light perfume that flavored her hair and made him want to bury his face in those thick tresses. Her body was satin. She'd given it so effortlessly that night. Even to this day when he thought of her soft flesh and the rustle of eager hands removing confining clothes and even more eager lips discovering secret hollows and curves...his damn body reacted like a horny adolescent's.

She'd told him she loved him over and over again. At first he'd soaked up the adoration like it was his due. Ego. He'd been lousy with it. J.J. Beckett, quarterback of the football team, most sought-after dream guy; God, it was miserable to admit, but he'd bought into the whole damn thing, hook, line and sinker!

When he first made love to Sherry, although every one of his senses had been aflame with desire, not once had he uttered words of love in return. She'd been hurt; he could feel how confused she was after that sweet, hot union, but he hadn't really cared. Not the way he should have. Not then.

He supposed, in a way, he was somewhat responsible for her next move. Hindsight was so incredibly clear. She'd turned to Tim to make him jealous and it had worked like the proverbial charm! He'd wanted to murder his old football partner. Turning to the solace of Caroline's arms hadn't been any answer, either. Caroline's coolness was so off-putting that even his friends' assurances that she was probably hot under all that ice could neither convince Jake nor make him want her.

So, he blamed Sherry totally and fought his feelings for her. And he just knew—the way he sometimes felt the weight of certainty about the future—that she was trouble for him. About as bad a match as could be made. And it didn't take his mother's continual haranguing about her to convince him, either—though Patrice was particularly eloquent on the subject of Sherry Sterling.

No, it was his own innate awareness of what would work, and what wouldn't. And he *knew* it wasn't ever going to work with Sherry.

Then she'd phoned him on Valentine's Day. And like the love-hungry fool he'd been, he'd met her for a soft drink and some stupid small talk and a ridiculous heart-shaped pizza. There was a lushness about her that never ceased to intrigue him; he could look at her for hours. And that sarcastic tongue was such a shock. Half the time he felt she was three steps ahead of him, but then he could read the desperation in her eyes and he sensed again the trap that he would fall into if he were to take those last steps toward her.

But it hadn't stopped him wanting her. He'd hated seeing her with Tim, even if it was just a chance word in the halls. He'd hated seeing her with any other guy.

"Another?" the bartender asked. Jake lifted his head. He'd ripped the bar napkin into strips. Gerald, who was more than amiably drunk already, was being coerced into taking a ride home with a friend. Jake supposed he should care what happened with his head "chef," but apathy seemed to have infected his every pore.

Nodding to the bartender, Jake expelled a sigh of

frustration, wishing it mattered as little as he would like everyone to believe.

There had been a time at the beginning of their senior year when they'd hung out as a sixsome—he and Sherry, and Matt and Roxanne, and Ryan and Summer. None of them had been really dating, although he and Sherry were connected at a primal level that had made him feel as if an engine was always humming inside his head. Then the night he and Sherry had first made love ended their group; *he'd* ended it. He'd wanted a different kind of relationship, although he'd been clueless as to what that different kind of relationship might be.

He had hurt Sherry. Had been unable to risk words of love and commitment and desire. He'd let his body do the talking and been proud of himself for his detachment.

Ha! Some detachment! He'd about gone crazy when she'd drifted toward Tim.

Dumb, dumb, dumb…

Then in May, after that tentative Valentine's Day truce and a throbbing need that wouldn't die, Jake had run for her like a dying man.

And she'd been waiting. He'd picked her up outside Bernie's, wrapped her in his arms, told her how much he'd missed her, how much he wanted her, and her resistance had melted like spring snow. They'd made love in the hammock all night while water dripped musically around the tree house. Only when the sun rose and Sherry remarked how she'd never stayed out all night before, did Jake start having those second thoughts. Terrible thoughts. Mean thoughts that should never have been voiced whether he'd believed them or not.

There had been rumors that she'd been sleeping with

Tim, too. There had even been talk that she was pregnant and not sure who the father was. That had nearly stopped his heart, considering that he was definitely a candidate! But he hadn't believed any of it. Not really. Well, sort of. Rumors flew through Oceantides High like the wind.

But waking up that wet spring morning, Sherry Sterling's warm nude body cuddled in his arms, Jake Beckett had asked himself in a cold, scared voice, *What the hell are you doing?* How could he keep making such stupid mistakes? He hadn't used any protection. Either time! And what did he know about Sherry Sterling, anyway, except that her home life was bad enough for her to want a ticket out of it?

With the benefit of hindsight, he could see what a bastard he'd been, changing from passionate lover to remorseful stranger in such rapid succession that Sherry was left stunned and wounded. She'd gazed at him through those huge, naked eyes and although he'd hated himself, he couldn't stop babbling on about Caroline and how, although he *liked* Sherry, they weren't meant to be together. Then his voice had dried up at the sparkle of tears in her eyes, tears left unshed. He'd wanted to drag her back into his arms and shout how much he loved her, but it was too late.

He told himself he'd done the right thing; there was no future for them.

He loathed himself like he'd never loathed anything before, or since.

The next few weeks had been the purest form of torture. Self-inflicted. He deserved every moment of it. Anguish gnawed at him. He'd been so cruel. He hadn't meant to be.

What the hell was he supposed to do?

Finally, unable to stand it anymore, he'd called Sherry but to his shock she was out with Tim! Fury licked through him, hot and nasty and evil. So, he'd been right, after all. She'd just been looking for a way out. If she couldn't have J.J. Beckett, she would settle for Tim Delaney.

Jake wanted to rip out Tim's heart. Instead, he concentrated on coldly learning to hate Sherry.

The same night he learned Sherry was dating Tim, Jake's parents were having a dinner party at their house and had invited the Newsmiths. Jake was supposed to behave like a proper gentleman. Caroline was there, of course, but all he could think about was Sherry—and Tim—and a seething, silent rage, careened his emotions out of control. He was less than worthless as a host— a glowering, furious maniac.

And then Sherry showed up at the house. Shaking, upset, panicked, she rang the front bell, a summons answered by his mother. Patrice strode into the salon where he half sprawled in a chair, a blatant display of arrogance and disrespect.

As if divining Sherry was somehow the cause, Patrice bit out frostily, "That trashy Sterling girl is here to see you, J.J. I had half a mind to tell her you weren't here. Make it quick."

Everyone stared. Jake took his time rising to his feet, but inside his heart hammered and perspiration collected along the back of his neck and palms. Nerves. God, she could turn him into mush.

Patrice followed him to the front door. "Don't invite her in. I don't know where Caroline gets her patience!"

"I'll handle this," he told her through his teeth.

"We have guests, J.J.," she implored.

Jake ignored her. He practically ran to Sherry's arms,

desperate for escape, his own anger and hurt turning him deaf, dumb and blind. But she was shivering and wretched, immersed in some inner turmoil that, as it turned out, had nothing to do with him....

"It was Tim," she whispered, staring down at herself in horrified disbelief.

Belatedly Jake noticed several buttons were ripped off her shirt. Her hair was mussed. A streak of dirt painted her cheek. Half-choked sobs issued from her throat and she ran shaking fingers through her tangled mane, embarrassment and fear turning her cheeks alabaster white.

He'd seen red. He left with Sherry, determined to beat Tim Delaney into an inch of his life.

"No," she'd moaned, one hand on his arm as he furiously wheeled his car onto the road, nearly sideswiping Mr. Newsmith's black Mercedes. "There's something else. I—I need to talk to you."

"You want to talk about something besides Tim's attack?" Jake demanded, insane with jealousy.

"He scared me, but I just—I just need to see you." Her voice was strangled, barely audible. "Please forget about Tim."

"Forget about him?" Jake bellowed. "Are you crazy?"

"I just had to see you."

He'd looked at her, then. Really examined her. And he hadn't liked what he saw. Could she have faked this whole "attack" story? A smudge of dirt on her face, a few ripped buttons, a shaking lower lip—it would be so easy to dupe someone as lovesick as J.J. Beckett.

Instead of feeling sympathy, he'd begun to wonder what was real. Near rape, or just a ploy to win his attention? How convenient that Tim had been so persistent! Or maybe she'd led Tim on and involving J.J. was her way of working on *him*.

He'd driven her to the beach, questions digging at his brain. She was shaking from head to toe, self-conscious about her blouse, huddled on the passenger side of the car.

"I need to know what your feelings are for me," she said in such a quiet voice he could scarcely hear her. When he didn't respond, she added, "I—I just can't go on like this without knowing."

"Without knowing what?" he'd asked, treading carefully. Who knew what diabolical plan was hatching in that beautiful head of hers?

"Do you love me...just a little?"

He'd gazed at her detachedly. It was a hell of a performance, but she had to think he was a complete moron to believe it. The Sherry Sterling he knew was confident and spicy and sarcastic, and this lost-little-girl stuff was just too much to buy.

"I don't believe you," he stated flatly.

"What...?"

"I don't believe you. You probably weren't even with Tim. You're just trying to get some sympathy."

"You—you—you think I did this to myself?" She gestured to her clothes, so utterly stunned that Jake realized he'd been wrong.

"No, I don't know. Maybe your father," he said feebly.

"Oh, God!"

She nearly ripped the door off its hinges in her fury to get out of his car.

"I didn't mean it," he apologized instantly. This was the truth. It had been a horrible thing to say. He had no basis of fact. It was all rumor about her family anyway.

He scrambled out after her. They faced each other with a warm May breeze billowing her hair around her pale, oval face.

"I hate you!" she declared in a voice packed with rage. "I really hate you! You don't know *anything!*"

"Look, I— I'm sorry."

"You are so stuck on yourself! Everything revolves around you. I can't believe myself. I was so blind!"

"If you say Tim did this to you, I believe you."

"You're incredible."

Her eyes were dark pools of resentment; her lush mouth now drawn tight. Jake knew he'd stepped over the line, yet a part of him was just as upset as she was. "I'll kill Tim," he growled.

"Too late." Sherry's voice rang with ugly sarcasm. "I don't want to see you again. Take me home!"

"Fine. But I'm going looking for Tim."

"When you find him, I hope he beats the living tar out of you!"

"He'll be lucky to get one punch," Jake snarled.

Her mouth worked. He expected round two. Instead, two tears appeared at the corners of her eyes, caught by the moonlight. She tipped her head back and inhaled a shaky breath, her breasts heaving with emotion. In that moment Jake was consumed by lust, his own body reacting to her vulnerability in a very male, very unacceptable way.

But he couldn't help reaching forward to catch a piece of her silken hair between his fingers.

She jerked as if he'd slapped her. Her eyes shot violet sparks of fury and she batted his hand away. "Don't touch me."

"Sherry..."

"If you're not taking me home, I'm walking." With

that she twisted away, half stumbling up the beach. It was the completely wrong direction and after a few silent swearwords, Jake took off after her.

He caught her halfway to the surf. "I'll take you home."

"No."

"Damn it, Sherry! I don't know what the deal is, but I can drive you home!"

"I'm not going there. I'm not going there ever again. And, *no,* my dad didn't do this to me. Oh, God." Hysterical laughter bubbled from her breast. "Maybe I did it to myself."

Something else was going on here besides Tim's pawing and her own need for him to admit his feelings. "What is it?" he asked, really wanting to know.

"Nothing." Her voice was flat.

"Tell me."

She opened her mouth as if to speak, caught herself, gazed at him long and hard, shook her head and silently walked toward his car, her steps weighted as if she were the oldest person living on the planet. Jake made one last attempt to talk to her, but she was deaf to him. She'd checked out, somehow, and only revived long enough to absolutely, totally and completely refuse a ride home.

He made some stupid comment—he couldn't remember what; something about her stubbornness—and she glared at him.

"I made a big mistake," she told him. "I made a big mistake in loving you."

"Sherry…"

"I hate you now. You don't know how much…."

Now, cradling his beer, Jake suddenly shivered, the memory ice-cold. Some said hell was a frozen waste-

land with no warmth. He could believe it. Sherry's glacial ending had been completely final. She'd never returned to school. And while Jake frantically tried to
reach her and make amends for his heartlessness and
lack of understanding, she was already on her way to
her new life—whatever that was.

He'd never seen her again until now, and the irony
of it was that seeing her again brought back the heat
she'd stolen from his life. He hadn't even really known
it had been missing. But last night, and this morning,
he'd felt a furnace blast of emotion and, yes, desire; and
although his head was clear, his body was all too eager
to jump in and get burned again.

"I'm sorry, he's not here," the pert young woman
behind the reception desk told Sherry, her brows lifted
inquiringly. "I'm not sure when he'll be back."

Jake's receptionist, Barb, as her nameplate read, eyed
Sherry with open curiosity. It occurred to Sherry that
Jake's small offices didn't invite a large crowd of cus-
tomers; it wasn't the nature of his business.

"Would you tell him that Sherry Sterling stopped
by?" The words were sawdust in her throat. "I'll call
him later."

"Sure."

Back on the street, Sherry reviled her continuing
cowardice. She was glad—overjoyed!—at the reprieve.
A bad sign. A bad, bad sign.

With time on her hands and nothing to do but wait,
she walked across the street to Crawfish Delish, instantly aware that some crisis was in full swing.

"The chef walked out," one of the waiters moaned
as Sherry took a seat.

"He's just a cook," another waiter sniffed. "And a drunk, too."

"The orders are backed up," the first one complained in a near wail. "I'm about to quit, too!"

"Need some help?" Sherry offered. "I run a deli in Seattle. I'm not bad at waitressing."

"Are you serious?" The wailer blinked twice, then rushed to the front counter where five minutes later a woman about Sherry's age came out to apologize to Sherry.

"I can't believe they'd go so far as to offer a job to one of our customers!" she declared, flustered.

They stared at each other. Slowly, Sherry realized that the heavyset woman with the bleached hair was none other than her old friend, Jennifer.

"Sherry?" Jennifer asked, blinking.

"Hi," she said a bit shyly. "I just keep running into people I know. I guess that's what happens when you return to your hometown."

"What are you doing here? Jeez, you look great." Envy and admiration were mixed together. "Everyone said you'd be a movie star, or something."

"'Or something,'" she agreed with a laugh. "Actually, I was serious about the job. I'm just in town for a while, but I feel so useless and when I walked in here, well..." She shrugged. "If you need some temporary help, I'd love to help out. I can cook a little, too."

"Well, Gerald'll be back after he gets his knickers out of a knot," Jennifer sniffed. "But hey, if you're serious, it'd be great!"

"Are you the owner?" Sherry inquired.

"Day manager. You'll love this, I took over Julie's job before she got married and left Oceantides. It really is a small world, isn't it?"

"Oh, yeah…" Sherry sighed.

"I'm divorced," Jennifer added, as if Sherry had asked. "How about you?"

"Single."

"I don't believe it. I always thought… Huh." She lifted her shoulders dismissively. "The guys all wanted you. I remember wanting to be you, senior year."

"High school's tough, isn't it?" Sherry blurted out, heartfelt.

"Hey!" the wailing waiter cried, and Jennifer grabbed Sherry's hand and led her through the few obligatory forms, hiring her on the spot. Sherry was taking orders by one o'clock and by five, she was in the kitchen, learning the chef's "secret" recipes, which were really basic seafood dishes prepared with spices that added flair. By six she was ignoring admiring glances from Dennis, the night manager, and by eight she'd befriended every employee and was a minor sensation at the small restaurant.

At ten she walked into a cold mist and turned as if by rote toward Bernie's Pizza. Ryan was at work and, spying Sherry, he saluted her with a flour-laden hand.

"You're still here! I'm glad. I told Kathy about you and she wants to see you."

I'll bet, Sherry thought, but she made appropriate interested responses.

"We should get the gang together again," Ryan added.

She remembered all the whispering after she and J.J. had separated at the end of football season. Ryan had always staunchly defended her to J.J. and his other buddies, but there was no way he could really understand how difficult the situation had been for Sherry. She would have done anything to win J.J.'s love, and she'd hated Caroline for being the girl for him.

Even now, hearing that Caroline and J.J. were engaged had the power to twist something inside her soul. Sherry hadn't forgotten J.J.'s stumbling speech on how he and Caroline were made for each other—*after he'd made love to her!*

And then she'd learned of her pregnancy. She'd still been reeling from that news when a drunken, overeager Tim Delaney had ignored all her signals and attempted to maul her. She'd run to J.J., expecting a white knight to ride to her rescue in more ways than one. After all, Tim's amorous attack had seemed ludicrous rather than frightening; it still did. It was the pregnancy that had her shattered and sobbing, but J.J.'s Neanderthal thinking had, naturally, traveled down one rut.

Enough, Sherry thought now, realizing Ryan was watching her curiously. *Enough introspection.*

"I saw Roxanne and Matt today," she told him. "They invited me to the wedding."

"Are you going?" Ryan was eager.

"I don't think I'll still be here."

"It's not that far away."

"I know, but...I've just got some things to take care of, and with any luck, I'll do that tonight."

"Yeah?"

"I'm going out to the Becketts'," Sherry revealed, making a face at the thought. "I tried to talk to J.J. today, but it didn't quite work."

"He's gotten a little cold," Ryan apologized instantly, ever the good friend. "Don't let it put you off."

"It didn't." She half laughed. "It's weird coming back here and seeing so many familiar faces. You always think things will change, but Oceantides feels like it's been caught in a time capsule.''

"Did Jake seem that way to you?" Ryan asked.

"Among others," Sherry half answered.

"Have you seen Caroline?" At Sherry's shake of her head, he said, "Looks great, like you," he added in kindly. "But she's... Well, she was *always* cold, if you know what I mean."

"I know what you mean," Sherry admitted, eyes twinkling.

"It would have been good for Jake to leave for a while, you know? I mean, try to imagine being a Beckett all your life."

Sherry actually laughed, her musical lilt catching the attention of several groups of people eating pizza at various tables. Encouraged, Ryan added, "Must be hell being a stuffed shirt, huh?"

"Hell," Sherry agreed, grinning.

"You and I never were."

"No, we weren't."

"Thank God," he muttered fervently. "It's a flat-out curse—that background. Jake's mother's enough to make you afraid to fall asleep at night."

"Dragon Lady."

"She's even worse now since Jake's dad died. The Becketts own everything in town, and Jake just gets unhappier with each purchase."

"Are you and—Jake—still close friends?" Sherry ventured.

"Naw. Not really. He doesn't come in here, and I'm busy with my family. Whenever we see each other we act like we're going to get together, but it never happens."

"That's a shame," Sherry murmured.

"Yeah... Well, things change." As if hearing how maudlin the conversation was becoming, he asked, "Hey, you hungry? Feel like a pepperoni?" He gestured to the row of sized, stainless-steel pizza platters hung on the wall.

"I just finished a shift at Crawfish Delish."

"A shift?"

"I'm their newest employee. Just for a while, until I...get things settled. Their cook quit today, and it was a madhouse. What?"

Ryan's face wore the most peculiar expression. "Did you meet the owner?"

"No. Why?"

He shook his head, opened his mouth, clamped his lips together, then shook his head again. After a few moments, he said, "The Becketts own Crawfish Delish, Sherry."

"What?"

"I told you they own everything."

Sherry was speechless. She was working for J.J.! Her little rescue mission had just made another tie between her and the Becketts. "Well," she said finally, exhaling heavily. "I guess when I see him, that'll give us one more thing to talk about."

"Good luck," Ryan said, and Sherry headed back out into the wind-driven night.

"Hey, wake up, Mr. Beckett. You're home."

Jake lifted his head and squinted through the windshield of an unfamiliar car. The vehicle was old and losing its muffler. The sound was deafening. Black rain streaked the windshield, then was swept away by scratchy wipers only to return in a thick, wavy sheath a moment later.

Jake's perception had been dealt a deathly blow. He was having a hell of a time remembering whom he was with. "What?" he asked thickly.

"You're home," one of the Tank House's barmaids reminded him with a gentle shake of his shoulder. "Your Jeep's still on the street. You were in it, but not moving, so I offered to give you a ride."

"Thanks," he muttered, meaning it.

"My pleasure."

He stumbled from the car, waved a thank-you, then fumbled with the front gate. Lord, when was the last time he'd been too drunk to drive?

The barmaid's car throbbed away, some dangerously worrisome metallic sound scraping underneath its hood. Serious auto work ahead, Jake decided hazily. Glancing down at his shoes, he noted the slippery mud oozing over the sides. *I'll have to take them off before I go inside,* he reminded himself dutifully, and just as quickly forgot it.

Swaying on the front-porch steps, he came to himself again. Damn it, he was at Beckett Manor, as Sherry Sterling would say. He should have asked her to take him to his condo. Too late now, though. Tomorrow there would be hell to pay, no doubt about it. But for tonight he didn't give a damn. Make that, he didn't give a *good* goddamn.

Headlights flashed around the corner. Jake squinted in the direction of the approaching car, decided he didn't give a good goddamn about them, either, and let himself into the house, half falling over the threshold.

Once in the foyer he remembered the mud on his shoes but it was too late. The gleaming patina of the polished oak was smeared with sloppy clumps of muck, and the fringed edge of the octagonal Oriental carpet was dark brown and wet.

"Whoops." Wrinkling his nose, he removed his shoes, nearly losing his balance in the process and swearing good-naturedly at his own drunkenness.

Sharp footsteps sounded like a rain of bullets. They approached from the rear of the house, Patrice's sitting room. Jake stood to attention, thought it might be amusing to salute, then found himself swaying in front of both Patrice and Caroline, hand at his brow.

Their mouths were twin ovals of horror.

Whoops again.

"J.J.!" his mother hissed.

"Oh, Jake," Caroline murmured, half turning away.

Suddenly he remembered he was supposed to meet Caroline tonight. Dinner, he recalled. Or was that last night? Nope, last night she'd been out of town.

"Sorry," he mumbled.

"Where have you been?" Patrice demanded.

"Out drinking?" he suggested. Thinking he was the epitome of humor, he started laughing, ignoring the heated silence from the two women in his life.

Two women in his life.

What's best for you.

He shuddered. And then the doorbell rang.

"Someone's on the porch," Patrice snapped, frowning. "Did you leave the gate open?"

Jake shook his head, then nodded, deciding, yes, he had left the gate open.

"Our reservation was for eight," Caroline reminded him a tad frostily.

"I don't think we're going to make it," Jake answered as a soft rap sounded on the front door. "I'll get it," he added magnanimously, but Patrice, after shooting him a look that could cut through steel, opened the door herself.

"Oh!" she said, surprised.

Jake peered behind him and nearly fell over. Sherry stood on the other side of the threshold, her hair wind-blown, rain darkening the shoulders of her black jacket, looking gorgeously wanton and refreshing as sea air.

"May I come in?" she asked, her gaze searching out Jake. Those violet eyes made contact and Jake felt his stomach seize up.

"By all means," he invited with a sweeping gesture of his arm that nearly knocked him over.

"J.J.!" Patrice hissed.

"Jake," Caroline entreated.

Ignoring them both, he said, "May I take your coat?" then reached forward to do so. Feeling her skin shiver beneath his fingers, he wondered suddenly if maybe he wasn't quite drunk enough to deal with the force that was Sherry Sterling.

"What brings you out so late?" Patrice asked her.

Jake blinked at her, wondering why his mother sounded so fearful. What was it about Sherry that sent Patrice into such a state?

"I think you know," was Sherry's mystifying answer before she turned to Jake and said, "Is there somewhere we could go to talk alone?"

Chapter Seven

"I don't think that'd be such a great idea," J.J. replied, one hand reaching awkwardly for the foyer wall for a means of support.

"J.J.'s not in any state to go out," Patrice declared tightly.

"I can make my own decisions, thank you very much," he told her amiably. "I'm going to head into the salon. Why don't you all join me?"

Sherry felt like crying in frustration as she watched J.J. move into the gilded room at the southwest corner of the house. She'd made a mistake. Once again. Although at least this time she could console herself with the thought that she'd had no way of knowing J.J. wouldn't be sober. Instead of relief, however, she felt annoyance and frustration. She wanted to unburden herself, and she wanted to do it now.

Patrice Beckett had aged. Little wonder; they'd all

aged. But the fire that had sustained her still burned. Sherry could practically feel its heat coming from the woman in waves of hate.

Or was it fear?

Patrice was in on this deception, too, Sherry reminded herself grimly. Patrice had guessed the truth and then had had the gall to try and direct Sherry which path to take.

As she looked at Patrice now, a flood of uncertain emotions poured through Sherry's veins. It didn't help to have Caroline standing behind the woman's shoulder, a lieutenant in this war with Dragon Lady, the autocratic general.

Oh, how it hurt. Sherry was surprised by the pain. She quivered inside, as much from J.J.'s unexpected touch when he removed her black jacket, as from the turbulent emotions plaguing her at the sight of her old nemesis.

Yes, J.J. had hurt her, too. Yes, he was the reason she'd fled without telling him she was pregnant. But it was Patrice—and Sherry guessed Caroline might be involved somewhere, too—who had turned Sherry's wound into a mortal one. It was Patrice who had ultimately forced Sherry to leave town.

She'd actually come to Sherry's home a few days after Sherry's ignominious appearance at the Beckett dinner party—shown up on a hot June night dressed in a lavender silk suit. She'd come from church, she said, although it was a Wednesday night and Sherry had never known Patrice Beckett to be an avid churchgoer. She'd come to offer Sherry money in order to drive her out of J.J.'s life forever. But the money was nothing compared to the pain of J.J.'s rejection.

So, now, with Patrice's blue eyes staring her down

and memories swirling like dust devils, Sherry remembered everything—the lies, the hurt, the money and the deception. And the guilt that had been eating at her lessened a bit because although she was partially at fault, she'd been barely *eighteen!* Patrice had been a grown woman who should have had some scruples, while Sherry had scarcely set a toe into the adult world.

Or so her guilty conscience tried to assure her.

"Are you coming?" J.J. asked from the doorway, looking disheveled in a frustratingly sexy way. His hair lopped forward and the grim lines around his mouth were replaced by a hint of dimples. He'd always been way too attractive—blessed by the gods. Wondering what she could possibly accomplish, Sherry took a step after him.

"Wait," Patrice muttered harshly. "You have no business being here."

Sherry eyed her adversary. "I have business."

"What kind of business?" Caroline asked, her eyes following J.J.'s progress as he threw himself onto a divan at the edge of Sherry's vision. Unhappiness had drawn fine lines around Caroline's mouth.

"You've been out of J.J.'s life for years," Patrice declared, picking her words carefully. So, Caroline didn't know. It was Patrice's own dirty little secret. "You can't come back now without some consequences."

"Consequences?" Sherry inched her chin upward, praying she could keep up her bravado. But a traitorous little shudder had begun in her lower limbs, a trembling she could not control although she desperately wanted to appear calm and cool. Patrice had that effect on her. She'd always had that effect.

"Caroline, would you mind giving us a minute alone?" Patrice asked.

Caroline looked from Sherry to Patrice. Clearly she was as confused as J.J. about Patrice's strange aversion to Sherry. Murmuring an assent, she headed after J.J., but as soon as she was gone Sherry wished her back. Alone with a viper. Dragon Lady. Sherry met Patrice Beckett's sharp gaze with hot defiance.

"We had a deal," Patrice said in a low tone.

"You and I never had a deal," Sherry replied.

She thought back to the ten thousand dollars she'd been forced to accept from Patrice once she'd left Oceantides, pregnant and alone. Her Aunt Elena had taken pity on Sherry and given her a home in Seattle while Sherry awaited the birth. But when the check arrived from Patrice and Sherry refused to sign it on principle, Elena had taken matters into her own hands and forged Sherry's signature. Sherry couldn't believe it, but she didn't stop it. Aunt Elena insisted they had to do it for Sherry's mother's sake. Cynthia Sterling had tried her best to keep the pregnancy a secret from her husband, but when Donald Sterling found out, his wrath was endless. The money helped Cynthia move closer to Elena and Sherry—and far from her abusive husband.

But of course, Patrice Beckett wouldn't understand that kind of desperation.

"You took the money," Patrice hissed. "If you rake this up now, I'll demand it all back."

"And I'll get it for you," Sherry answered tautly.

Patrice snorted. "You can't possibly pay it all back."

"I don't have to discuss this with you. It's J.J. who needs to know the truth."

"You can't talk to him now. He's drunk." Her mouth said the word as if it tasted bad; her expression seemed to suggest J.J.'s lack of sobriety was entirely Sherry's fault. "Go home and think about what you're doing. I mean, *seriously* think about it."

"I've thought about it for fourteen years." Sherry pushed past her on her way into the salon and J.J.

Caroline was perched next to him on a burgundy divan that looked old and beautiful and expensive, probably a one-of-a-kind antique. J.J. sprawled, legs out, hands dangling between his knees, his eyes half-closed with sleep. Sherry hated to admit that Patrice might actually be right: now wasn't the time to tell him about Mandy.

"So, how long are you in town?" Caroline asked, smoothing her palms on her dress.

"I'm not sure," Sherry answered, wondering how many times she'd been asked that question since she'd resurfaced in Oceantides.

"Sherry," J.J. sang unexpectedly. "Sherry, baby..."

Sherry didn't know which of them reacted the more violently—herself or Caroline. Caroline flinched so hard she half jumped up from the couch, but Sherry's intake of breath was a gasp of shock. Patrice, who'd stepped into the salon's archway, looked ashen and old, but J.J. seemed completely unaware of his devastation.

"Still haunting the neighborhood, I see," he muttered, his gaze narrowing on Sherry in a way that momentarily panicked her. Was he more sober than he let on?

But no, his head flopped toward Caroline, his temple touching one tense shoulder. She reached up to touch him but it was a curiously reluctant gesture, as if she were unfamiliar with the feel of him—her fiancé. There was absolutely no naturalness about Caroline Newsmith at all. She wouldn't meet Sherry's eyes, and Sherry, for reasons she didn't want to examine too closely, felt her chest constrict painfully.

"It's been a long time," Caroline murmured, her smile forced.

"A lifetime," Sherry agreed.

"So, you wanted to see Jake?"

"Well, yes...among other people," Sherry added, realizing her small lie was to save Caroline embarrassment. Why she cared, she couldn't say, but Caroline's petty meanness in high school seemed far away and remote right now; practically nonexistent, as insubstantial as fairy dust.

High school itself was an ancient memory and Sherry marveled that such a brief span of her life, a time spent wallowing in teen angst and infantile emotions, had produced such a rage of continuing torment.

It had produced Mandy, she reminded herself. And Mandy was the reason everything mattered so much to this day. Mandy was a product of intense feelings, and maybe that was why she appeared so intense herself.

"It's really great to get all misty-eyed over high school, isn't it?" J.J. declared ironically.

"People move on. Grow up. Change their lives." This was from Caroline, surprisingly, who seemed to suddenly feel the need to justify her position. "Did you know Roxanne Matherbury is marrying Matt Hudson? On Valentine's Day," she added, unwittingly sending a frisson up Sherry's spine.

Mandy's birthday.

"I heard this morning," Sherry admitted. "Roxanne invited me to the wedding."

Caroline's eyes flared. "Are you going?"

"I...think so," Sherry said, wondering what devil had possessed her.

"So, you're staying in Oceantides, then," J.J. said. Beneath his thick, inscrutable lashes she couldn't tell if he was watching her or not.

"My business partner wants to make a trade. I take a few weeks off now, she takes a few weeks later."

"Kind of like a reunion for you," Caroline suggested. She looked none too happy with the arrangements.

"It's more like a pilgrimage," Sherry admitted.

A cool breeze swirled through the room and everyone looked to the doorway where Patrice stood like a statue. Sherry's fanciful mind wondered if the stirring air was created by her own cold fury, but she could see the front door had cracked back open, and the breath of sea air was welcome in these close confines.

Examining J.J., Patrice demanded, "How long have you been drinking?"

J.J. shot her a glance that would have set a lesser person's knees to quaking. But Patrice was made of stern stuff. "Not long enough," he told her. "I'm still conscious."

"I'm sure you're making a wonderful impression on our guest."

"Don't worry about Sherry," J.J. said before Sherry could object herself. "She escaped early. Ran right out of town."

Patrice's hands fluttered. "It's not like you to do this sort of thing."

"Really," J.J. drawled. "What *is* like me? Living here with you? Letting the Beckett empire swallow me up whole?" He threw out his arms, nearly overbalancing. "I shoulda up and split, like Heather."

Patrice inhaled sharply. "There's no point in this."

Sherry had come to the same conclusion. "I'll go."

"No, don't." J.J. struggled to his feet.

"I'll...call you," Sherry told him as Caroline got to her feet, too, as if she were afraid to let him do anything on his own with Sherry in the room.

"You wanted to see me alone. Now's a great time. Maybe I can catch a ride home with you."

"I'll take you!" Caroline quickly offered.

"This can wait," Sherry agreed. "I'll be around for a while, and there's bound to be a better time to talk." Sherry meant her words. Now that she'd made her decision to stick around Oceantides a bit longer, the pressure was off. She would call the Craigs tonight, she decided, and tell them what was happening. Mandy would want to know.

"What are you going to do?" Patrice demanded, clearly unable to help herself. Small wonder. She had a lot to lose.

"Go to bed," Sherry said, deliberately misunderstanding. Then a mirthful sprite inside her suddenly said, "Oh, I took a job while I'm here. It's just temporary, but it's a lot of fun. At Crawfish Delish."

Patrice gasped. Caroline's jaw dropped, and J.J. stared at her in a way she couldn't quite fathom. Sherry wouldn't have been human if she didn't enjoy the moment a little. They deserved it—the whole lot of these "on the water" snobs.

"Then maybe I'll see you at work," J.J. drawled, a grin lightening his face. He, at least, saw the humor in the situation.

They stared at each other, and Sherry, sensing that he'd somehow joined her "side," at least for the moment, decided it was a good time to leave. With some muttered goodbyes, she hurried out of the house, holding her breath until she was inside her rental car, then letting it out on a sigh of release as she closed her eyes.

"Hey..."

Knuckles rapped against her window. Sherry jumped, her eyes flying open. J.J. stood outside, hunkered against the driving rain and wind. Twisting the ignition, Sherry waved a goodbye at him, but her escape attempt wasn't quite fast enough because he threw open the passenger door and climbed in beside her.

"What are you doing?" she demanded.

"What are *you* doing?" he answered right back. "You've got something to say, just say it."

"I don't want to talk to you like this."

"You'd rather I was sober?"

She could smell the liquor, but more than that she could smell the rain on the shoulders of his damp denim shirt. His hair glistened with droplets and when he shook his head, some of the moisture hit Sherry in a soft spray.

Her hands tightened around the wheel. "I've got to get back," she said through tense lips.

"To work? I happen to know the shift's over at Crawfish Delish. And don't tell me you didn't know I own the restaurant."

"I didn't when they hired me."

"But you did before tonight."

Sherry shrugged. "Ryan told me."

"Ah..."

She didn't like the way he said that. Too knowing. Too sure of what she was all about.

"Is it a problem?" she asked, feeling strained.

"Ryan's still your number-one fan. I remember that. He'd never let anyone say a bad word about you."

"They managed to anyway," Sherry murmured lightly.

"I don't care if you work at the restaurant," he said, switching topics. "I don't care if you stay in Oceantides for good."

"Well, I'm not."

"But I've got this feeling that I'm in the dark about something important." He brushed his hair back with one hand, his face taut and serious. "Patrice is scared of you for some reason. That doesn't make a whole lot of sense unless there's some reason more than high school." He glanced at her. "Gonna enlighten me?"

She could almost believe he was sober enough to hear the truth. Staring at him, she gathered courage. "There is something I need to talk to you about," she admitted. Her heart began pounding once again, slow and heavy, feeling as if it would beat right out of her chest. "But I'm not sure now's the time."

"That bad, huh?"

"Or that good," she whispered, dry-mouthed.

"So, when is the time?"

"Later. When you're sober and I'm...ready."

"I'm pretty damn sober."

"Not enough."

"You're just not ready," he guessed, his eyes narrowing. The sweep of his lashes against his cheek was too seductive, too appealing. She had to look away.

"I'll call you."

"Will you?"

She nodded.

"When?"

"I think I'll stay until Roxanne's wedding," Sherry said. "So, we've got a lot of time."

"Then I'll see you at the wedding," he replied, re-opening the door and stepping back into the rain.

"Oh, we'll talk before then," she assured him.

"No." He was positive. Leaning against the frame of the open door, he ducked his head inside to meet her confused gaze. "I'm going out of town. So, now's your chance. What's the big secret?"

There was never going to be a good time, Sherry thought with frustration. Might as well just dive in. "All right. I'll just say it. It's about you and me, and what happened between us. A lot happened between us," she reminded him, searching his eyes.

"We had a relationship," he agreed amiably enough.

"An intense relationship."

"Jake!" Caroline's voice was an unwelcome intrusion. Sherry gritted her teeth, inwardly groaning as she spied his fiancée coming down the front steps, and the silhouette of Patrice in the doorway like the overprotective mother she was.

"Say it," J.J. urged, frowning in annoyance at Caroline's interference. "Quick!"

"I— It's— We had—"

"I'll give you a ride," Caroline declared, reaching earshot just then and spoiling the moment. "I want to talk to you anyway."

In frustration J.J. held Sherry's gaze. She stared right back, unable to break that fragile contact between them. He seemed about to blow Caroline off, but she heard herself say in a low voice, "I'll see you at the wedding, okay?"

"We'll get it all straight then," J.J. agreed, reaching her wavelength.

Sherry nodded thoughtfully and as J.J. slowly closed the door, she put the car in gear, glancing back in her rearview mirror at him and Caroline who stood side by side in the rain. It seemed inevitable, somehow, that the truth about Mandy would come out at a wedding. A wedding on Valentine's Day. On Mandy's birthday.

How ironic. It added a poignant sting to an already sensitive issue.

But somehow it felt right.

Valentine's Day was on a Saturday, and Roxanne's wedding was slated for five o'clock in the afternoon. With J.J. out of town and the pressure off, Sherry's days sped by in a blur until suddenly it was the Friday evening before, with Sherry serving shrimp dishes prepared by Gerald, the "chef"—who, for reasons unknown, decreed her fit to work in his restaurant and who was doing his damnedest to get her to stay on, although she'd let him know in no uncertain terms that this would be her last day.

Since that last evening with J.J., she'd been content to just fill in the hours and wait for D-Day. Mandy, however, had not been so understanding when Sherry called down to the Craigs to let her know there would be a bit of a delay in meeting her father.

"He's out of town and can't meet you yet," Sherry had said truthfully. "And I'm—uh—reacquainting myself with him, so it's going to take a little more time."

"Next Saturday's my birthday," Mandy revealed, sending a quiver up Sherry's spine.

"I know," she said softly.

"My mom and dad said I could come to Seattle if I wanted to. Will you be back by then?"

"I don't—think so." Sherry ached to be with her daughter on her birthday, but telling J.J. the truth was more crucial. *Maybe next year,* she fantasized. "Your father's best man in a wedding that day."

That gave Mandy pause, but she recovered quickly. "He doesn't want me in his life, does he?" she said in her direct way. She had a knack for expecting the worst. *Like mother, like daughter,* Sherry thought. *That way it doesn't hurt as much.*

"Just because he's busy doesn't mean he doesn't want you," Sherry told her.

"What's he like?" Mandy suddenly interjected, as if she couldn't help herself.

"He's—great," she answered, struggling. "Strong and decent. He's engaged to a woman we both went to school with." *Now why did I say that?* Sherry asked herself.

"Engaged? You mean, to be *married?* When?"

"I don't know. Sometime soon, I guess."

"Do you like her?"

"Mandy!" Sherry half laughed in exasperation.

"Well, you knew her in school. What's she like?"

Sherry had gazed out her motel window to the gray waves sliding over the darker gray sand. "She's perfect for him," she said, unable to keep the bitterness out of her voice.

And Mandy, with a keen sense of awareness that Sherry was just beginning to appreciate, stated flatly, "I hate her."

"You don't even know her."

"You don't like her. I can hear it in your voice."

Their communication amazed and thrilled Sherry. Having gotten over her own initial shock, she'd discovered that she and her daughter talked the same language. It was incredible, and although she knew this just might be Mandy's way, and that she might simply be reacting to her daughter's frankness, Sherry truly believed their ability to get past all the rhetoric was because of blood. They were related, mother and daughter, and it mattered.

Whatever happened with J.J., Sherry had a chance with Mandy now. A chance she'd never really expected. She'd dreamed of it, when she allowed herself to dream, but she'd been unable to imagine her dreams might be realized. She wanted so badly for everything to work out between her and Mandy. In her most fanciful moments, she dreamed of them living together as mother and daughter, with J.J. at least accepting his daughter at some level. But even if that could never be—for Sherry was completely aware that the Craigs loved her daughter to distraction—she and Mandy had the chance for a real relationship.

As long as she handled this J.J. thing right.

"When can I see him?" Mandy had asked.

"I'm working on it. Soon, I think. Be patient."

She couldn't tell her J.J. didn't know about her; that would sever their delicate connection in one second flat! No, better to put Mandy off until she told J.J. about his daughter.

His daughter...

Sherry shivered. Fleetingly she considered how J.J. would react when he realized she and his mother had kept the secret all these years. And she would pay Patrice back every penny of that ten thousand dollars. She should have done it years ago except that she'd always felt it was better to let sleeping dragons lie. But Patrice was awake and breathing fire now, so Sherry, who had a decent relationship with the banker who'd helped put the deal together to buy her share of Dee's Deli, had already set the wheels in motion to get her a loan for the money. She couldn't wait to drop a cashier's check in Patrice's lap—with interest!—and wash her hands of the whole dirty deal. For her mother, she would do it again, but that didn't make the idea of accepting Beckett money any more palatable.

"Hurry," Mandy urged, sounding incredibly young.

"I'll do my best," Sherry assured her softly, aching inside. She'd hung up the phone feeling oddly moved. And she realized how badly she wanted to have her child in her life. There was still time. Still a chance...

"You going to stand there daydreaming all day?" Gerald burst into her thoughts, yelling from the bowels of the kitchen.

Sherry came to with a start. She'd been standing at the kitchen swing-door, a million miles away. "Oh, stop your bellowing," she teased.

"Come out tonight with me—after the kitchen's closed."

"Forget it, Gerald. I never date co-workers. It's a rule."

"It's a bad rule. We'll go have a drink somewhere."

One of the waiters gave her the "look." Sherry had learned during her short employment that Gerald was closing in on alcoholism, amiable drunk that he was, and he used his supposedly volatile temperament as an excuse to go out and throw back a few too many. Although she liked Gerald, she suspected he was not long for employment. He was just too reckless and undependable. Fortunately for him, J.J. Beckett appeared to be a fairly hands-off employer.

And this was Sherry's last day, for tomorrow was the wedding. And afterward... Well, she might have to get out of Dodge fast after she and J.J. had it out.

Skin tingling with apprehension, she hurried to serve

several plates of Gerald's fabulous shrimp pasta to a young couple holding hands by the front window.

"Why can't we go together?" Caroline asked, twisting her opal ring on her right ring finger. It was a gift Jake had given her not long after he'd graduated from college. Blinking, he suddenly couldn't remember what the occasion had been. "What?" Caroline demanded, seeing him stare at her ring.

They were at her condominium, a stark glass-and-concrete building jabbed onto the cliffs above the beach, a monstrosity that even Jake had protested against at city council; he preferred the cozy, rambling beachfront dwellings that dotted the coasts of Washington and Oregon. Beckett Enterprises might own real estate, might even build and develop, but Jake had a strict code of aesthetics that other developers did not.

The developer who'd built these condos could have used a lesson in keeping with the beauty of the area. It bugged Jake that Caroline had chosen to live here, of all places; but then he hadn't wanted her to reside in one of his own units, either—something that he'd never voiced but suspected she'd picked up on.

"Why are you staring at my ring?" she asked again, spots of color highlighting her cheeks. She was more upset than he'd ever seen her, and for the life of him, he couldn't figure out why.

"Was it your birthday? I can't remember what it was."

"What?" She blinked. "You mean, why you gave me the ring? It was our five-year anniversary, Jake!"

Memory flooded. Of course. They'd been dating for five years—if you didn't count the time he was seeing Sherry senior year in high school. Caroline had decreed that their anniversary was coming up, and she'd hinted how special it was. He'd picked out the ring between exams one Friday before he came home from college. As he recalled, she'd been slightly disappointed in the gift. Maybe she'd wanted an engagement ring.

He wondered if he should ask her what the actual date of that "anniversary" was again, looked at her unhappy face, and decided not to.

"Why can't we go to the wedding together?" she asked, returning to her theme. "I want to go with you."

"I've got too many things to do first. I've been out of town for a week, and I don't want to go early. Let me meet you there."

"You're the best man! You have to go early."

"I'll get there in time," he assured her.

"What were you doing out of town?" she asked suddenly. "Why all of a sudden?"

"Looking at property on the Oregon coast. I told you," he growled.

"For a week?"

Jake gazed at her in frustration. How could he explain that what had originally been a jaunt—more vacation than business—had become a good excuse to get away and think? And how could he tell her that he'd spent the week running on the beach, trying to exorcise Sherry from his thoughts, scared spitless that upon his return to Oceantides he would find her mysteriously gone, never to return?

Hell, he couldn't even explain it to *himself!*

"I wanted to go with you," she revealed. "My job is demanding, and I don't get to spend enough time with you as it is."

Caroline worked as right-hand woman to the owner of a small, successful electronics firm that had grown too large for its modest roots in Oceantides and was now based in Seattle. So far, the owner hadn't asked her to make the move; she spent a lot of her time at trade shows and conferences and wasn't in the office anyway. But the company was in the process of hiring a marketing agency and Caroline's job description was sure to change. With that change would come a move to Seattle; the writing was on the wall.

But Caroline wanted to chuck it all and marry Jake.

"I needed some time alone."

"Why?" Her eyes flared with alarm.

"I just did. And I still do," he admitted, not wanting to hurt her but unable to lie.

"Oh, Jake." She swallowed hard.

She couldn't mask her unhappiness, but Jake was through with trying to make everyone happy and therefore making no one happy. "This isn't working," he said softly. "We both know it."

"It's her. Ever since she came back, you've been different."

"It's mostly us," Jake disagreed. "You and I. There's something missing."

"Something you can get from her?" Caroline asked angrily.

"Caroline—" he began, frustrated.

"No, don't. Don't say it!" she interrupted. "Just go with me tomorrow and everything'll be okay. The weather's supposed to be terrible, for Pete's sake! Rain—possible snow! Cold as the devil. Don't make me drive."

Caroline was normally as independent as a tiger; this sudden insecurity had to be a ploy. And that bugged Jake, too.

"I thought you were catching a ride with Ryan and Kathy."

"I want to go with you."

"I'll meet you there!" Jake told her in exasperation. "But don't make me get dressed up sooner than I have to. And I'm leaving right afterward. I hate receptions. I hate weddings!"

"You don't have to yell." She turned away, twisting the ring so hard her skin stretched white before turning red.

"I'm going to work out first," he reminded her, as if that had anything to do with the real crux of their argument.

"Do you have to run every day? My God, you spend so much time racing along the beach, people will think you're a fanatic."

"I hardly ever run." Jake gazed at her in amazement.

"You're just never around! I'm tired of being your 'sometime' fiancée! Make me a priority, Jake, or forget it. I can't stand this much longer. I'm so upset I just want to—spit!"

Jake's jaw dropped. This was more passion than he'd ever seen. "Is that an ultimatum?"

She waved her arm, frowned, then shook her head. "I just want to walk through the door of the church with you."

"Oh. Appearances."

She flushed. "Damn you. You think it's so easy for me. Well, I won't be here forever. If you want me— yes, this is an ultimatum—you'd better make room for me."

She swept out ahead of him, toward his Jeep. He followed behind her, frustrated and uneasy and wishing *something* would change.

"I hate this thing!" she suddenly cried, slamming the palm of her hand on the driver's door.

"I love it."

"Can't you just do one thing for me?" she cried. "Just one?"

"What the hell do you want, Caroline?"

"Marriage. I'm sick of waiting. But it's like your feet are stuck in concrete. You won't do anything. You won't change. And Sherry Sterling's appearance just made things worse. Now you talk like you and I have a problem."

"We do."

"No, it's *you.* It's like you're *waiting* for something! Well, I've got news for you, it's not coming. And I just can't wait forever."

Yanking open the door of the Jeep, she climbed inside, swishing her long black skirt around her legs. She wore a white silk blouse and a black wool overcoat. Jacketless himself, Jake levered himself behind the wheel, glanced down at his own jeans and navy corduroy shirt, and suddenly realized the incongruousness of their disparate life-styles.

"I can't be what you want, Caroline," he said, gesturing to his clothes. "For better or worse, this is it."

"I'll take you as you are," she responded instantly. "But it's got to be soon. You think about that when you're running on the beach tomorrow. When we meet again at the wedding, I want a real commitment, not some phony half-baked engagement. Please," she added, laying a hand on his.

Jake nodded, thinking it was time everything got straightened out. Besides, Sherry was going to talk to him tomorrow and Roxanne and Matt were getting married. It was the perfect day for endings and beginnings.

* * *

Saturday dawned in dark, dank misery. Sheeting rain, followed by hail popping against an already frozen ground, complemented ice-crusted pools of rainwater and other treacherous, frozen patches on the highway to make driving a hellish torture.

Sherry had brought one nice dress with her, a black double-breasted sheath with white trim. A little sober for a wedding, but she didn't have anything else. She'd almost left it at home. What need was there for a dress in Oceantides? Now, she smoothed the skirt over her hips and wondered what the hell she was doing.

The wedding was at five. The skies were already leaden and closing to night fast as Sherry climbed into her rental and negotiated out of her lot and onto the two-lane road toward the church where the nuptials would be held.

She was late—mainly by choice, she decided ruefully, since she was really dreading this affair.

Therapy, she reminded herself. These past two weeks in Oceantides had been good for her, in a way, for she'd found a part of herself she'd locked away and hidden, and it wasn't so bad, after all.

About a mile from the turnoff she spied a sight that set her pulse rocketing. A black Jeep had skidded off the road and it was listing to one side.

"There are tons of black Jeeps," she said aloud. "And J.J. would already be at the wedding since he's the best man."

But the words were still hanging in the air when she recognized J.J. Beckett himself standing beside the vehicle. In a black tuxedo and white pleated shirt, he looked incredibly handsome. She saw, then, that his axle was bent.

He glanced up, recognized her, his expression dark as a thundercloud.

"Need a lift?" she asked.

Without a word, he climbed into the passenger seat of her car. "I'm late," he said.

"They'll wait for you."

"I don't want to go."

"You have to." Sherry actually laughed.

"Marriage is a wasted institution. They don't last. They're never happy. Somebody always gets hurt."

"What a cynic," she declared, wondering what was eating him. "They never should have made you best man!"

"You got that right," he growled.

"What happened to your car?"

"Daydreaming." He yanked on his bow tie, thought better of it, and glowered at the rain splattering on the windshield. "Be careful, it's a skating rink."

As if hearing him, Sherry's compact suddenly jumped over the center line as if leaping out of her hands. Deftly and gently, she dragged the steering wheel back but she overcompensated and the little car swirled around in a wild circle, whipping them around until they were facing the way they'd come.

"Oh, my God!" she breathed.

"You okay?" J.J. asked, his hand touching her shoulder.

Sherry's attention instantly changed to the feel of his hard fingers through the shoulder of her dress. She wore no coat. Her black jacket had seemed too sporty and she'd figured she could run from the car to the church and back again. But now she fervently wished she'd thrown it in the car.

"I'm kind of scared to put my foot to the accelerator again."

"Want me to drive?"

She shot him an amused look. "Because of your skill with the Jeep?"

He grinned, shocking her to her socks because she thought she might have offended him. His dimples did her in, and she found herself unable to tear her gaze from his face. "I am not going to make this wedding," he said, more relaxed now.

"Yes, you are."

She threw the car into reverse and slowly touched the gas. The rear end of the car suddenly ran for the ditch as if it were in a race. The next thing Sherry knew they were staring up the slope of the shoulder, her headlights tilted skyward toward an unforgiving sky, the engine humming and tires churning as her foot had slammed on the accelerator instead of the brake.

She released the gas and the car slid backward, idling as contentedly as a friendly, panting dog, waiting for its next command.

"You are not going to make this wedding," she said on a sigh.

J.J. broke into laughter, and after a moment, Sherry followed suit. They laughed until tears starred her vision, and when she swiped them away she turned to look at him, and the look on his face made her stomach flip.

"I promised Caroline I wouldn't talk to you," he said into the uncomfortable moment that followed.

"What?"

"She didn't want me to talk to you, but it was a promise I couldn't keep."

"Why didn't she want you to talk to me?" Sherry asked, her heart pounding heavily.

J.J. stared out the window into the gathering gloom. Running his hand through his hair, he drew a deep breath. "We're going to have to walk," was his ambiguous answer. "Here."

He extended a hand, helping her from the car. Sherry felt his cool fingers clasp her sweating palm, but that was the least of her worries. Wet, slapping weeds attacked her nylon stockings and she felt the fabric snag and run up the side of her leg as she worked her way to the edge of the road.

J.J.'s hand was still close by, hovering somewhere around the small of her back in case she should lose her balance. Sherry was too concerned with keeping her footing to be unnerved by his closeness, and anyway, she was beginning to accept and relax around him a bit.

Face it. You like it!

They slogged through the rain in the direction of the church, their conversation concerned with their predicament. By the time the front steps of the little clapboard building with picturesque spire were in their sight, Sherry and J.J. were both drenched to the skin, their teeth chattering.

From inside, organ music boomed outward, mixing with the pattering rain. The sound was mournful and powerful in the fading light, resonating inside Sherry in a way that made her feel short of breath.

"My kingdom for a shot of brandy," J.J. muttered, clasping her elbow and leading her up the steps. He grabbed the front-door handle, twisted, opened the door a crack and groaned.

"What?"

"Come around to the side." Her hand still held

tightly within his, J.J. urged her around the porch toward a side door. "They're all in there, waiting. And they're dry!"

Sherry grinned, but her mouth was too cold to do more than grimace. "I can't feel anything."

"Hurry."

He ushered her through the side door, which led to a small hallway used as a means to enter the back rooms behind the altar. The door closed with a sigh behind them and it was dark, but dry. Music swelled, filling her head. Sherry gingerly reached forward into the suffocating darkness, her fingers finding the wall. "I should be out there with the crowd," she murmured.

"Can you feel anything yet?"

"Just the wall."

"No, I mean, on your body. Have you got any feeling back?"

His breath blew hot against her wet hair. "Not much," she admitted, a frisson slipping down her spine.

"Do you remember the rain on the tree house?" he asked suddenly, unexpectedly.

Sherry didn't know how to answer. She could hear his even breathing and as time passed, her eyes began to adjust to the dim light. There was light beneath a doorway at the end of the hall, but J.J., standing beside her, seemed tall and huge and inordinately male. "Yes," she whispered.

The music rose to a crescendo, then faded away. A woman's voice, pure and sweet, took its place as she sang a hymn of joy.

And J.J. did the unthinkable. He leaned forward, his right hand softly groping along the slant of her jaw. Sherry shrank backward, but it was no use. J.J.'s mouth touched down on hers, as cool as silk. Startled, Sherry gasped, her breasts lifting to brush lightly against his chest.

His tongue sought hers, softly, questioningly. Sherry stood immobile. She hadn't kissed a man in years and never with the passion with which she'd once kissed J.J. She couldn't have this, but she wanted it, she realized vaguely. Wanted it so badly it was all she could do to keep from wrapping herself around him in the intimate little hallway.

Slowly, agonizingly slowly, he drew back. His breath fanned her face, uneven and warm. The singer's voice reached a peak, ran back down the scale, then returned to another high. Sherry ached for J.J. to kiss her again. Her lips remained parted. Desire danced in her head.

"You taste like rain," his voice murmured.

"So do you."

"I want to see you," he stated harshly, as if he were mad at himself for the admission. "While you're here," he said, "I want to see you."

He kissed her again before she could protest, turning her knees to water. Her hands climbed over his shoulders, her wanton body quivered. He pulled her close, molding her to him, his mouth possessing hers. Sherry moaned low in her throat, unable to stop herself.

"After the wedding," she whispered when his lips relinquished hers to travel along her jawline.

For an answer, he reluctantly set her away from him, then his hand held hers tightly as he led her the rest of the way down the hallway and into the lighted rooms behind the door.

Chapter Eight

She didn't remember the wedding ceremony. She sat in the back row, wet and silent, but inside she was heated by her own churning thoughts. Roxanne and the rest of her wedding party had greeted her and J.J.'s arrival with cries of worry and surprise, then she'd been bustled to a rest room and was toweled off by, of all people, Summer, who'd grown fat and happy, but no less wise.

"Still with J.J.!" she declared, rubbing down Sherry's hair. "My God, I thought you'd escaped this dreary hamlet."

Sherry couldn't explain. There was no time. She was hustled right out again and directed back to the dark hallway, then outside onto the covered porch and finally through the front door to sneak into a pew at the rear of the church.

J.J. appeared moments later with the other groomsman, his hair still wet but combed into place. His suit was soaked, however, and the crowd murmured in amusement as he stood near the altar, his back to the audience.

Roxanne made a beautiful bride, her hair bound up and adorned with tiny white flowers; her dress a flowing, lacy cape with a long train. Red tulips and roses abounded. Valentine's Day.

With a jolt Sherry realized that J.J. had kissed her on Valentine's Day. Coincidence. Symmetry.

Her gaze was reserved for only him. Throughout the ceremony it was his broad shoulders Sherry watched; the back of his black hair, the hem of his waterlogged jacket. It was there—this *thing* she had for him—alive and beating still. One kiss and she remembered all those luscious feelings from high school. It was like an addictive drug, dangerous and upsetting and wrong, yet tempting beyond belief.

It was why she was here. *No!* she reminded herself. She was here for Mandy. Only Mandy. J.J. hadn't loved her when she was seventeen; he didn't love her now.

And he would hate her when he learned the truth.

Shivering, she closed her eyes. Emotions swarmed, scorching her like hot lava. *I want him.*

How could this be? Sherry couldn't credit it. For years she'd felt nothing for any male but friendship, or contempt, or just general lack of interest. Her customers at Dee's Deli had earned her friendship; overardent admirers her contempt; and the rest of the lot, her general lack of interest. She'd done nothing—*nada*—to encourage any man, and the few kisses she'd received since J.J. had been stolen ones from an overpersistent date who had felt it was payment for services rendered.

She'd begun to wonder if her sex drive was tepid at

best. High school didn't count, she told herself on a regular basis. One was too young at sixteen, seventeen and eighteen to make those decisions. It was all wrapped up in anxiety, anyway; worrying about popularity and who was cool and all that claptrap she'd disdained ever since.

Now she realized she'd been kidding herself. Those feelings *had* been real. They were here now. They'd just been hiding beneath her skin, biding their time, waiting to leap out and expose themselves.

But *J.J.?* He was the last person in the world she should want. Not now! Not when she'd gotten her life together. Not when Mandy had resurfaced and there was a chance for them to be a real mother and daughter.

Was that it? Sherry asked herself, delving painfully into her own soul. Was it thinking that they could be a *family* that had brought this on?

"You're not that stupid," she whispered.

"Pardon?" The woman in the wide royal blue hat sitting next to Sherry peered at her from beneath the oval brim.

"Talking to myself," Sherry assured her, throwing a glance at J.J.'s wide shoulders and slim hips. She could practically feel the blood rushing lightly through her veins.

"Beautiful, isn't it?" the woman said in an aside.

"Mmm." Sherry's gaze wandered to Roxanne and she forced herself to think about her friend instead of her own problems. What would it be like to embark on your own marriage? To plan to share your life with the man you loved?

Tempting thoughts. Ridiculous thoughts. Dangerous thoughts.

As soon as the ceremony was over the wedding party

gathered for pictures. Standing toward the back of the church, Sherry could still hear the amused laughter and comments about J.J.'s wet tuxedo. But Roxanne, true to form, merely urged everyone into place and proceeded as if the fact the best man was dripping puddles everywhere was of no consequence, which it wasn't. "Something to tell the kids," Roxanne said with a dismissive wave of her hand, her face glowing with rapture. Nothing could spoil her day.

A pang of something like jealousy filled Sherry's breast and she glanced away, wondering if she should skip out. But Summer was here, and nostalgia was like a long beckoning finger, drawing Sherry forward even while she wanted to melt into the woodwork.

She was as bedraggled as J.J.; worse, really. Lank, wet tendrils of hair were sticking to her neck. Glancing down, she could see her nipples standing at attention through the black sheath. Shivering a little, she crossed her arms.

"The reception's downstairs," Ryan said, near her ear.

Startled, Sherry turned, glimpsed Kathy's closed face, then smiled a thank-you at her friend. "I'll be right down."

"We're all going over to Roxanne's parents' place afterward," he added. "Ya coming?"

"Uh...I don't know."

"If ya don't, Roxanne and Summer will send a posse," Ryan predicted.

"We'll see," was her noncommittal answer.

"There's Caroline!" Kathy interjected, leaving her husband's side to meet the cool blonde in the taupe silk dress. What was it about her? Sherry mused to herself. Caroline had always possessed that same touch-me-not

look, and now, years out of high school, it seemed a
hundred times worse.

The memory of J.J.'s hot kiss swept over Sherry
again, a wave of excitement that left her slightly breathless. Did he kiss Caroline the same way? Did Caroline
possess these *feelings?*

Kathy and Caroline stood in the center aisle as the
church emptied toward the stairways on either side of
the main altar. Sherry edged her way to the side aisle
and walked quickly downstairs, her skin prickling as she
imagined the two women watching her departure.

A cup of punch and I'm out of here.

"Sherry!" Summer caught sight of her just as she
reached the stairs. "Wait for me!"

"Sure," Sherry agreed. Her eyes met J.J.'s for one
brief millisecond, but it was enough to send her pulse
skyrocketing. She knew he was thinking about the kiss,
too; she could read it in his tense, passionate expression.

Inwardly groaning, she took a deep breath and fought
hard to tamp down these feelings—feelings she
shouldn't have for Caroline Newsmith's fiancé. Feelings
she shouldn't have—period.

Downstairs, she suffered through endless small talk
until the wedding party joined the group. The ritual
cake-cutting and reception line felt like an excruciating
wait. Twisting the handle on her cup of punch and trying, unsuccessfully, to look inconspicuous, she nearly
choked when J.J. detached himself from the group and
walked straight toward her.

"Mark's got studded tires. He said he'd drop us off
at my place and we can figure out how to rescue our
cars."

"Shouldn't we wait by the cars?" Sherry suggested.

"And freeze to death?"

"What about—Caroline?"

"What about her?"

Sherry shot him a cool look.

"She came by cab, and she's going back with Ryan and Kathy." J.J. clearly didn't want to talk about her. It bothered Sherry deeply, because she felt that old, familiar sensation of somehow being the "other woman," the secret affair, the "not good enough" girl.

But who was she kidding? She needed time alone with him to have their "talk," and this was her opportunity. What Caroline would think of it was not Sherry's problem. As soon as J.J. learned he had a daughter, the situation would be so incredibly different that no one would give a damn about who'd left with whom anyway.

"All right," Sherry murmured with a taut swallow.

He nodded a goodbye then, to return to his best-man duties. At the same moment Summer grabbed her arm and Sherry was introduced to her husband and two bright, redheaded children. One, a boy, was just a few years younger than Mandy. His grin was huge and he shook Sherry's hand vehemently, as if the harder the shake, the better the greeting. Summer's little daughter had no front teeth, and she smiled as widely as her brother. A pang shot through Sherry as she thought about Mandy's sober, almost-angry persona.

But I have a chance now to make things better for her. A real chance.

"So, what's the deal with you and J.J.?" Summer asked.

"What do you mean?"

"He can't take his eyes off you, and you're just as bad."

"What?" Sherry inwardly squirmed with embarrassment.

"Oh, come on. Clue me in. I've only got a few hours to catch up on all this stuff, then we've gotta hit the road for home. I deserve the whole dirt!"

"There is no dirt."

"Oh, right. You just happened to appear back in town a few weeks before Rox's wedding, looking like a million bucks, I might add. Except you're kinda wet right now," she added humorously. "But something's up. Is it J.J.? Still?"

"I haven't seen him since I left school. And it's 'Jake' now, or so I've been told."

"Well, whatever his name is, he can't help staring at you every free moment. See that? He's looking out of the corner of his eye."

"Oh, stop!" Sherry half laughed.

"Everybody's thinking it. I just say it."

"I came to town to set some things right," Sherry told her, picking her words carefully. "One of those things that needed to be set right had to do with J.J.— Jake."

"Hmm." Summer looked thoughtful. "I always thought you really loved him."

"I was a teenager, for heaven's sake!"

"Doesn't matter. Do you know the things we find attractive in a person never change? I read this article about it. The reasons you're drawn to someone are the same throughout your life. So, it stands to reason that someone you loved in high school is someone you're still going to love when you're older."

"High-school romances don't last." Sherry was blunt.

"Some do."

"People mature. They change. It doesn't last."

"Who're you trying to convince? Me?"

"I know I was attracted to J.J. because he was such a big deal. Mr. Quarterback, Mr. Popularity, Mr. Everything. I was shallow, I admit it."

Summer threw back her head and laughed, surprising Sherry. Eyes twinkling, Summer declared, "That wasn't why you liked him. You liked him *in spite* of all that! Good grief, Sherry, this is Summer you're talking to. I *know* you."

Sherry was about to refute everything she'd said but the words shriveled in her throat when Caroline suddenly broke from her tight group of friends and approached Summer. Sherry stepped slightly away, but it was Sherry Caroline apparently had come to talk to because she ignored Summer completely, her clear blue eyes cautious but determined. Summer's red brows lifted and she gave Sherry a "Can you believe this?" look from behind Caroline's right shoulder.

"I didn't really get a chance to talk to you the other day," Caroline began. "It's been such a long time."

"Years," Sherry agreed.

"I think having you around has thrown Patrice for a loop," Caroline said, smiling. "But she's always overreacted where Jake's concerned."

Sherry wasn't certain what she was supposed to say to this.

"I tried to assure her that this wasn't high school, and there's no need to worry so much. Jake's a man now. He makes his own decisions."

Sherry nodded, wondering where this was going.

"So, how is it, working at Crawfish Delish?" Caroline asked, apparently not as focused as Sherry had originally thought.

"Yesterday was my last day."

"Oh?" She looked surprised. "Didn't it work out?"

"It was fine. It's just that I'm almost ready to leave Oceantides." Sherry didn't want to talk to her. Caroline's comment about Patrice had turned up her stress level, reminding Sherry how tenuous her relationship with J.J. was—and how she foolishly wanted it to be stronger.

"You make it sound like you have an agenda." Caroline lightly touched her lips with her fingertips. Did she know about Mandy now? Sherry wondered. Had Patrice told her? And how would Patrice have done it without throwing herself in a bad light?

"I've got to straighten some things out, then I'm history."

"With Jake?" Caroline asked quickly.

"Uh…yeah," she admitted, tired of all the deception.

Caroline's expression changed to one of anxiety if not out-and-out fear. Sherry almost felt sorry for her.

Out of Caroline's range, Summer cleared her throat and started signaling Sherry frantically. But it was too late. From somewhere behind Sherry's right shoulder, J.J.'s familiar voice drawled, "So, are you ready to go and get our cars?"

"Cars?" Caroline asked, thinking he was talking to her.

"Sherry and I each drove off the road trying to get here," Jake explained. "Matt's ready to take us before he goes to Roxanne's parents' house for the reception. Unless you wanted to go there first…?"

"No," Sherry said instantly, as Caroline drew a sharp breath.

"Well, I'll see you at the reception later, then," Caroline told him in a voice that brooked no argument, but the look on J.J.'s face suggested she might not see him there at all.

In the front seat of the tow truck, the radio blasting away as the driver whistled tunelessly, Sherry glued her eyes to the companion tow truck leading the way, the one that had dragged J.J.'s car from the ditch and would be hauling it into town. Matt had driven her and J.J. to their vehicles to wait for the tow trucks, and now the drivers were taking them to J.J.'s condominium before hauling their cars to the auto-body shop.

Through the truck's rear window, Sherry could see J.J.'s shoulders and the back of his head. She knew without a doubt that neither one of them would make the reception. This was the time for her revelation.

As the two trucks and their sad-looking fender-mangled cargo headed toward J.J.'s beach condominium, Sherry made another decision: no more kisses; no more fleeting dreams; no more nostalgia.

Just the truth. It was all she could afford to give.

But once she and J.J. were both unloaded and the twin trucks had headed away, she found she was as tongue-tied as when he had confronted her at the wedding reception.

"You look like you could use a drink," he said thoughtfully, leading the way inside.

She walked on legs that felt like water as she followed him through the front door and down a short, black-tiled hall to a room with thick cream carpet and a wood-beamed ceiling. A river-rock fireplace climbed up one wall and Japanese glass floats in shades of aquamarine and royal blue filled a wicker basket on the hearth. Treasures from J.J.'s youth, Sherry thought with a pang. She walked straight to them and cradled one between her palms.

Her heart beat heavily. She heard the clink of a bottle against glass and then J.J. was offering a goblet of dark red Burgundy that glinted seductively in the soft lamplight.

Sherry reluctantly accepted the drink, took a swallow, then held her breath for as long as she could. J.J. stood nearby, neither moving away nor coming any closer. With an effort, she lifted her chin.

"I've got some things to say. Some *thing* to say," she corrected herself.

He wasn't listening. He was gazing out the back windows toward the silvery stretch of beach and the ebony waves cresting against the sand, their frothy edges sliding forward, then slowly receding.

"I feel like I'm in a dream," he said, his voice sounding as if he found the idea slightly confusing.

"How so?" she asked, sipping the wine.

"I don't feel like I'm thirty-three and that it's been almost fifteen years since graduation. I especially don't feel that way now—because you're here."

"I represent high school to you?"

He thought about that a moment, shrugged and nodded. "In a way. It just feels like everything stopped."

"Stopped?"

"Maybe not for you, but, well, look at me. I slid into the family business and I never wanted to. I didn't *not* want to enough, I guess," he added with characteristic honesty. "And I've resented the hell out of my mother and Caroline ever since. God, my mother...!" In a gesture of frustration, he ripped off his bow tie and tuxedo jacket, flinging them across a chair. The white shirt looked cool and seductive against his dark flesh, and unwillingly, Sherry's eyes feasted on him.

"She's been crazy since you got back to town. I always thought she was over the top on a few things, but now she's way over."

Sherry's fingers clung tightly to the stem of her wineglass. "Really."

"She's been grilling me like I'm sixteen again."

"About me?" She took a long swallow of wine, fighting the tiny tears collecting in the corners of her eyes.

"Well...yeah, as a matter of fact," he said, shaking his head as if he were completely to sea, which in fact, he was. "I swear, it's like a recitation. 'Did you see her? What did you talk about? What did she say?' It's nuts!"

Sherry could well imagine. Patrice knew she was going to tell J.J. about Mandy and that meant revealing Patrice's involvement. Sherry had half expected J.J.'s mom to beat her to the punch and direct all the blame to her somehow, but there was really no way to do that without revealing her own duplicity—something Patrice was undoubtedly loath to do.

"But that's her problem. My problem is that I've never moved on. Just stayed in the same rut, waiting for something to happen." His gaze shifted to her face, making Sherry feel suddenly vulnerable and transparent. "Well, something has."

"What?" she asked a trifle breathlessly.

He didn't answer and Sherry was forced to look away first. Complications. The situation was rife with them! But, oh, it felt good to see the yearning in his eyes, the same yearning she felt.

"Caroline told me not to see you. She made me promise," he added ironically. "Now, I know why."

"J.J., this is getting away from what I want to say," Sherry began, but he cut her off.

"You know, I always blamed you for throwing me off track, so that I ended up here, wasting my life."

"You haven't wasted your life."

"The hell I haven't. I chose the path of least resistance. Isn't that wasting it? You were right, back in high school. The silver spoon was so far down my throat I let it choke me."

"I never said that," Sherry muttered uncertainly.

"You didn't have to. I always knew what you thought of me—deep down. All those sarcastic remarks. You wanted me to recognize how full of crap I was. So self-important. And all I wanted to do was..." He hesitated, inwardly struggling. With a deprecatory snort, he finished, "All I wanted to do was sleep with you."

Silence pooled in the warm room. His honesty cut like a knife. Sherry stood speechless, weakened by those simple words. Gazing at his familiar face, she unknowingly let every feeling she possessed flood her smooth features.

I want you, she thought, her pulse beating hard and ever faster. *I love you.*

"Don't look at me like that," he whispered. "I don't have the strength to resist, and you didn't come here for this."

"I came to tell you something important," Sherry responded, her gaze sliding to his mouth.

"Tell me."

"When we were together..."

"In high school," he prompted.

"Yes. In high school." She swallowed. "I loved you very much," she said in a small voice.

"I loved you, too," he answered.

Shock registered in every fiber of her being. The words had come so naturally, so perfectly. Unrehearsed. From the soul and heart of him.

Her lips parted. Naked emotion filled her eyes. J.J. was powerless against her and with a muffled oath, he took two ground-devouring steps toward her and gathered her close, burying his face in the tangled glory of her hair.

"I always loved you!" he grated harshly. *"I still do!"*

If there had ever been a time in Jake's life when he needed self-control, this was it. All day. Hell, all week, month—whatever it had been since Sherry had reentered his life—he'd denied and fought feelings that wouldn't do him any good. And now she stood before him in innocent splendor. Truth to tell, he'd been unable to look at any other woman at the church—even the bride!—and all he could think about was their kiss in the darkened back hallway.

I love you had slipped past his lips as naturally as daybreak. He did love her. He always had. Her distraction only added to her mystique. Whatever mission she was on, whatever secrets and decisions she wanted to reveal, he didn't give a damn. Recklessly, foolishly he only wanted to take her in his arms and kiss and caress her until the hot beat of desire was assuaged.

"J.J...." she murmured in soft protest.

And even that stoked the flame of his overheated senses. Memories. Lustful, passionate memories of a careless, reckless time. She was the only person who could get away with calling him J.J. and make him feel like more than a little boy.

Her uncertainty was an aphrodisiac. He could feel the beat of her heart and the uneven tenor of her breathing. Jake inwardly groaned, wanting, *needing* to passionately join himself to her. But this was not the time. Not while something hung on her mind and prevented her from feeling every emotion he was feeling.

Carefully he released her from his urgent hug. She gazed at him, but her eyes had a faraway look, almost as if she were in a dream. He could relate. It *was* a dream. One he never wanted to wake up from.

Gently he took her drink away from her and set it on the mantel. Sherry's lips quivered, as if she wanted to say something. Jake waited, watching her with eyes that devoured the sight of her. Something in his expression must have registered with Sherry, reaching a kindred spirit within her, for she seemed to melt in front of him, all womanly armor falling away without a word spoken.

He reached for her, holding her at arm's length for a moment as he studied her.

"Do you want me?" he muttered. "Damn, I want you!"

Her answer was a soft expellation of breath. Slowly, inexorably, he pulled her to him again. She didn't quite resist, but she didn't quite come willingly, either.

Her palms were pressed against his chest. She couldn't miss his galloping heart. She looked down, at her hands, as if surprised at the feeling beneath them. He saw her eyelashes flutter. It was too much.

"Sherry," he whispered, bending his head until his lips were near the soft, escaping tendrils of thick brown hair that swung like a curtain to her shoulder.

"I...don't...can't," she struggled.

She turned her head but not before his lips grazed the corner of her mouth. His own body's reaction was unmistakable and suddenly he wanted her to feel his sex, to know what she was doing to him. It seemed incredibly important; or maybe lust was making him crazy. He certainly felt crazy.

His hands crept down her back to the curve of her spine. He wanted to grab her rounded bottom and press her against him. She was a perfect fit. She'd always been a perfect fit. It had just taken years for him to understand it. Hell, he didn't understand it yet!

As if his thoughts, not his conscience, controlled him, he did as he wanted, letting his palms slide over the delicious curve of her hips. His mouth crushed hers at the same moment he pulled her to his hardness and her slight protest was more a meow of pleasure—at least to his biased ears and inflamed senses.

Her own hands betrayed her, fluttering ineffectually somewhere near his waist, then softly pressing against his chest, then crawling up his back to clutch the fabric of his shirt between damp fists.

Memories were long gone. The moment was now. His tongue slid into her mouth, hot and seeking. Almost afraid, she reacted by sucking gently. Emboldened, he held her as tightly as he could, melding her to him possessively. She made no protest now. Her legs separated to accommodate him. Jake groaned, masochistically refusing to take advantage of the moment and press her against the wall to relieve the ache between his thighs.

"I want you," he admitted thickly, against her hot humid breath.

It was redundant, he realized. She had to know. She hesitated, inhaling light and fast, her chest rising and falling against his in rapid succession. His hand crept upward to cup her breast, just as lightly, which sent her breathing into warp zone. She wore no bra. He could feel her raised nipple through the weak shield of fabric. Jake, drunk with desire, leaned down and sucked her breast through the black dress, eliciting a groan of pleasure from Sherry that sounded like sweet torture as she threw her head back, exposing the vulnerable curve of her throat.

"I can't," she whispered, holding on to him for dear life as if afraid he might actually heed her words.

"You want to."

"Oh, J.J...." Sherry's eyes were squeezed closed, her expression one of intense need. Her hands had found the back of his neck, where his overly long hair lapped his collar.

With no thought for anything but how he felt at the moment, Jake swept her into his arms, luxuriating in her warm flesh, wanting to devour her as if she were some sweet delicacy he'd been long denied. Vaguely he realized he hadn't been this hot since high school—a situation that mildly worried him in some dark, neglected recess of his mind.

"What—what are you doing?" Sherry asked in alarm.

"Taking you upstairs."

This was trickier than he'd thought, considering the stairway was narrow with a carved wooden rail leading from the tiled entry below and Sherry was fast becoming an adversary instead of co-conspirator.

"I can't," she said in a louder, more controlled voice, all the while clinging to his neck while Jake, fueled by potent ardor, determinedly made his way around the landing and up to the bedroom loft.

"I can't! Oh, mercy. Put me down. Jake, for goodness' sake, this isn't the tree house and we aren't teen-agers!''

He set her on her feet in the middle of the room. Now her hand was at her throat and she darted looks around the room like a scared rabbit. Watching her, he read her reaction as her eyes noted the smooth pine walls, recessed lighting, huge braided rug that nearly covered the wooden floor, and the massive king-size bed with its deep, forest-green spread and collection of decorative throw pillows.

"I know it's not the tree house," he snapped.

"I don't just go to bed with men. It's not—what I do."

"I don't just go to bed with women, either."

"You—you have Caroline." Her distraction merely fanned the flames of his desire. She was so beautiful, auburn hair flowing loosely around her shoulders, shadowed eyes seeking some escape while pride rooted her firmly to the floor. She wouldn't run, although she wanted to.

"We're not engaged," Jake stated flatly. "We're just...together."

"You don't sleep with her?"

Jake hesitated. "Not much," he admitted, the truth tough for him to admit aloud. But Sherry clearly didn't believe him. Her expression took on that superior look he remembered so vividly from high school.

"I didn't ask for quantity."

"You don't know a damn thing about it!" he declared with heat, tired of the hypocrisy.

"You're not engaged and you don't sleep with her—much. Maybe it's because you're so damned good at seduction." She gestured to herself. "Case in point!"

"I have not slept with any woman but Caroline for

almost a decade. And I couldn't tell you the last time I slept with her!''

Sherry stared at him, registering the hammering honesty of his words with silence.

''But I want to sleep with you,'' he admitted. ''I have since the moment I saw you outside the gates. Hell, maybe even before that. I've got my fantasies like anyone else. You were the girl who made love to me, then ran away. I've lain awake nights wondering what it would be like to have you again, then I've spent my daylight hours pretending I never, ever thought of you. Sometimes I almost convinced myself.''

Sherry swallowed. ''Because I was the one that got away. The only one who couldn't resist you.''

It was a question. A hope? Or maybe a worry. Jake didn't care. He was only interested in the truth and making love to her. ''The only one *I* couldn't resist,'' he corrected softly. ''I want to make love to you so bad it hurts. I love you, Sherry. I always have.''

Tense fingers raked through her hair. She shook her head vehemently. ''You can't seduce me with words. I won't let you!'' Terror ran like a river beneath her words.

''What is so wrong with taking up where we left off?''

''It's been fifteen years!''

''Who the hell cares?'' he demanded frustratedly.

''I do! I'm not a kid anymore. I'm a woman, with responsibilities.''

''Coulda damn well fooled me! You've been here what? Weeks now, with no sign of returning to this other life you talk about! You took a job at Crawfish— *my* restaurant—and you've jumped back into my life. What are these other responsibilities? No, don't answer," Jake finished, crossing to where she stood once more, taking her trembling hands within his. "I don't care. I don't want to talk."

"J.J.," she protested with a sigh, "I have to talk."

"Then talk," he murmured, ducking his head to capture her lips one more time as he gently pushed her backward to the end of the bed. Her knees buckled and she slid onto the green comforter, with Jake fitting himself atop her. "I'll do the rest...."

Sherry's senses were aflame. Hot as lava. Sensitive as a new blossom. This wasn't the way she'd planned things. *Oh, be honest,* she berated herself ruefully. *You didn't plan things! You just let them happen.*

And let them happen she did. From the moment she'd kissed J.J. at the church, those things she hadn't planned began springing up like uncovered popcorn, flying at her wildly with no advance warning.

And now J.J.'s mouth was sensuously rubbing hers until her lips felt swollen and sensitized, begging for more. His body lay on hers in a position of intense intimacy, as if he were meant to be there.

He'd said I love you!

She moaned and twisted with desire beneath him. Her fingers skittered up his back to cling at his hard, muscled shoulders. The little sighs that issued from her lips were an invitation; she could hear *that* even above the furious pounding of her heart in her ears. It would be so easy to make love to him. The thrust of his manhood between her legs was an irresistible invitation, and without thinking, she moved to accommodate him.

Worse than when she was a teenager. Much worse. Her own desire humbled her. She was putty. *Putty!* And no amount of berating herself seemed to matter.

Slowly, slowly, he was seducing her. Touching her, breathing in her ear, moving sinuously against her. But even so he was waiting—waiting for her to make that final decision, holding back until she was completely, utterly ready.

"I love you," she murmured, shocked that she'd actually voiced the words she'd said only to him.

His answer was a kiss full of promise and a groan of release. His lips traveled to her neck where his tongue made crazy circles that fueled her desire until she was limp and throbbing. She sighed in sorrow for she knew it wasn't going to last; she couldn't let it last.

He was moving against her. "I missed you," he murmured. "I missed you so much."

"J.J...."

"I know it's crazy. It's always been crazy. I feel like I've been living in purgatory for *so long*." His breath feathered her flesh as he kissed her throat, her chin, her mouth, her eyes. And all the while his body moved, hard and seductive in a way that left her powerless, weak and wanton.

He was so masculine and she'd shied away from men ever since her ill-fated affair with him. Now she wanted to indulge herself like a glutton. She pulled his errant mouth back to hers and plunged her tongue inside. His groan sent shivers down her spine, infusing her with new power. She wanted to be possessed by him. His kiss hardened and lengthened, thrilling her, seducing her with its own need. He thrust against her and she arched, glorying in his hardness, making them both aware how slight a barrier their clothing was, how quickly it could be shed.

And putting that thought to action, J.J. suddenly twisted away to remove the rest of his clothes. The tiny buttons on his shirt gave way beneath anxious fingers, hers and his, and when his chest was bare, she slid her fingers through the dark, crisp hairs and over the sculpted muscles.

He unbuttoned her dress and slid it from her shoulders. As soon as her chest was free, his tongue moistened the flesh at the base of her neck until she squirmed with desire. In slow motion, she felt him undress her and only when a cool stirring of air brought goose bumps to her skin did her long-sleeping conscience awaken.

"J.J.," she whispered. And when that elicited no response apart from a movement of his mouth to her nipple that left her shivering, she said a bit louder, "Jake."

That caught him off guard. He lifted his head, gazing at her with passion-drugged eyes. "Jake?"

"I can't let this happen, without telling you why I left Oceantides before."

"Oh, Sherry," he whispered. "It doesn't matter now that you're here."

"It does matter."

As if he refused to recognize the ill wind that swept over them, he redoubled his efforts to make love to her. Sherry struggled to find words, struggled to keep focused on Mandy and her real reason for coming home.

But suddenly he was poised above her, the tip of his shaft seeking her warm sheath. She knew, without a doubt, that he would hate her for not telling him first; that he would feel used.

But she also knew this wouldn't happen again unless she let it happen now.

"I love you," she whispered, gasping as J.J. thrust himself inside her and they both succumbed to the rhythm of love and seduction, the moment spinning out of time and space, gone from reality.

In the darkness that followed, Sherry counted her heartbeats, waiting until they were at a normal enough pace that she could trust herself to speak with reason. J.J. was sprawled across her, in total abandonment to pure sensation.

"Birth control was never my strong suit," she whispered with deepest irony.

He lifted his head, eyes flaring in alarm. "God, a condom!"

"No, it's okay. I'm not completely crazy. I won't get pregnant at this point of my cycle. I have learned one or two things over the years."

He expelled a breath, gently disengaging himself from her but holding on tightly, his arms and legs surrounding her as if he never wanted to let go. "Apparently, I haven't. We've been really lucky," he added thoughtfully.

Sherry drew a breath. "Yes, we have. Really lucky."

Her tension transmitted itself to him. "What is it?" he asked.

"Oh, J.J. It's what I came to Oceantides to tell you. We *were* lucky. Lucky enough to have a beautiful daughter."

His gray eyes held hers, confused.

"I was pregnant, J.J. With your baby. That's why I didn't make it to graduation!"

Chapter Nine

Sand squeaked protestingly beneath his running shoes—a rhythmic, familiar noise that normally blended with the dull roar of the waves and the plaintive cries of the gulls. Today, however, he was so self-absorbed he heard nothing but the echo of Sherry's shocking announcement.

I was pregnant, J.J. With your baby.

He'd called his sister, Heather, at four o'clock this morning, as soon as he'd woken, which was a laugh because he'd never fallen asleep. Sherry's words hadn't really penetrated for what had felt like eons. He could visualize her flushed face, the sparkle of unshed tears in her violet eyes, the rosy blush of her exposed flesh, last remnants of their lovemaking.

He'd backed away. He'd been doused with ice water. He hadn't heard right. It was a joke. A cosmic prank.

He'd spent so much time congratulating himself on

not "knocking up" Sherry Sterling, as his friends so eloquently put it. And he'd been so proud of the fact that he wasn't like his father—Rex, with his philandering ways and lack of responsibility; Rex, who'd cared only about football and himself, and not necessarily in that order....

Heather had been surprisingly empathetic. "It's not your fault. You didn't know. Take it from the here and now. But you'd better ask yourself what she wants."

"What do you mean?" His head crashed as if he were recovering from an alcoholic binge.

"Well, everyone's got a personal agenda. It must not be money, or she would have hit you for that when she found out she was pregnant. How old is this child? Did you say it was a girl?"

"A daughter. She's fourteen. Just had a birthday."

Valentine's Day.

His mouth was dry. His breathing rasped. He could hardly think. All the information about Mandy had come tumbling past Sherry's lips, a torrent that had nearly drowned him. Truth was, he couldn't recall much of anything she'd said except the basic, salient points.

"Why did Sherry come and tell you now?" Heather asked him.

"Because—because Mandy wants to meet her father," he answered her thickly, sounding like a stranger to himself. He *was* a stranger. The Jake Beckett he'd lived with for thirty-three years didn't really exist. Gone in the light of one incredible revelation.

"So, meet her."

"I can't," he answered with painful honesty. "I don't want to."

"Why not?" She was impatient.

He had no answer. He just knew he couldn't. His

feelings were a jumble. He wasn't prepared to be a father. He didn't feel like a father. *He didn't want to be a father!*

Somewhere during last night he'd roared as much at Sherry: *I don't want to be a father!* She'd flinched as if he'd hit her. He was so furious, so consumed with outrage, that he'd lost his mind for a few moments. He'd awakened, as if from some deep sleep, minutes later to stare down at hands clenched so hard they still ached today. Sherry had stood shivering before him, her own hands covering her nakedness, too destroyed herself to reach for the clothes they'd so heedlessly tossed on the floor, heated moments earlier.

He wasn't proud of it, but his initial reaction had been pure horror. The explanation fit so perfectly he didn't doubt it for an instant. She'd left because she was pregnant. With his child. And that was one truth he didn't bother questioning; he knew Mandy was his. He could sense it in some inner part of himself that grabbed hold of what she was saying and processed it inside his soul.

She'd wanted comfort—or at least, understanding. As she slowly dressed, her movements heavy with exhaustion, he'd known that all he had to do was reach out and touch her and everything would be okay. Okay? No. Nothing would be okay, but Sherry would have felt better.

She'd left within a half hour of dropping her bomb, stumbling away although he'd insisted he would call her a taxi. She'd refused. Nothing in Oceantides was beyond walking distance, and she'd headed south down the beach to the motel room—part of Beckett Enterprises—where she was staying. Before she disappeared she said something that made him realize much later that Mandy, the child in the picture she'd given him, hadn't been living with Sherry all these years. In the heat of the announcement, she'd somehow forgotten to convey that to him, and he had to admit part of his fury had been that she'd carried off such a deception for so long without a thought to his feelings.

But after he'd sorted through the words again, his gaze focused squarely out the window on her footsteps that were rapidly being eaten away by the greedy waves, the echo of her meaning finally reached his dulled brain.

"She told me she wanted to meet her father," Sherry had said in a choked voice. "She wanted a picture of you, but I didn't have one. I'd made sure there was nothing from those years. I never dreamed she would show up one day and ask for something about you!"

It was only when her footsteps were completely washed away that he'd realized Sherry had been through this same shock he was feeling now. She'd obviously given Mandy up for adoption, and Mandy must have looked her up only recently. Her deception had been self-protective, but not completely without regard for his feelings. She'd come to him with the truth after Mandy had come to her. And she'd been too upset tonight to realize she hadn't made the situation clear.

If he'd known she hadn't raised Mandy herself he might have shown more compassion. He would have believed her decision to keep him in the dark had been more altruistic; made for their daughter's benefit, so that she could have a life with two loving parents—not a pair of mismatched teenagers. But all he'd seen was the fact that Sherry had run away with her secret and taken away his choice.

He'd wanted to kill her for that!

I might never have known, he thought with an internal shiver.

But did he want to know now?

Jake covered his face with his hands, raking his fingers through hair grown far too shaggy and long. How could *he* be a father?

His lungs burned from exertion. His legs were like water. His arms hurt. How long had he been running? An hour? Two?

"God..." With an expellation of air that was almost a sob, he flung himself onto the wet sand, sweat pouring from him. The internal shiver hadn't stopped and he trembled as if from palsy.

Heather had spoken to him slowly and clearly, as if he were half-deaf, which, in his distraction, wasn't that far from the truth. "Take a deep breath. Take a run on the beach. Take a few days off work. Get yourself together and then sit down and talk it over rationally. This is an opportunity, J.J.," she'd added kindly. "It's not your fault you didn't know."

Then why did it feel like his fault?

Jake rolled onto his back and stared up at the low, thick gray sky. Mist from the ocean dampened his face, cool against his overheated flesh. He would probably die of exposure, he thought, his mouth twisting ironically. No Sherry to save him this time.

Sherry... Sherry, baby...

If he were honest with himself he could admit he'd reacted like a child. He'd practically stuck his fingers in his ears and screamed and stomped his feet. Well, not literally, perhaps, but he'd certainly closed himself off to everything but his own emotional outrage, cocooning himself against Sherry's own pain and torture to protect himself.

Some hero.

"You bastard," he whispered to the stiff breeze.

Feeling a hundred years old, he climbed to his feet and staggered back up the beach toward home.

It would be nice to take Heather's advice but he couldn't afford the time. He had to see Sherry and learn more about his—their—fourteen-year-old Valentine's Day child....

"Thank you for coming back today. You are the best thing that happened to this place!" Gerald enthused heartily.

"I'm just saying goodbye," Sherry reminded him.

"Ha! You are an angel!"

Sherry smiled wanly. She'd stepped in to smooth the feathers of a customer who was infuriated that she hadn't gotten her dish just the way she wanted it after asking them to change the recipe until the garlic-dusted scallops had been smothered in sherry and cheese and ended up with about a thousand calories more than normal.

"There oughta be a law," Jennifer sniffed, casting a glare over her shoulder at the disgruntled woman.

"It's unimportant," Sherry answered indifferently. She'd been an automaton since the evening before, when J.J. had taken her to the peak of ecstasy before dropping her into a chasm of despair.

He'd hated her for delivering the truth. He'd hated her for lying to him. He just hated her.

And it hurt. So much so, that she'd had to relearn how to breathe, since every intake of breath sounded like a sob and choked her swollen throat.

She hadn't cried. She'd gone past that into some strange state of nothingness where her feelings were deadened. Of course, they'd come screaming back sometime in the middle of the night, a night so pain-filled she'd curled into a ball and rocked herself to sleep like a newborn babe.

Her sleep had been a walk through nightmares. She'd awakened to the knowledge that Mandy might not be able to meet her father because Mandy's father wasn't interested in being one.

It had ripped her heart in two.

So, why was she here? Because sitting alone with her thoughts for company was the purest form of torture. She didn't know what to do now.

"You okay?" Gerald asked as Sherry sank down on one of the stools in the kitchen.

"Fine."

"So, the wedding was beautiful, huh?" Jennifer asked. She'd hinted around about it all afternoon, ever since Sherry had shown up for work. It was so pathetic, Jennifer's desire still to run with the popular crowd of Oceantides High—a crowd that had been forced to accept Sherry by virtue of J.J.'s attraction to her. Sherry remembered her own subsequent disinterest in everything associated with popularity and social status.

It was so pathetic and small it was almost funny, but Sherry had never felt less like laughing. "Beautiful," she agreed with a sigh. "A beautiful wedding."

"Leave her alone," Gerald scolded. Jennifer darted him a black look, then shrugged and returned to her duties. Gerald laid a thick, reassuring palm on Sherry's shoulder, and it was all she could do to keep from weeping. One tear did escape from the corner of her eye and Gerald whispered softly in her ear, "Go home. Whatever it is will be better tomorrow."

She should have taken his advice, but once outside

Crawfish Delish, she beelined toward Bernie's Pizza as if it were a magnet. As she pushed through the doors, the familiar scents of pasta and tomato sauce, Italian spices and pepperoni and just everything of comfort swirled around her, enveloping her.

And as if he'd known she needed him, Bernie himself was behind the counter, his face splitting into a grin at the sight of her.

The tears she'd fought poured out like a tidal wave.

"Sherry, *bella!*" Bernie cried, throwing open the counter and coming to her with comforting flour-dusted arms. He embraced her warmly, hugging her hard.

"I'm so sorry," she muttered through her sobs.

"No, no. Get it all out." He patted her back.

Knowing she was making a spectacle of herself, Sherry struggled to pull herself together, eventually managing to slip free of Bernie's arms, but not of his concern.

"What's the matter, honey?" His normally jovial face was creased with worry. "You are so unhappy."

"It's been an unhappy kind of day," Sherry admitted.

"Ryan said you were in town. I said, 'When does she come see me?' and he says that you have important things to do."

"They're done," Sherry said.

"Ah... Did they turn out badly?" he asked kindly.

"Something like that."

"Want a root beer?"

She laughed, swiping away her tears. "I'd love a root beer."

"Want to tell Bern your troubles?" he asked, as he headed for the soft-drink machine and pulled her a foamy glassful.

She shook her head. "Not especially. But it's great seeing you," she added, warmly.

"Then let me tell you about me...."

As Sherry positioned herself at a nearby table, Bernie launched into tales of his grandchildren. Sherry let the warm words soak into her skin, as if Bernie's love for his family was a tonic for her, as well.

"You never tied the knot, then, huh?" he asked when he came to a slight break in his stories.

"No. Not even a serious relationship."

"I know nobody appreciates advice, but you should give it a try. A girl like you is going to want children sooner or later. Tick, tick, tick! That's the biological clock, and sooner or later you're going to hear it." He pointed a finger at her nose, grinning.

Sherry smiled faintly. What could she say?

Bernie suddenly glanced up, his brows lifting at something he saw through the glass doors behind her. "It's Jake Beckett," he said in wonder. "He hasn't showed up here in years."

The hair on Sherry's arms rose in tandem with her suddenly galloping heart. She twisted around. Sure enough, J.J. was coming across Bernie's parking lot in a straight line from Crawfish Delish's front door. His head was bent against a spate of rain, his black hair lopping over his eyes and obscuring his face.

He knows I'm here, she thought half-hysterically, her eyes desperately searching the room for escape.

"You don't want to see him." Bernie eyed her thoughtfully, wiping his hands on his apron even though they were clean.

"No, I don't," Sherry admitted. Then, hearing herself, she added with a sigh, "But I have to."

"Hmm."

That was all Bernie got out before J.J.'s strong arm pushed open one of the glass swing-doors and his gaze collided with Sherry's. He looked worse for wear, she realized with a guilty pang: tired, drawn, and grim. The ultimatum was here. There was no more sand in the hourglass.

Unknowingly, Sherry squared her shoulders and took a deep breath, preparing herself for round two. As he spied her reaction, J.J.'s mouth turned downward and he shook his head slowly.

"I've got to know more," he said by way of apology.

"All right," Sherry answered uncertainly.

"Come with me for a drive. I've got a car over by Crawfish."

It was more a command than a request, but who was Sherry to argue? She'd come to Oceantides for this specific purpose. Soon, it would all be over.

Or just beginning...

She followed him into the rain and climbed into the passenger seat of his rental. Remembering yesterday's intimacy, she shuddered involuntarily, drawing J.J.'s gaze her way. She met his eyes. He looked—shattered.

"You said she's fourteen," J.J. began as soon as they were on their way. His gaze was fastened on the winding road in front of him, his hands gripped tightly around the wheel.

"Yes. Her birthday was Valentine's Day," Sherry reiterated.

"And she's been living with...?" He frowned, unable to dredge up the data she'd thrown out at him the night before.

This, Sherry could understand, so she began again, more cautiously this time in case J.J. should react as he had the night before. She could scarcely blame him.

She'd hidden the truth and if the situation were reversed, that sin alone would be unforgivable.

"I made a lot of stupid decisions that I wouldn't now," Sherry confessed with a faint smile. "But putting Mandy up for adoption wasn't one of them. The Craigs, her adoptive parents, love her. She's just at an age where she's questioning everything, and it's really hard."

She told him about her visit from Mandy, and how their daughter had demanded to meet her father. She specifically related the facts unemotionally; J.J. could fill in the blanks if he wanted to without much effort.

He listened in silence until Sherry had given him every bit of data about Mandy that she could think of. When she was done, she realized belatedly that he'd parked the rental car in the same turnaround she'd found him in the night he'd nearly frozen to death after swimming in the ocean. Mariner Lane. Glancing around, she saw the same, though slightly more dilapidated, closed-up snow-cone shop that had been there in her youth.

Night was falling. The sky, already pewter, seemed to darken and sweep down around them, creating an intimacy Sherry would have liked to avoid. J.J.'s profile, so sharp moments before, began to blur in the dimming light. He hadn't turned to glance at her once during the dissertation, so she was surprised when he suddenly twisted in his seat to give her a good, long look.

"I hate it that I didn't know," he told her.

"I couldn't tell you."

"Why not?"

"Oh, J.J...." She gazed out the side window, needing some space. If this went on much longer, she would choke on the lump in her throat all over again.

"All right. Forget it. I understand."

"You do?"

"I was a jerk and we were so young. But even so, you should have told me," he added, unable to forgive.

"Will you see her?" Sherry asked, her hands knotted into fists.

"Of course, I'll see her. I just can't believe it! It's—incredible. And I don't know how to feel."

"You made your feelings pretty clear last night," Sherry said softly, remembering his horrified reaction to the news that he was a father.

J.J. sucked in a sharp breath. "Okay, I deserved that. But you hit me in the gut."

"So, what are you saying?" Sherry turned to gaze at him.

"You really think I wouldn't want to know my own daughter?" he asked in disbelief, searching her face.

"But you said…"

"I know. I lashed out. At you. I'm still having trouble getting it all straight, but I want to meet my daughter."

"You mean it?"

"Yes, I mean it. Just tell me how."

"I— Well, she's in Seattle this weekend for her birthday. Let me call and see if she and the Craigs can stay over, so you can meet her."

A long moment passed while J.J.'s jaw tightened and relaxed several times, as if he were struggling to get something out.

"What?" Sherry asked.

"I'd like you to be there with me, when she and I meet."

For an answer, she placed her hand over his.

With a feeling of unreality still dogging him like a bad smell, Jake let himself into the Beckett home, his footsteps loud in the hallway. His entry didn't go unnoticed. He heard animated voices suddenly hush from behind Patrice's sitting-room door.

No time like the present for delivering unpleasant news, he thought, recognizing one of the voices as Caroline's.

They say revelations happen to us all, and at that moment, Jake Beckett had a revelation—and that revelation was that he was chock full of bull. He'd made himself believe that he and Caroline were a perfect match when in reality they were completely wrong for each other. Together, they were colorless and empty, and Jake finally recognized how hard he'd hung on to this delusion because he hadn't wanted to really face the future.

He couldn't believe himself. Good grief! It had been Sherry from the beginning. From the time they were barely older than kids. Could love really last that long? Be that enduring despite such a brief, shaky start?

His inaction for so many years suddenly felt like a betrayal. He wanted movement. Change. A leap toward an uncertain but exciting future. All this time spent half at his place, half at the family home. He'd been waiting for the break. Wanting something to come along and slap him on the head—and it had!

Without knocking, he flung open the sitting-room door. Patrice gazed at him over the tops of her glasses, her ubiquitous crossword puzzle folded neatly on her lap. Caroline stood at the window, her hands clasped in front of her, her expression hard to read. Jake didn't care. He was emancipated, and in his emancipation he spoke what he felt.

"I've been with Sherry."

Caroline stiffened and a sound of protest slipped past

her tight lips before she could hold it back. Recklessly, Jake added, "She told me I'm a father. I have a four-teen-year-old daughter with her."

Caroline's regal jaw dropped. She gaped at him in pure shock. Jake felt a pang of regret that quickly changed to wonder and fury when he realized Patrice betrayed no emotion whatsoever.

"You knew," he said softly. "All these years, you knew."

She didn't deny it. Nor did she look the least little bit remorseful. "It was the only reason that made sense that she left," she stated primly.

Jake reeled. "You didn't tell me!"

"Would it have made a difference? You were a child!"

"I was eighteen!"

Caroline slumped onto the window seat, staring dazedly at the floor. Patrice threw her an impatient glance, as if annoyed by her lack of backbone. But it was Caroline whom Jake suddenly wanted to comfort. Her reaction was at least real and heartfelt. His mother was alien to him.

"I don't believe this," he muttered hoarsely.

Patrice was furious. "I knew that's why she came back. Just to torture you and turn your life into a circus!"

"Caroline," Jake murmured, moving toward her as if in a fog.

"Did you spend last night with her?" Caroline asked stiffly.

Jake couldn't deny it. "Yes."

"Did you come here to tell me it's over between us?"

"He did not!" Patrice answered for him, throwing

the crossword to the floor and rising to her feet in a tower of fury.

"I can't have the two of you run my life anymore," was Jake's form of reply. "That's over. I'm going to meet my daughter. I'm going with Sherry."

Patrice stared at him as if he'd grown reptilian scales. "J.J., I—"

"Don't say it. I don't want to hear it."

"You can't just leave. The business needs you!"

Very succinctly, he told her what she could do with the business.

Twin spots of color flared in his mother's cheeks. "She took money, J.J. That's what she wanted, you know. She chased you down because you could give her a future. She got herself pregnant to ensure that future."

"Stop it." Jake was terse.

"I gave her ten thousand dollars the first time. And she's collected damn near a hundred thousand over the years! Yes, I should have told you rather than let her blackmail me, but damn it! I knew your ridiculous chivalry would create a worse problem!"

"Wait a minute. You gave her money? You bought her off! You *knew*, really *knew?*"

Patrice hesitated for a moment, realizing she'd overplayed her hand. Shrugging impatiently, she barreled on, determined to have her say. "Did you hear how much money I'm talking about? Do you get it?"

"Damn you to hell!" Jake roared, so incensed he could scarcely think.

"I'll show you the canceled checks. I've got every one of them."

She walked to a drawer in the antique, rolltop desk, pulling out a neatly arranged pile of checks. Holding them in front of his nose, Patrice lifted her chin, but the desperation in her eyes gave her away.

Jake wanted to throw the checks in her face. He didn't care. He didn't give a good goddamn. He had a daughter and all the deceptions didn't matter.

But they did....

Snatching the evidence of Sherry's materialism, his heart shattered at the sight of her signature on the back of each and every check. Patrice hadn't lied about the amount. Sherry had feathered her nest with about a hundred thousand dollars of Beckett money.

"You were a fool to let her take you," he snarled, stomping out of the house and the most vulgar scene of his life.

Chapter Ten

Patchy blue Seattle skies greeted Sherry and J.J. as they drove his newly fixed Jeep toward Sherry's apartment. Sherry's tension mounted with each mile that passed beneath the tires, drawing them farther from Oceantides and closer to Mandy.

The Craigs had stayed beyond the weekend and were waiting in a kind of strained limbo for both of Mandy's biological parents to arrive in Seattle. Sherry had spoken to Mandy briefly but most of her conversation had been with Gina Craig, who'd sounded as distracted and lost as Sherry felt.

"Mandy wants to stay, so we'll stay. She can make up her classes. She's a good student. She's a good kid. She's just got some things to sort through right now and it's hard for her." Gina had drawn a shaky breath. "But it's good for her to close this chapter—or open it," she added quickly, hearing how that had sounded. "It's important. Is—is her father anxious to meet her?"

Sherry understood the question. J.J. had been more of a phantom all these years than she had. "Very anxious."

"Then we'll see you on Wednesday," Gina said, reiterating what they'd already discussed.

In the past few days Sherry had had little contact with J.J. She'd expected him to stop by or call. Their last moments together had been surprisingly tender, with J.J. struggling to come to terms with his fatherhood. Since then, she'd sensed a withdrawal that had left her a little baffled.

In their last conversation, in fact, J.J. had been terse to the point of rude.

"I'll pick you up at noon on Wednesday, or as soon as I get the Jeep back."

"Okay," Sherry had agreed.

"Goodbye," he'd responded shortly and she'd been left staring at the receiver in her hand, wondering what in the world had happened. J.J. seemed to yo-yo from acceptance to rejection with each passing hour. She never knew what to expect next.

Now, she stole a sideways glance at him. His jaw was set and his eyes were locked on the freeway, as if daring to meet her gaze would blind him or worse! When he'd picked her up this morning he'd uttered less than ten words, and apart from a pleasant "Hello" to one of the motel's maids whom Sherry half remembered from high school and who was also, therefore, an employee of Beckett Enterprises, J.J.'s face hadn't altered one iota from its unforgiving frown.

But it was not her problem. She was a mass of nerves anyway. She hoped, *prayed*, their coming meeting would be a joyous occasion, not a confrontation. Maybe J.J. was as nervous as she was. Maybe that was it. Whatever the case, meeting Mandy was the first step toward the rest of all their lives. She had no idea what would come after.

"Turn here," she directed, and J.J. silently guided the Jeep to the off-ramp and through the series of streets that led to Sherry's apartment complex.

She had no feeling of coming home. The apartment, she realized distantly, meant as little to her as the colorless years of her life since high school. She'd been more alive and vibrant since Mandy had come into her life and she'd been forced to return to Oceantides. It was as if she'd been on sabbatical all these years. Absolutely everything had changed.

As soon as the Jeep was parked, Sherry slid out the passenger door, glancing at the cars in the lot, wondering if one of them belonged to the Craigs. But no, she and J.J. were early. Mandy wouldn't be here until dinnertime.

J.J. didn't follow her to her door. "Are you coming?" she asked. He shook his head. His tension was palpable, and she felt a wave of empathy. "I can make coffee and sandwiches."

"I'm not hungry."

"Neither am I."

She let herself inside, flicking on lights against the growing darkness as night fell outside. Shivering a bit, she turned up the heat just as J.J., apparently reconsidering, stepped across the threshold and closed the door.

"I'm not hungry, but I'm freezing," she said, plugging in the coffee maker.

J.J. stood at the edge of the cabinets that separated her U-shaped kitchen from the rest of the apartment.

His silence unnerved her, and she kept her gaze on the coffee maker, watching steaming water gurgle through the filter. Now it was her turn to be unable to look at him.

"I know about the money."

His voice could have chilled the Sahara. Sherry shivered and asked automatically, "The money?"

"That Patrice gave you."

Sherry gazed at him in anguish. An unfathomable ache filled her chest. She was beaten. Aunt Elena had signed the check and she hadn't stopped her. Sherry may have given her mother her life, but it had cost her J.J.

"Aren't you even going to try to deny it?" he asked hoarsely.

"I told Patrice I'd pay her back."

"Oh, God..." His words were a soft prayer. He sagged against the counter. Automatically she moved to help him but he jerked away and Sherry stopped short, stunned by his withdrawal.

"I'm sorry," she murmured on a half sob.

Betrayal filled his eyes. "I always told myself you were different. All these years, at some level I believed you were the one. I lied to myself about it, but then suddenly, here you were! *And I believed in you!*"

Sherry couldn't answer him. No excuse was good enough.

"You know I expected you to tell me it was all a trick. Something my mother managed to pull off. I never knew why she hated you so much. I couldn't understand." His voice broke and he stopped himself.

"J.J..." She reached a trembling hand to him.

"Don't call me that!" His voice shook with loathing. "I told you I loved you, but it's a lie. It's all a lie!"

"Mandy isn't. She's real."

"You're a lie."

The buzz of Sherry's apartment bell felt like an electric jolt. J.J. shuddered. Sherry walked to the door, her legs lead weights. It took every ounce of willpower she possessed to twist the knob.

"Hi," she greeted Mandy and Gina and Tom Craig. "We've been looking forward to seeing you...."

Sherry sat in an armchair, too exhausted to do more than cradle her cup of coffee and watch the proceedings as if she were an uninterested party. Tom and Gina Craig sat on the love seat that flanked her left side. J.J. and Mandy stood tensely near the counter that divided the kitchen from view. They clearly did not know what to do with each other, but their fascination was obvious. From the moment Mandy had crossed the threshold, she and J.J. hadn't taken their eyes off each other. Having gone through the same experience so recently, Sherry could well understand their absorption and shock.

As for her, there was another kind of turmoil inside her breast. He hated her. She'd taken the money and he hated her. Why, in all the worry over their secret love-child, had she never considered that this would be the mortal wound?

Gina leaned toward Sherry. "They look a lot alike, don't they?"

"Yes." Sherry attempted a smile.

"It's all so difficult...."

Sherry nodded.

"I've worried for years," Gina confided. "As an adoptive parent you know that someday your child's going to ask questions. We never hid her adoption from her, but we didn't encourage a lot of discussion, either. It was too hard.

"And then when Mandy wanted to find you, I resisted a little. I guess I was afraid she'd love you more."

Sherry nearly choked on her coffee. Her gaze was on Mandy's expressive face. Although Mandy tried to hide it, her delight in meeting her father was self-evident. Her cheeks were flushed and her blue eyes sparkled. She smoothed back one of her braids, her fingers twisting the rubber-banded end, a self-conscious gesture that displayed none of the defiance she'd shown when she'd first met Sherry.

"He didn't know, did he?" Gina guessed, throwing a look at J.J.

"Pardon?"

"About Mandy. You told him after Mandy found you. That's what took so long."

"No, he didn't know," Sherry admitted.

"He's not going to tell her. At least, not now. He's going to protect you."

Sherry laughed without humor. "He wouldn't protect me. He'll protect Mandy."

"In time, it will all work out." Gina smiled. "I really did worry a lot before. I was so afraid she would meet you both and all of a sudden you'd be this happy family, and Mandy would be gone."

Tom reached over and silently clasped his wife's hand. It was then Sherry realized that Gina was trembling; that this whole scenario was so incredibly hard on her.

"You never had to worry," Sherry blurted out. "You're her parents. You raised her. I can't deny I haven't had those same dreams, but that's not the way it works."

"When she got so belligerent, I blamed myself," Gina murmured, tears developing in the corners of her eyes. "I wanted to just hold on and keep her home!"

"You can't do that," Tom muttered, as if he'd said it a thousand times before, which he probably had.

Gina nodded. "No, you can't. But it's *so hard!*"

"You've been really wonderful," Tom interjected seriously. "Gina was so afraid, and so was I, that meeting her parents would backfire and Mandy would be more angry."

Sherry twisted her cup in her hands and flicked a look at J.J. His animosity toward her was carefully veiled, or with any luck, momentarily forgotten, as he talked quietly with Mandy. "I think it's a good thing."

"Oh, it is!" Gina nodded. "I'm so glad!"

"I guess we're all wondering what the future will bring," Tom said, and at that moment there was a lull in J.J. and Mandy's intimacy.

"Mandy says you're not flying back until this weekend," J.J. said to Tom and Gina. "If that's the case, I'd like to invite you all to Oceantides, where I live."

Mandy's bright face turned eagerly to her parents. Tom and Gina looked uncertain, and the pain in Sherry's breast swelled to drastic proportions. She wanted to be a part of this. She wanted to be invited, but she knew there was no hope.

"All right," Tom agreed.

For a split second J.J. glanced at Sherry. His thoughts were unreadable, but the slant of his jaw told a story of its own.

"I'm driving home tonight," he suggested. "Why don't I take you to your hotel and we'll pick up your luggage and go...."

* * *

The yearbook tumbled out of her closet as if it had been waiting for just the right moment to surprise her. Stuffed beneath a mass of belts and jewelry, she'd taken it to be part of the shelf during her search. Her eye had traveled over it a dozen times while she'd concentrated on more hidden areas where she'd assumed the yearbook must be.

Now, when one of her belts had lopped down and impeded the closet door, she'd yanked the offending article out and the yearbook had followed. A sense of premonition ticked icily down Sherry's spine. Frozen for a moment, she almost reluctantly picked it up and carried it to the bed.

J.J. and company had been gone less than an hour, and in that time she'd desperately tried to put them out of her mind. Thinking about them was dangerous. She'd always wanted a family and for the second time in her life she was the uninvited and unwelcome interloper. Couldn't she be a part of it? Couldn't she?

She'd called Dee at work, but Dee had been unable to talk because she was working alone and there were just enough customers to keep interrupting their conversation. Sherry had offered to help, but Dee had absolutely insisted she stay home and "work through this." Sherry thought working might be a better antidote, but she could sense how weary she was. So, she'd prowled around the apartment in misery and frustration and then the yearbook had popped into her possession.

With slightly unsteady fingers she opened the gilt-edged cover. Memories from high school flooded her vision. Jennifer and Julie and Roxanne and Summer, and most of all, J.J. Beckett. Casually she turned the pages, lingering on his senior picture, consumed by how young he looked. How young *she* looked! It was all well and good remembering, but it struck Sherry how incredibly long ago and far away it was.

His football pictures brought back an extra tingle of resentment. She'd been blamed, after all, for the team's floundering in the play-offs. But seeing him drawn back for a pass, right hand in the air, his uniform mud-spattered, a surge of players surrounding him, Sherry suddenly wondered what all the fuss was about. Why had she cared so much? Why had everyone? It was silly, really. A silly game. A silly time of her life. There was absolutely no reason to waste all this energy on something that, in the end, mattered so little.

Closing the book, Sherry flopped down on her bed. The images stayed in her head. And in her soul was the deepest heartbreak she'd experienced to date.

A tear trickled from the corner of her eye and she clenched her hands into the comforter.

The floorboards of the tree house were mushy with rot. Jake stepped gingerly across them to the window. It was a strange feeling, being here, but yesterday Mandy had insisted on climbing inside and Jake, fearing for her safety, had accompanied her and they'd spent a pleasant afternoon together.

Mandy was gone now. He'd driven her, Tom and Gina to Sea-Tac airport this morning. But her memory lingered and Jake couldn't help the chuckle that erupted from him now as he glanced toward Beckett Manor.

Mandy had taken Patrice by storm!

Not that he hadn't been in a state of delayed shock himself; meeting his full-grown daughter had left him speechless and locked in amazement. But when they arrived in Oceantides and Patrice got a look at Mandy—

and narrow-eyed, Mandy regarded her grandmother
right back—the fun began. Woe to anyone who tried to
mold Mandy Craig, and Patrice jumped right in to do
just that. Patrice might not like Sherry, but Beckett
blood was Beckett blood and she'd been determined, by
God, to win her granddaughter to her side. Being her
usual forceful self, Patrice had taken over, dragging
Mandy through the house and yammering madly about
what it meant to be a Beckett. What Patrice didn't count
on was that Mandy was Beckett through and through;
she wasn't about to be coerced, cajoled or forced into
anything. And Mandy said so, in no uncertain terms.

Patrice's response to this was to make a sideways
comment about Sherry. Jake's chuckle deepened in his
chest. Sparks had flown then! Mandy might have just
met Sherry, but Patrice had slurred her *mother!* Swords
were drawn, so Jake had quickly hustled the slightly
befuddled Craigs outside to view the ocean. When
they'd all returned it was to absolute, total silence, with
Patrice at one end of the room and Mandy at the other.
Mandy then slid him a look of "I've had enough already" and Patrice stood iron straight, lips thinned with
fury and disappointment—a posture he knew only too
well.

The tree house had been Mandy's way to get her
father alone, Jake realized after he'd scrambled up after
her. She couldn't know the memories it evoked for him.
Jake hadn't set foot inside the place since that last time
with Sherry, and he'd had to fight stirring emotions he
wanted to quash forever.

He and Mandy had been forced to share a section on
the far side of the structure that had escaped the worst
of the rot, but that was okay with Mandy. Although she
hadn't said so, he could tell she enjoyed the tree house

as only a kid can. For that, fighting his own feelings was worth it, and he'd settled against the hard slats at his back with a strange feeling of contentment.

Of course, Mandy had had other ideas. "What's *her* problem?" she'd demanded right away, jerking her head in the direction of the house.

"Patrice?"

"Yeah," she'd snorted, flipping back a braid and staring at him through huge blue eyes that were more like his than Sherry's but reminded him of Sherry all the same.

"You mean, besides egomania?"

Laughter filled those gorgeous orbs, held in check, however, since he was still the enemy, too. That, he'd figured out right away. Mandy might want to meet her parents but she was reserving judgment on whether to love them or not.

Love... Such a difficult word and one that seemed to come so easily to him all of a sudden. For years he couldn't face it, or voice it, or believe in it. Now, within the space of a few weeks, he realized he'd loved Sherry all along and that he loved Mandy immediately, no holds barred.

Except he didn't love Sherry anymore, he reminded himself.

"Was she always like that?" Mandy asked curiously.

"To varying degrees."

"I wouldn't trust anything she said. She wants to get people."

It was Jake's turn to stare. He couldn't deny it, but her perception got to him. "She's difficult."

"She hates my mother, doesn't she? She didn't come right out and say it, so I said it."

Jake frowned. "What do you mean?"

"I said, 'Why do you hate my mother so much? What did she ever do to you?' and she got all testy and puffed up."

He could picture Patrice, ready to explode. "I'll bet!" he muttered with feeling.

"Why does she hate her?"

"Because..." Jake hesitated, picking through his words.

But Mandy wasn't one to wait. "Because?"

"Because I loved her," he decided after a long moment. "Patrice sensed something I didn't even know, and she did everything she could to keep us apart."

"I thought you wouldn't marry her."

"It never came to that."

Mandy nodded and murmured, "Ah..." in understanding. Staring down at her hands, a line forming between her brows, she asked softly, "You didn't know about me, did you? Patrice made a crack about you not knowing."

As angry as Jake was at Sherry, he didn't want to hurt her further, but neither did he want to lie. "No, I didn't."

"What happened when she told you the truth?"

Thinking of that night, Jake made a face. He'd let Sherry down. He'd let himself down. "I—freaked out. Totally lost it."

That had made her grin. "I'll bet," she'd echoed with his identical inflection, and then they were both laughing.

And for a shining moment Jake had been thoroughly and completely happy. He couldn't recall ever being so happy, in fact, except for the hours he'd spent with Sherry.

Now, as he gazed out the makeshift window toward

the beach and watched faint streaks of sunlight peek between the gray clouds, he searched his feelings and realized he was going to have to get over thinking about Sherry and concentrate on Mandy instead. She was his family now. No one else. Not even Patrice.

Drawing a deep breath and exhaling carefully, Jake reached into his back pocket and pulled out the series of canceled checks that Patrice had given him. He looked at them daily. He had to constantly remind himself of Sherry's treachery or he would go back to her like a big, stupid puppy, desperate for love.

But his love was for Mandy. Only Mandy. He would see her as much as possible and she could absorb all his love. He didn't need Sherry. He didn't need anyone else.

Her signature scrawled so boldly and defiantly across the back of the checks infuriated him. He crumpled the checks with his fist. His hand hurt. He wanted to crush them to pulp. But then the spurt of rage and betrayal slipped away, turned to emptiness—a vast wasteland of nothing.

He just wanted to lie down and die.

He wanted to hate her forever, but his chest throbbed with pain.

"Damn you, Sherry," he muttered, swallowing hard. "Damn you..."

"Since when do you want to sell me your partnership?" Dee demanded, glaring at Sherry as if she were a recalcitrant child.

Sherry put the finishing touches on a five-foot-long hero sandwich that was being made for one of their customer's kid's twelfth birthday party. "Since I decided to move on. My daughter lives in California and—''

"You're planning to move to California?" Dee gasped.

"Not immediately. I don't want to alarm the Craigs. But I think I'll start making some changes. I've got some money saved—enough to get by on for a while. I do have a debt to pay back," she added ironically, "but I should have some left over for some traveling. Maybe I'll move to Hawaii for a few months and lie around in the sun and drink mai-tai's.''

"You'll go crazy," Dee predicted.

"Probably.''

"Sounds like you want a change. You don't have to sell, you know. I can get someone to work for a while, so you can go find yourself.''

"Find myself! I've found myself. Finally!" Sherry declared. "After years of being in limbo it's all over now, and I can get on with my life. When Mandy showed up on my doorstep, that started it all.''

Dee examined Sherry thoughtfully as Sherry wrapped the hero in plastic wrap. Then they worked together to lift it to the top of the counter just as their customer walked through the door with about ten boys to help her haul it out to the car.

When they were alone again, Dee questioned, "What about Mandy's father?''

Sherry shrugged. "What about him?''

"What's his role in all this?''

"I haven't talked to him." Sherry was blasé.

"Ah...''

"Okay, what's that mean?" Sherry asked.

"Sounds like there's still unfinished business. Oh, I know, I know!" she said, lifting her hands to ward off the protests already forming on Sherry's lips. "You told me what happened between you. I heard. But it ain't over till the fat lady sings, and to my mind, she's been pretty quiet."

Sherry didn't want to argue with her, but she couldn't let that one go by. "He thinks I took that money for myself, Dee!"

"Yeah, so? Of course, he does! All you have to do is tell him the truth."

"I took the money for my mother. I did take it."

"Your Aunt Elena took it."

"For *my* mother. I could have stopped her. I could have found another way to make everything right."

"Oh, honey." Dee suddenly put her arms around her, surprising Sherry. Unwanted tears sprang to her eyes in spite of herself.

"Anyway, I'm paying Patrice Beckett back," Sherry said, her voice quivering. "I've got the cashier's check already."

"You did what you thought was right for your mama, and no one can blame you for that," Dee said kindly.

"Oh, yes, they can." Sherry's voice was low with emotion. She had to get out of this conversation fast, or she was going to break down altogether. "I can't decide whether to send it, or give it to her in person."

"Oh, in person!" Dee was definite. "Make sure you look that bitch right in the eye and tell her it's over."

Sherry managed a half laugh. "Thanks, Dee."

With a last, hard hug, Dee let her go. "Well, I'm not letting you sell out just yet. And you owe me my vacation in August! So, go do what you have to do, but you're still half-owner until I say differently."

"Okay."

"And you let Mandy's father know about this payment to his mother. The way you describe her, she might not tell him."

"Oh, I'm sure she won't. But believe me, it won't matter. It's over between us forever." The finality of her words hurt, but Sherry fought back a new set of tears.

"Well, it'll buy you back your self-respect. And that can get you anything," Dee said, sounding sage.

Sherry smiled sadly. She knew better. J.J. hated her for taking his family's money, and that was that. All she could hope for now was that he wouldn't poison Mandy's mind against her, too.

"Thank you, Jake," Jill Delaney said for about the fiftieth time. "Thank you so much!"

"You're welcome," he answered into the receiver, "but it's Jennifer Seeley who hired you."

"But it was only after you stopped by this morning that I became a full-time employee!" she reminded him.

"It's Crawfish Delish's gain," he muttered, wishing he could get her off the phone. He didn't do well with gushing enthusiasm. It always made him feel like a fake, somehow.

But Jill wasn't about to give up. "It's like Christmas in February! My mother's come to stay and take care of the kids for a while and Tim's actually been trying to catch up on some back payments. I can't believe it! Everything's just about perfect. When I think where I was just a few weeks ago... Well, you never know, do you?"

No, you never do.

"I'll stop by tomorrow with this month's rent and a little extra." She actually laughed with delight. "You may own everything in town, but you're one heck of a nice guy, Jake Beckett!''

Her words should have cheered him up. They should have at least registered. But since Mandy's exit he'd been in a blue funk that couldn't be lifted, no matter how much he berated himself.

Maybe it was time for another run on the beach. Maybe it was time for a change. *Something...*

Jake was bent down to change his shoes when his intercom buzzed. ''Someone to see you,'' his receptionist announced.

If it's Caroline or my mother... Jake thought savagely, jerking to attention. Since the night Patrice had given him the checks, he'd scarcely spoken to either of them. Yesterday, Caroline had left a message on his answering machine saying she was finally considering taking the job in Seattle. He'd felt a pang of remorse then; Caroline deserved better. But it quickly faded away because it was all for the best, anyway. It would never work between them, no matter what happened.

As for Patrice... They hadn't communicated in any form since Mandy had left. A blessing, Jake thought, less and less convinced his mother's machinations were to benefit the family and more than a little sure she was only looking out for her own best interests.

What's best for you...

Jake shuddered—footsteps walking on his grave. Preparing himself for a battle of wills if his unexpected guest should turn out to be Patrice, and a battle of unwanted emotion if it should be Caroline, Jake faced the door...and was surprised when a strange woman stepped across his threshold. She was vaguely familiar-looking, however, and he fought to place her. He'd seen nearly everyone in Oceantides at one time or another. Hell, he'd probably gone to high school with her!

"Mr. Beckett, you don't know me," she began uncomfortably, "but I work at the Seacliff Motel. I'm one of the maids."

Memory surfaced. When he'd picked up Sherry to take her to Seattle, she was the maid who was cleaning rooms. A Beckett employee, he thought ironically. "I remember you from the other day."

She seemed pleased he'd recalled her. "That's right. I was there when you came to pick up Sherry Sterling."

Jake's brows lifted. She knew exactly who Sherry was.

"My name's Lindy," she explained hurriedly. "Annie Winters is my sister. Caroline's friend from high school…?" She waited for Jake to make the connection. He remembered Annie but he hadn't seen her since graduation, so he merely shrugged and waited for Lindy to go on. "I was a few years younger than you guys. My dad kind of got in financial trouble and we lost our house, so we all moved away, but I came back. But none of that matters," she added, apparently realizing she was rambling on. "When I saw Sherry I wondered if you two still had a thing, but then everyone said you and Caroline were engaged."

Jake waited. What the hell did this have to do with the price of tea in China? Lindy rushed on. "Of course, it's none of my business, but I was cleaning up one day and I dumped out her wastebasket and, well, your name just jumped out at me."

"My name?" Jake asked, confused.

Reaching into her purse, Lindy pulled out what looked like a letter, all ripped up and taped back together. Shyly, she handed it to Jake.

"It was powerful information. I didn't know what to do, so I just kind of kept it awhile, but now that she's gone I thought you'd better have it, in case she never told you...."

Jake accepted the letter and glanced down at the pages. Then he looked again, harder. Distantly, he heard Lindy say, "I just thought you should know, y'know...."

Pregnant... Our daughter...Mandy... Wanted to tell you so badly... So sorry...so awfully sorry...

Blood pounded in Jake's head. Lindy kept talking but he only caught the gist of what she was saying, which was mainly about how she didn't know whether to tell him or not. But Jake was too focused on Sherry's words to pay much attention and when he finally surfaced, she was gone. Silence filled his office, a strange backdrop to the turbulence inside him. He read the letter again, although there was nothing in it he didn't already know.

When he was finished he sat back in his chair and tried to summon the strength to go running. He couldn't move. He felt zapped, enervated, destroyed. It was like being dunked underwater every time you surfaced. Over and over and over again. And he was powerless to kick himself free.

Shadows lengthened outside his window and the pink neon crab and scripted letters of Crawfish Delish! came alive in the gathering gloom. Jake clenched his teeth together. It hurt. It hurt like hell. So what if he knew the contents of the letter, it still hurt every time he was reminded of Sherry's betrayal and treachery. Slowly, slowly he was coming to terms with why she'd hidden Mandy's existence from him...*but not the money!* He could never forgive her that. Her cold avarice ripped at his soul.

"I'm going home now," his receptionist's voice called over the intercom. "Can I get you anything?"

"No, thanks."

Moments later he was alone. The letter lay between his hands. He crumpled it, just as he'd crumpled the checks a few days earlier. He wanted to crush her words from his sight and rip her memory from his mind's eye.

A jolt. His heart somersaulted painfully. Realization drove the blood from his brain and set up a hard hammer inside his veins.

He smoothed out the letter, examining it carefully.

"My God," he murmured, shocked.

He examined her words again, reading between the lines this time to something Sherry would never have suspected he could see. He waited, making sure, asking himself if he might not just be playing the fool because he loved her so much.

But no, the truth was there.

With a lighter heart and firmer resolve, he slammed out of the office, taking the stairs three at a time as he raced to his Jeep.

Late-afternoon sunlight slanted over Oceantides, like an arrow pointing the way home. Caught in its glow, Sherry opened her car door and was immediately met with a puff of brisk ocean breeze. Her hair whipped around her face and she pulled back the errant strands and breathed deeply, closing her eyes and turning her face into the cool wind, listening to the distant roar of the surf.

On her way to the Becketts' and Patrice. The final stop on this tour of destiny.

But first, a walk down memory lane at Bernie's Pizza.

"Sustenance," she murmured, hurrying across the street and through the front doors.

Jukebox music blared—something in the alternative-rock line that was faintly memorable but even less melodic. To her delight, Bernie was there, along with Ryan.

"Hi!" they both called in unison.

"Hey, there," Sherry greeted them. "A root beer," she ordered before either of them could ask. "I need a shot of courage."

"You look better," Bernie decreed, his eye skimming over her discerningly.

"I'm at the end of a long, hard journey."

"Going to see J.J.?" Ryan guessed.

"Jake," Sherry corrected. "But no, I'm checking in with Madame Beckett."

Bernie's face twisted into a look of comical horror. "Her?"

The Dragon Lady herself. "Yep."

"You take care of yourself," Bernie warned. "She's a mean woman with a tongue that could cut glass."

"Dad!" Ryan half laughed.

"She's lucky her son's like his father. Oh, Rex had his faults." Bernie waved off any protests either she or Ryan might make with both hands. "He liked a good time too much, maybe. But he wasn't mean. He liked people and he loved his children. He had a nice daughter, too, but she had to leave for good because that wife of his was full of acid, heel to scalp. Picked out Jay's wife before he was even born and did everything she could think of to get rid of anyone else!" He shook his finger at Sherry's nose. "Don't think I don't know. I always knew! She hurt you, and she'll keep right on doing it."

"She can't hurt me anymore," Sherry said quietly, touched by Bernie's concern.

"No?" He didn't believe her.

"No," she assured him.

He frowned and blinked at her, wanting to concur but unable to. She loved him for that. Holding out her arms, she gave both of them big hugs before she reluctantly eased away.

"You come back here if she beats you down. You come back to Bernie's! We're your family, you know!"

"I know." Sherry struggled to smile, then slipped out the door to her dance with destiny.

Beckett Manor loomed large and bleak even with a watery sun trying to fight its way free of clinging gray clouds. Sherry climbed from her car and marched to the intercom, pressing the buzzer with a slightly unsteady finger.

"Anybody there?" she demanded, sure Patrice was sitting in her web, just waiting.

For an answer the gate buzzed open. No verbal response, just an eerie, silent admittance that made Sherry's throat go dry in spite of her bravado.

But that was all it was, she could admit now that she was away from Bernie and Ryan's support. Bravado. No substance. A blustering facade that lacked any real conviction. Patrice had wronged her, but somehow Sherry knew *she* would be the villain. Patrice would twist and turn and blame and nearly convince Sherry that it was all her fault anyway!

But, so what? There was no other option, no other path to pursue.

Wind slapped at her face and slid cold fingers beneath the collar of her black jacket. Her boots slipped a bit on the damp stone walkway. Infuriated by her whipping hair, she yanked it back into a ponytail and held it with one hand. Inelegant, perhaps, but too bad.

With her free hand she rapped on the door. Would Patrice magically open it, as well?

But it was Jake who twisted the handle and slid the well-oiled oak door open. The chandelier cast sparkling shadows on the floor and across his face. In low-slung jeans, a torn denim shirt and toting a hammer, his hair tousled, a smudge of dirt near his chin, he looked strong and vulnerable at the same time. All the vinegar went out of Sherry and she stood in shock, consumed by the desire to throw herself into his arms and beg him to believe in her.

"Jake," she said through numb lips.

His mouth twisted. "No more J.J.?" he asked, sounding faintly sad.

"I thought you didn't like it anymore."

He shook his head, his eyes hooded so she couldn't read his expression.

"I—I talked to Mandy," she said as he closed the door behind her, creating an unintended intimacy that crawled across her skin like a premonition. "I think she really enjoyed being here with you."

"She's a great kid."

Sherry's eyes searched his face, her heart skipping a beat. "You think so? I mean, I do. I can't believe I missed all that time with her, and now I just want to hold her and tell her how sorry I am."

The way his eyes stared into her soul silenced her tongue. She wanted to cry. He wouldn't understand. He would be the *last* person on earth to understand. "I just love her so much," Sherry finished awkwardly.

"Were you looking for my mother?" he asked,

frowning at the floor, as if continuing to look at her was too much effort.

"Uh, yes..." The urge to throw the money in Patrice's face had disappeared. Now she just felt tired. "I need to—pay her back."

"She's in Seattle. We had words and she decided she needed a little vacation."

"Words?" Sherry asked, instinctively knowing it concerned her.

"Do you want to give me the check? I promise I'll see that she gets it."

Sherry didn't know what to do. It seemed so anticlimactic, somehow. Reluctantly, she reached into her purse for the envelope with the cashier's check. "I added interest on. If it's not enough, I'll be happy to pay more."

A spasm crossed his face. For a moment she thought he was going to refuse the envelope, but then he snapped it from her fingers and boldly ripped it open. He stared at the check for a long moment. "How much money did you borrow?" he asked.

"I—didn't I tell you? Ten thousand dollars." She craned her neck to look at the check. "Why? I said I'd pay more if it's not enough."

"My mother had checks written to you for over a hundred thousand dollars."

"*What?* My God! She didn't! I took ten thousand dollars for my mother, and I shouldn't have, but I—" Sherry swept in a harsh breath, shaking all over. "*She lies!*"

"It's not a lie. I talked to—"

"You—you can't believe that I took—I took—" Sherry stumbled over the words, hurrying them out. "I didn't. I couldn't! I wouldn't be able to live with myself."

"Wait—"

"No, no." She threw up a hand, warding him off.

"Sherry!"

Tears blurred her vision. "Take the check!" she gulped. "We're even!"

"For God's sake, *I know* you didn't take the money," Jake hissed through his teeth, grabbing her arm. Sherry pulled at his fingers, but his words finally penetrated. She glanced up at him, her eyes full of questions.

With a groan, he suddenly pulled her close, until she could feel the light beating of his heart beneath her tense fingers. "Then what?"

"Come here," he muttered roughly, his arms surrounding her, his breath tickling the hairs near her ear. "Let me hold you."

Time seemed suspended. Sherry drank in his scent like a sweet elixir, letting it fill her head. She wanted to collapse against him, but she didn't dare. What did he mean?

Without a word, he drew back, gazing down at her in a way that made her heart skip a beat. "Come out to the tree house," he invited roughly.

Tree house? Sherry let him lead her to the base of the tree where a ladder had been securely lashed to the trunk. Jake climbed up and reached a hand down to her. Glad for her own jeans and sneakers, Sherry climbed to the newly laid floorboards of the famous tree house, scene of reluctant memories of her youth.

"So, that's what the hammer's for," she murmured, smelling the new wood.

"Mandy wanted to be here. I hadn't climbed up since high school and the place was rotten."

"And you decided to save it?" Sherry asked, dozens of more pressing questions flying inside her head, unable to voice any of them.

"I thought it was worth saving."

The hammock swayed softly. A new hammock. Not as big as the other. Big enough, though, she thought inconsequentially.

"You look scared," Jake said softly.

"I'm thinking about Patrice."

He threw back his head and laughed. "Liar," he said.

"I'm thinking about the money," Sherry exclaimed. "And that reminds me of Patrice."

"The money Patrice sent Elena."

Sherry's jaw dropped. "What do you know of Elena?"

"I know she's your aunt and that she endorsed the original check Patrice sent you for your mother. I know she endorsed at least ten other checks as well, all made out to you and equaling ten thousand dollars each. I know she deposited them in a bank under your name."

The ground rushed forward. Sherry's head buzzed. It suddenly was too heavy to hold up. "Wha-at?" she whispered, as J.J.'s arms suddenly closed around her, supporting her, guiding her to the hammock where they both fell in a tangle of arms and legs that normally would have embarrassed Sherry, but right now she couldn't think!

"It's all right. She saved it all. Took it from Patrice for you and your baby. Kept right on taking it without a qualm. Proud as a peacock about it, as a matter of fact."

"You—talked to her?" Sherry's tongue was too fat for her mouth. Everything circled in slow motion. Telling herself she just needed the support, she buried her face in J.J.'s warm neck.

"I talked to everybody. Elena, Patrice, Dee…" He let that one sink in but Sherry was too undone to react. "When I figured it all out, I headed straight for Seattle. I ran into Dee, first, and she told me you were going to pay off your debt and she didn't want me screwing it up."

"She said that?" Sherry gasped.

"And a lot more, besides," he added with feeling. "So, I tracked down Elena, then came back and waited. You took your sweet time getting down here. I've been hanging around this place for days."

"You've been waiting for me?" Sherry repeated.

"Yes." He chuckled.

She couldn't take it all in. "Elena took more money from Patrice?" she asked now, horrified.

"I was ready to turn her in to the authorities for blackmail," J.J. admitted, "but I decided to confront her first. It was a good thing. Gave me a different perspective. And then when I had it out with my mother, well, a few more things came to light."

"Like what?"

"Patrice is a control freak. She's always wanted to direct my life, and she wanted you out of it. Somewhere in her warped mind, she thought if she kept on paying you off, you'd look worse. The more money you took, the more evil you would be."

"God," Sherry murmured, shivering.

"It almost worked," he said flatly. "I reacted just the way she expected, but then I realized the signature wasn't yours."

"How?"

"Providence," he admitted, then pulled a piece of

paper from his pocket that had been pasted together. Sherry blinked in lack of understanding as she recognized the letter she'd written to J.J. when she'd first arrived in Oceantides. "This is a small town," he reminded her with a laugh. "The maid thought I might like to read what you had to say. She gave it to me after I got back from meeting Mandy."

"Oh, J.J.!" she breathed, holding him tightly.

"I love you," he answered, his lips soft against her cheekbone. "I've always loved you. And I don't want to wait anymore."

"Do you mean it?" Her voice quivered.

For an answer he fit her body snugly against his masculine contours. "Could you stand to live in Oceantides again? Could you stand to be a Beckett?"

So much information. Too much. Too fast! Her senses swam with delight. *Wait,* she warned herself. *Be smart. Think. Don't rush.*

"If you're asking me to marry you, the answer's yes," Sherry replied, disregarding every bit of her own advice. "That is, if you and Caroline have called it quits..."

"It was quits before it ever started," he admitted harshly. "And yes, *you know* I want you to marry me!"

Before she could respond he swooped in for a kiss. Sherry's lips parted in surprise and J.J. slipped his tongue inside her mouth.

The kiss was long, hot, and filled with pent-up desire. Sherry's fingers wound in his hair. Her tongue danced with his and then she couldn't stop the laughter that bubbled up from inside her. "I love you!" she told him. "I always have."

"We have a daughter. I know she's happy with the

Craigs, but don't you think she'll be happy for us? I mean—"

"I know what you mean. Of course, she will. She can be with us some of the time. The Craigs want what's best for her."

"So do I," he answered soberly.

"She brought us together again," Sherry said.

They stared at each other for a long moment, savoring the rediscovery, then Jake took it upon himself to remind her of what the tree house had meant to them, his mouth moving down her neck as his fingers undid the buttons to her blouse.

And that was how Mandy came to have a sister, Angela, born on Christmas Day.

* * * * *

THE POWER OF LOVE

*is an exciting new mini-series
which begins next month,
only in Silhouette Special Edition®.*

Mail-Order Matty *by Emilie Richards
will be on the shelves in March 1998.*

Here's a sneak preview...

MAIL-ORDER MATTY
by
Emilie Richards

Matty had been fine but now she was nervous.

"We can't get married right away, Damon. There's the license."

"That's all a formality, but you're right. You'll still have a few days to decide once we're there."

"And so will you."

He looked down at her from his six feet of solid masculinity. "I'm not going to change my mind. I know everything I need to know about you. I wasn't advertising for a wife, and you weren't really applying to be one," he said. "But, Matty, I'm in a desperate situation here, and I don't know where else to turn."

Damon gestured to a baggage carousel that was slowly circulating, although by now there were only a few pieces left on it. "Point out which are yours when they come around and I'll get them off."

Matty glanced at him from the corner of her eye. He

was wearing dark slacks and an ivory dress shirt unbuttoned at the neck.

"Your hands seem to be full, Damon."

He looked down at the bouquet of carnations he had been choking since she'd first turned around to face him. Then he looked up at her and grinned. "They're for you. I'd completely forgotten I had them." He held them out.

"They're lovely." Actually, they might have been lovely once, but the white paper stapled around them was crumpled now from fingers that had gripped it too tightly, and Matty suspected the stems were mangled.

"I'm sorry," he said. "Maybe I'm not as calm as I thought."

"I'm sure that if there was a handbook on mail-order marriages that would be on the first page. I guess our palms are supposed to sweat and our hearts are supposed to beat double time."

"Is yours beating double time?"

"Triple." She heard her voice waver. She had talked herself into coming here with a bravado she hadn't even known she possessed. She had marched in to her supervisor at Carrollton Community Hospital to give her resignation, and she hadn't even considered the immediate promise of a pay raise if she would just rethink her decision. Without a backward glance she had rented her house to friends and said her goodbyes.

And somewhere along that path she had used up all her stores of courage.

Damon took her hand. The gesture so surprised her that she froze. She knew her eyes gave her away. She excelled at warm good cheer, at encouragement and empathy, but right now she needed someone to give all those things back to her.

"Matty..." His voice was kind, even kinder than she

remembered. "I'm not going to pressure you. I know I'm asking too much. Let's just get to know each other today. One step at a time. Okay?"

"Damon, look at you. There have to be a dozen women who would have said yes to marrying you, women you know well, women you're attracted to. I'm nearly a stranger. Why me?"

He had answered that question before, but he seemed to sense her need to watch his face as he explained once again. He linked his fingers with hers, and her heart skipped erratically.

"Not a dozen. But I do know some women who might have said yes. None of them could offer what I really need. The only question is whether you need Heidi and me enough to take this step. Do you?"

The answer was yes, of course. Perhaps there had been a thousand possibilities for her future, but somehow, after Damon reentered her life, she had only glimpsed two. She could continue at Carrollton Community taking care of other people's beautiful babies, continue living in the house and town she had lived in all her life, continue wondering what the world was like outside that small frozen speck on the map. Or she could accept Damon's astounding offer of marriage and motherhood and a new life on a distant tropical island.

In the end the choice had been easy, because the second possibility had come attached to Damon Quinn, a man she had once loved with unrestrained passion. And this gift of Damon in her life once more, even under these strange and unromantic circumstances, had been too tempting to reject.

"I'm here," she said. She would not reveal more of her heart than that.

He seemed to think it was answer enough. "Let's get your suitcases, then we'll go somewhere for lunch." He squeezed her hand before he dropped it. She felt absolutely alone when he was no longer touching her, but she lifted her chin and managed a smile.

* * *

Don't miss **Mail-Order Matty**
by **Emilie Richards**, *available next month
in Silhouette Special Edition®.*

COMING NEXT MONTH

THE 200% WIFE Jennifer Greene

That Special Woman!

Abby Stanford always gave everything she did 200%—particularly her job. But now she wanted the love of a good man, too. Where could she find one of those?

MAIL-ORDER MATTY Emilie Richards

Matty Stewart had a champagne celebration on her birthday and she ended up winging her way off to the Bahamas to get married and become a mother! Better still, her new husband was none other than Damon Quinn, the subject of more than one midnight fantasy!

THE EIGHT SECOND WEDDING Anne McAllister

Channing Richardson couldn't believe that his mother had found him a wife! Even the proposed bride thought it was ridiculous. So certain were they, that they agreed to spend the summer together...

A HERO'S CHILD Diana Whitney

Parenthood

Rae Hooper's love had marched off to glory a decade ago, never to return. But at ten, their child had found herself a father figure—a mysterious drifter who drew Rae just as much as he affected her daughter. *Could it be...?*

MOTHER NATURE'S HIDDEN AGENDA Kate Freiman

Lily Davis didn't plan on falling in love with a rugged single father. But Blake Sommers *was* irresistibly sexy.

SEVEN REASONS WHY Neesa Hart

She had seven reasons to accept Zack Adriano's marriage proposal; her foster sons' futures were at stake. But exactly *why* had the cynical, too-smooth lawyer asked her to marry him?

COMING NEXT MONTH FROM

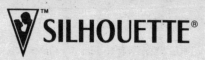 SILHOUETTE®

Intrigue
Danger, deception and desire

THE CASE OF THE VANISHED GROOM
Sheryl Lynn
ALIAS: DADDY Adrianne Lee
ONE TOUGH TEXAN M. J. Rodgers
SWEET DECEPTION Susan Kearney

Desire
Provocative, sensual love stories for the woman of today

WHISPERS IN THE DARK BJ James
COLTRAIN'S PROPOSAL Diana Palmer
HUSBAND: OPTIONAL Marie Ferrarella
TALLCHIEF FOR KEEPS Cait London
MATCHMAKING MONA Diana Mars
WEDDING PLANNER TAMES RANCHER!
Pamela Ingrahm

Sensation
A thrilling mix of passion, adventure and drama

I'M HAVING YOUR BABY?! Linda Turner
A MAN WITHOUT A HAVEN Beverly Bird
BABY BY DESIGN Paula Detmer Riggs
RECKLESS Ruth Wind

DALLAS SCHULZE

Home to EDEN

Some temptations can't be denied

Kate Moran's perfect life threatens to disintegrate
when she falls in love with her fiancé's brother.

*"a love story that is both heart-warming and
steamy...with an unexpected twist that will keep fans
going well into the night."*—Publishers Weekly

MIRA®

1-55166-290-6
AVAILABLE NOW IN PAPERBACK

HEATHER GRAHAM POZZESSERE

If Looks could Kill

Madison wasn't there when her mother was murdered, but she *saw* it happen. Years later, a killer is stalking women in Miami and Madison's nightmare visions have returned. Can FBI agent Kyle Montgomery catch the serial killer before Madison becomes his next victim?

"...an incredible storyteller!"—LA Daily News

1-55166-285-X
AVAILABLE FROM FEBRUARY 1998

4 FREE

books and a surprise gift!

We would like to take this opportunity to thank you for reading this Silhouette® book by offering you the chance to take FOUR more specially selected titles from the Special Edition™ series absolutely FREE! We're also making this offer to introduce you to the benefits of the Reader Service™—

- ★ FREE home delivery
- ★ FREE gifts and competitions
- ★ FREE monthly newsletter
- ★ Books available before they're in the shops
- ★ Exclusive Reader Service discounts

Accepting these FREE books and gift places you under no obligation to buy; you may cancel at any time, even after receiving your free shipment. Simply complete your details below and return the entire page to the address below. *You don't even need a stamp!*

YES! Please send me 4 free Special Edition books and a surprise gift. I understand that unless you hear from me, I will receive 6 superb new titles every month for just £2.40 each, postage and packing free. I am under no obligation to purchase any books and may cancel my subscription at any time. The free books and gift will be mine to keep in any case.

E8XE

Ms/Mrs/Miss/Mr..................................Initials ....
BLOCK CAPITALS PLEASE

Surname ....

Address ....

....

....Postcode...................................

Send this whole page to:
THE READER SERVICE, FREEPOST, CROYDON, CR9 3WZ
(Eire readers please send coupon to: P.O. BOX 4546, DUBLIN 24.)

Offer not valid to current Reader Service subscribers to this series. We reserve the right to refuse an application and applicants must be aged 18 years or over. Only one application per household. Terms and prices subject to change without notice. Offer expires 31st August 1998. You may be mailed with offers from other reputable companies as a result of this application. If you would prefer not to receive such offers, please tick box. ☐

Silhouette® is a registered trademark of Harlequin Enterprises used under licence by Harlequin Mills & Boon Limited.

JOANN
ROSS

NO REGRETS

Three sisters torn apart by tragedy each choose a different path—until fate and one man reunites them. Only when tragedy strikes again can the surviving sisters allow themselves to choose happiness— if they dare pay the price.

"A steamy, fast-paced read."
—Publishers Weekly

1-55166-282-5
AVAILABLE FROM FEBRUARY 1998

Karen Young

SUGAR BABY

She would do anything to protect her child

Little Danny Woodson's life is threatened when
he witnesses a murder—and only his estranged
uncle can protect him.

"Karen Young is a spellbinding storyteller."

—Publishers Weekly

MIRA®

1-55166-366-X
AVAILABLE NOW IN PAPERBACK

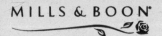

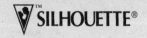

SPECIAL OFFER
£5 OFF

FLYING FLOWERS

Beautiful fresh flowers, sent by 1st class post to any UK and Eire address.

We have teamed up with Flying Flowers, the UK's premier 'flowers by post' company, to offer you £5 off a choice of their two most popular bouquets the 18 mix (CAS) of 10 multihead and 8 luxury bloom Carnations and the 25 mix (CFG) of 15 luxury bloom Carnations, 10 Freesias and Gypsophila. All bouquets contain fresh flowers 'in bud', added greenery, bouquet wrap, flower food, care instructions, and personal message card. They are boxed, gift wrapped and sent by 1st class post.

To redeem £5 off a Flying Flowers bouquet, simply complete the application form below and send it with your cheque or postal order to; **HMB Flying Flowers Offer, The Jersey Flower Centre, Jersey JE1 5FF.**

ORDER FORM (Block capitals please) Valid for delivery anytime until 30th November 1998 MAB/0398/A

Title ....Initials ....Surname ....

Address...

....Postcode ....

Signature..Are you a Reader Service Subscriber **YES/NO**

Bouquet(s)**18 CAS** (Usual Price £14.99) **£9.99** ☐   **25 CFG** (Usual Price £19.99) **£14.99** ☐

I enclose a cheque/postal order payable to Flying Flowers for £...or payment by

VISA/MASTERCARD ☐☐☐☐☐☐☐☐☐☐☐☐☐☐☐☐ Expiry Date........../.........../.........

PLEASE SEND MY BOUQUET TO ARRIVE BY........./.........../........

TO Title ....Initials ....Surname ....

Address...

....Postcode ....

Message (Max 10 Words) ....

....

Please allow a minimum of four working days between receipt of order and 'required by date' for delivery.

You may be mailed with offers from other reputable companies as a result of this application.

Please tick box if you would prefer not to receive such offers. ☐

Terms and Conditions Although dispatched by 1st class post to arrive by the required date the exact day of delivery cannot be guaranteed. Valid for delivery anytime until 30th November 1998. Maximum of 5 redemptions per household, photocopies of the voucher will be accepted.

The
Christmas
Connection

The
Christmas
Connection

Discovering a Relationship with God

J.John

Authentic

16 15 14 13 12 11 10   8 7 6 5 4 3 2

Reprinted 2010
First published 2010 by Authentic Media Ltd
Milton Keynes
Company Registration No: 7101487
www.authenticmedia.co.uk

British Library Cataloguing in Publication Data
A catalogue record for this book is available
from the British Library.

ISBN: 978-1-86024-799-6

Cover design by Chris Jones
Illustrations by Louise Neumann
Thank you to Liza Hoeksma for her editorial expertise
Printed in Great Britain by J.F. Print Ltd., Sparkford, Somerset

Introduction

God wants to communicate with us.

He could have shouted from heaven in a loud voice, but instead he came to earth as a baby, born in a stable.

He couldn't make himself any bigger to impress us, so he made himself smaller to attract us.

He came into the world we know, so that we can reconnect with him.

This Christmas do you want to know more?

There are so many good things about Christmas: family, friends, food and presents. But what's underneath all the Christmas wrappings? It can be easy to relegate the Nativity to simply a play performed by thousands of school children; to think of the baby Jesus as nothing more than a character in the 'Silent Night' carol. But that would be missing something absolutely crucial that can impact and transform our entire lives.

Christmas is so incredible, it's been celebrated for 2,000 years. The essence of it? God wanted to communicate with humankind, but he knew that many were struggling to understand who he was and what he was all about. So he didn't sit back and complain about it – he came to earth to reveal himself to us.

Christmas is the time and place where God pulls back the curtain so we can see his face. The invisible God becomes visible; the unknowable God becomes knowable.

If it was me I'd have been tempted to put on a bit of a show to impress people, given them a display of my power that would have people in awe. But Jesus came into the world as a helpless newborn baby, as reliant on his mother as we once were on ours. By living as a human, God wanted us to see what he looked like and how he acted, but most importantly he wanted us to know how much he loves us.

So who is this God? We all have different ideas of what God is like. Many of us imagine him as a stern old man, ready to point the finger and tell us off, or as the 'Great Architect' who set the world in motion then sat back and observed us from a distance.

This Christmas why not look beyond all the trappings and discover something more about who God really is and exactly how he feels about us. Find out how we lost our connection with God and how our connection can be restored.

Losing the Connection

The night is darker now
And the wind blows stronger
Fails my heart, I know not how,
I can go no longer.
('Good King Wenceslas' by John Mason Neale)

In theory, making the connection with God ought to be natural. God wants to communicate with us. He is everywhere, all the time. This means that he is never out of range. There is nowhere on earth that we cannot get through to him.

Sometimes at Christmas we find it easier to feel his presence and be aware of him, perhaps when we listen to Christmas choirs or attend a carol service. Yet the reality is that the rest of the year many people find establishing a connection with God very difficult. They may call, but find that the line appears to be dead. There is only silence. So where is he? Is he only there with the candles and carols? The teaching of Christianity is that God is there all the time and is willing to answer, but there are some blockages that need to be overcome.

Let's get some background clear first.

In the beginning there was perfect communication between human beings and God. When God created the world, he made it perfect. He created men and women to live under his authority and guidance and to enjoy a relationship with him. God's instructions were meant to protect humanity and provide a life of harmony, joy, order and peace. They connected to him in the best possible ways, but this didn't last very long. Instead, human beings chose to ignore God's instructions and to put themselves, rather than him, first in their lives. The brief and blunt biblical word for this is 'sin'. Notice the middle letter of that little word. As the French atheist Albert Camus put it, 'It's the story of my whole life.'

Sin is not just a specific act but also an ingrained selfishness. Sin is the stubborn tendency we all have for choosing to do, say or even think all manner of things that we know are wrong. This pattern of rebellion that started in the distant past has continued in an unbroken pattern to the present day. Every human being that has ever lived – except one – has committed sin. As the Bible says, 'everyone has sinned; we all fall short of God's glorious standard'.[1] That is at the heart of the problem.

We need to realise that sin is deeper, wider and more persistent than we might think. It is *deeper* than we think because we tend to consider issues of good and bad as simply being about visible actions: about those things that we do. But sin is deeper than we realise, because it includes words, attitudes and thoughts. Sin is also *wider* than we think, because it is not just a private, personal matter, but something that affects our relationships with each other and with the world. You only need to see the news to be reminded that all too often people make choices on the basis of selfishness, cruelty or greed. Sadly, too, we have to admit that sin is more persistent than we imagine. Sin is a reality that is so deeply embedded within human nature that no amount of effort or education will remove it from us. It is all-pervasive within us, affecting every part of our being – thoughts, feelings and actions.

How does sin break that precious connection with God? Imagine you had a mobile phone but it didn't work. Firstly, it could have something to do with the contract. Sometimes our failure to get a signal on our phone has the very simple explanation that we have either broken or ended the terms of our contract. Perhaps we haven't renewed it, or perhaps we have just gone beyond some agreed limit. Now the Bible teaches that God made a similar contract with human beings. The contract

had conditions and terms and by rebelling against him all of us have broken it. The line is dead because, by sinning, we broke the contract that made the connection possible. The Bible states clearly that breaking this contract is so serious because the breakdown in communication is a symptom of something far worse: the danger of eternal separation from God for those who have failed to keep the contract. It is that finally we shall *perish* or fail to fulfil the purpose for which we were created.

he line is dead because, y sinning, we broke the contract

Secondly, there could be something blocking the signal. Have you ever tried to make a call from your mobile, perhaps from indoors, and found that you couldn't get through? So you step outside, maybe walk around the corner of the building and suddenly you have a signal. It happens because the obstacle has been removed. Something – a wall, a building or a hill – has blocked the transmission. For human beings sin is that big obstacle that gets in the way between us and God. Our sin has become a barrier between us and God. While it remains, a connection is impossible.

Any way you look at it, as a breaking of a contract or as the creation of a barrier, sin has got in the way between us and God and we know the connection is broken. Worse still, we can do nothing ourselves to solve the problem. No amount of good works will help!

2

God's Reconnection Remedy

Joy to the world, the Lord is come!
Let earth receive her King;
Let every heart, prepare him room
('Joy to the World' by Isaac Watts)

So if sin is the problem, what can be done about it? *We* can do very little about the breakdown in relationship. It's too major and too complex. On our own we cannot restore the broken contract or remove the barrier that blocks our vital connection to God. But what we cannot do, God can and does do. The Good News is that God himself has acted to remedy the problem and restore the connection. But it cost him.

The Bible refers to God as Father, Son and Holy Spirit existing in community of being. God is three in one: God is the Father lovingly watching over us; God is the Son walking alongside us; God is the Holy Spirit living in us.

In order to reconnect something that is broken, it is essential to have someone on either side of the breakage. So in a dispute, you may have a meeting between representatives of both sides acting as mediators or negotiators. When it came to re-establishing the connection with human beings we see God adopting the same principle. That's why we celebrate Christmas, because God himself came to earth. God literally humbled himself and became a human being and was born into this world. He came as Jesus the perfect mediator, someone who was both fully God (and could represent God) and fully human (so could represent humankind). It's like a bridge over an uncrossable chasm: if he was not God, then the bridge is down at the other end; if he was not truly human then the bridge is down at our end. But he was fully God and fully human and as such he was entitled to represent both sides.

The four accounts of the life of Jesus that begin the New Testament show from different perspectives how Jesus lived on this earth. The Gospels recount what Jesus said and did. Right from the start he showed the kind of God that he is. He didn't arrive with flashing lights and a huge parade: he was born to a young girl and his first bed was in a stable among the animals. Jesus came in complete humility. But there were many signs that he wasn't just an ordinary baby. The King of the time, Herod, was so troubled by Jesus' birth that he commanded all children under the age of two to be killed to try and destroy him. Wise men visited Jesus and brought him gifts of gold, frankincense and myrrh. The precious gold symbolised that this baby was a King, the frankincense was a sign he was a Priest and the myrrh indicated right from his birth the significance of his death.

As an adult Jesus claimed to be the Messiah or 'Christ', God's long-promised deliverer. He accepted supreme titles without protest, like 'Son of God' and 'Lord', and his works – his teaching and his healings and miracles – as the work of God. He did the things that only God could do: ruling over nature, disease, disaster and death. He claimed final authority in all matters of religion and he pronounced the forgiveness of sins – bypassing the temple, priests and rituals that were supposed to convey this – on his own authority alone. He set out the highest morality the world has ever seen and, uniquely, he kept that standard totally. No substantiated accusation has come down to us of any inconsistency between what he taught and how he lived – he practised what he preached. He alone of all the human beings who have ever lived was without sin. He kept the contract with men and women, which we have all broken. He was, quite literally, perfect.

sus kept the contract with men and omen, which we have all broken.

Yet being perfect in an imperfect world is tough, provocative to others, and Jesus' own people rejected him. The religious leaders of the day couldn't handle the idea that Jesus might actually be who he claimed to be (the Saviour God on earth). Like many human beings, they did not care to get too close to moral perfection. Eventually, the religious leaders created charges against Jesus and, with the aid of political pressure, persuaded a vulnerable but willing foreign ruler to execute him through nailing him to a cross and leaving him to die in the most shameful and dishonourable way possible. And as Jesus died, the Bible tells us, almost everybody, friends and enemies alike, thought that this was the end of the story.

Yet it wasn't. On the third day after the crucifixion, Jesus' tomb was empty and reports began circulating that he had appeared bodily and physically alive to his followers. The appearances were of a solid, living, resurrected human, a being who was now beyond death. The Bible records that Jesus appeared to more than five hundred people after his resurrection from the dead, over a period of forty days. His followers then and now have seen in the resurrection the living proof that Jesus was everything that he claimed to be: Son of God,

Messiah, Lord, the sinless one and the conqueror of death and evil, reversing all the negative verdicts of his enemies against him. After promising his disciples his continued presence through God's Holy Spirit, Jesus returned to heaven after forty days, with his glorified human body – so there's a human in glory, the first of many who will come through death to live again.[2]

The rest of the New Testament tells the amazing story of people who came to God through Jesus. Each person had their story of how God touched their lives in a way that was personal to each and every one. The writers of the New Testament all agree that Jesus' death was no tragic accident, but the very goal of his life. Jesus was born to die. 'Why did Jesus die?' you ask. In that terrible, bloody execution God was, in some extraordinary way, restoring the connection back to himself by fixing everything again.

Perhaps one of the easiest ways of understanding what Jesus achieved on the cross is to think of our serious communications problem. Think first about that illustration of the broken contract. Jesus kept the contract and through his death on the cross, restored the signal. By being both God and man, Jesus could represent and link both sides of the broken communication chain. The only one who had ever kept the contract took the rap so that the many who had broken the contract could be forgiven and reconnected. Jesus took the penalty that our selfishness deserved. In Jesus, God himself took on all of human sin and suffered death so that you and I might be forgiven, escape eternal death and have life forever with God. Through the cross, the contract is renewed for all eternity: we can now have a lasting and secure peace with God. The Bible says: 'Therefore, since we have been made right in God's sight by faith, we have peace with God because of what Jesus Christ our Lord has

Through the cross, the contract is renewed for all eternity

done for us'.[3] And again: 'Christ suffered for our sins once for all time. He never sinned, but he died for sinners to bring you safely home to God. He suffered physical death, but he was raised to life in the Spirit'.[4]

Now think about that second idea: our sin as a barrier to meaningful communication. One of the many ways of thinking about the cross is that somehow Jesus was taking upon himself the sins of the world. He was confronting the barrier between us and God and demolishing it by his own death. Here the Bible states: 'You were dead because of your sins and because your sinful nature was not yet cut away. Then God made you alive with Christ, for he forgave all our sins. He cancelled the record of the charges against us and took it away by nailing it to the cross'.[5]

3

Getting Reconnected

Peace on earth and mercy mild,
God and sinners reconciled.
('Hark the Herald Angels Sing'
by Charles Wesley)

We have seen that God has done everything he can do to restore the links between himself and us. He has himself stood in the gap between us, personally suffered all the penalties of the contract we have broken and cleared the barrier of sin away to allow a new relationship to commence. The fact that God has done everything for us in such a free and generous manner is what the Bible calls 'grace'.

One thing – and only one thing – is needed: we must respond to his grace offered to us. Consider the phone again. Imagine that the problem you have is now fixed: your contract is renewed and the barriers to communication have been taken away. Is that enough? In one sense yes – but it does you no good until you pick up the phone and use it. Or think of a great Christmas present – it may be everything you've ever wanted, but if it's left in its wrapping under the tree, what use is it to you?

Now at this point you may hesitate. Perhaps deep down you believe that you are not good enough for God to want to hear from you. You may feel you've made too many mistakes in life and perhaps you've let yourself and others down

Think of a great Christmas present – it may be everything you've ever wanted, but if it's left in its wrapping under the tree, what use is it to you?

badly. Be encouraged – no amount of sin is too great for God to forgive. He loves you deeply and is eager to welcome you into his family. Consider this Bible verse: 'For God loved the world so much that he gave his one and only Son, so that everyone who believes in him will not perish but have eternal life'.[6] Notice who it is addressed to: *everyone*. That 'everyone' definitely includes you.

Perhaps, though, you feel that if you were to try to follow Jesus you'd soon end by giving up. As you look back over your life you see far too many failures: diets, New Year's resolutions, promises to yourself and to others. How could this be any different? Well, God knows our frailties and weaknesses and he has given his Holy Spirit to those who have decided to follow Jesus. If you do become a Christian and genuinely put your trust in Jesus Christ then God promises he will give you the Holy Spirit to live within you and strengthen you.[7] You can now face the world and all its temptations and problems, not on your own but with God's own power to help you. It is the task of the Holy Spirit to help us each day to become more like Christ. He guides us, empowers us and sometimes rebukes us so that we become more like Christ. And remember this is not like a New Year's resolution: it is the beginning of a new relationship.

You now might be thinking, 'What must I do practically to be connected to God?' There are three simple steps . . .

4

Making the Connection

O holy Child of Bethlehem
Descend to us, we pray.
Cast out our sin and enter in
Be born to us today.
('O Little Town of Bethlehem' by Phillips Brooks)

If you do indeed want to make a connection with God, you need to take three steps: admit, commit and submit.

1. Admit

Either silently or aloud, admit that you have been disconnected from him: that you have broken the contract, and that you have allowed the barrier of sin to separate you from him. Tell God specifically about those areas of your life where you've messed up. Remember there is no point in blaming others or trying to conceal anything. He knows everything already. He just wants you to own up to it. So, tell God how sorry you are. Then pray these words (which I have amended and personalised) from the carol 'O Little Town of Bethlehem' by Phillips Brooks, which clearly and concisely capture the essence of the Christmas Connection:

O holy Child of Bethlehem
Descend on me, I pray.
Cast out my sin and enter in
Be born to me today.
Amen

2. Commit

Think about Jesus, dying on the cross for you.
Remember that he bore the responsibility for the
contract you broke and that he took upon
himself the barrier of sin you had created, and
then demolished it. Through Jesus, God has
dealt permanently and completely with your sin.
You can now be totally forgiven for everything
you ever have done and ever will do wrong.
Thank God for what Jesus has done for you and
tell God that you accept his forgiveness, and
that you commit your life to him for him to
remake and fully restore it. This includes calling
you to discover his will for your life now, and the
part you'll get to play in restoring his broken
world and other people's broken lives too.

He took upon himself the barrier of sin you had created, and then demolished it.

3. Submit

Thirdly, choose to submit the whole of your life to the God of love. You are beginning a new relationship with him, and with others, in God's new community. Ask him to help you to live out this relationship day by day. Submitting to God involves choosing to live a life that pleases him and starting to behave in right ways. Remember that submitting your life to God and living for him is not something that you are expected to handle alone. God knows that we would find this an almost impossible task and that is why he gives us his Holy Spirit and his Church – restored power and restored people just like you.

A prayer

Let me suggest this prayer

**Thank you, God, for loving me
before I ever loved you.**

**Thank you, Jesus,
for dying on the cross, for me.**

**Thank you that I can get connected to you
now because you are alive today.**

**I admit that I have lived my life without you
and have messed up.**

**I ask for your total forgiveness
and I commit myself to you.**

**Help me to submit my life to your teaching
and direction from now on.**

**I receive you into my life and ask you
to fill me with your Holy Spirit.**

Amen

5
Staying
Connected

And he leads his children on,
To the place where he is gone.
('Once in Royal David's City' by C.F. Alexander)

Being a Christian is not just something to think about at Christmas. It's the beginning of a lifelong adventure. The Bible talks about the experience of coming to faith in Christ as being 'born again'.[8] That's a great image, but no one wants to stay a baby. The key thing to living the Christian life is to keep growing in your relationship with God.

We have used the analogy of phones in this book because it's important to get your priorities in line with God's priorities. You would be a pretty sad person to rate your phone as being more important than the friends you use it to contact. People and relationships are always much more important than things. It's the same with the Christian life: it's the relationship with God that is the important thing. Now that you are reconnected, you need to *stay* connected. Let me suggest one basic principle and four vital practices to help.

A basic principle

The way the Bible explains it, becoming a Christian is not like signing up with a phone company, it's more like being adopted into a new family.[9] We were once far away from God, completely separated from him by our sin and failure to keep the contract. But now, thanks to what Christ did for us, we are God's children and he is our perfect heavenly parent. That is an absolutely essential principle that we need to hold on to because it gives us confidence in our relationship with God. A company might disconnect you, a club might kick you out but no good parent would ever reject their child and certainly not God, the perfect parent. He is now our loving and totally committed Heavenly

Father, unlike some earthly fathers who may have failed and disappointed us. We are his and we will stay his forever.

The principle that Christianity is about being adopted into God's family should guide you in how you live. You don't have to do good deeds to keep God's interest or involvement in you. You don't have to earn his love, or top up your credit with him by behaving in 'religious ways'. God loves you because you are his and he will never give up on you. There is a great phrase about God in Psalm 136 that is repeated 26 times: 'His faithful love endures forever'.

God, the perfect heavenly parent, delights in giving good things to his children. In this life and the next you are likely to be constantly surprised by God's goodness to you and his surprise gifts and generosity. Don't forget to thank him.

Four vital practices

There are four ways to build our relationship with God. We can read about him in the Bible, we can communicate with him through prayer, we can meet with others who follow him and we can share what we know about Christ with others. These four things are vital to keeping that good relationship.

d loves you because you are his
d he will never give up on you.

1. Reading the Bible

The Bible is a library of 66 short books, in one volume – some history, some prophecy, some poetry and some letters to individuals and communities – all written over a period of fifteen hundred years by many different authors. Christians believe that there is a dual authorship to Scripture: men and women spoke and God spoke through them – an authentically human yet fully divine word from God. Perhaps the best summary of what the Bible is about comes from the Bible itself: 'All Scripture is inspired by God and is useful to teach us what is true and to make us realise what is wrong in our lives. It corrects us when we are wrong and teaches us to do what is right. God uses it to prepare and equip his people to do every good work'.[10]

Although originally written in Hebrew, Aramaic and Greek, the Bible has always been translated into other languages for access to all. I urge you to have a good and modern translation, such as the New Living Translation or the New International Version, and begin a good habit of regular reading. If you are not familiar with the Bible, the Gospel of John in the New Testament is a good place to start. The other Gospels and the New Testament letters are also books that you should read. There are a number of good Study Bibles with insightful commentaries and notes that help you understand the background and meaning to particular passages, and these can be very valuable. As you read the Bible it is a good idea to pray that the Holy Spirit would help you both understand what you are reading and apply it to your own life.

Above all, treat the Bible seriously.

The Bible is the world's best-selling book for good reason: through it we hear God communicating directly with us. Read it attentively and your life will be transformed.

2. Praying to God

No relationship flourishes without communication and our relationship with God is no exception. Prayer needs to be regular, honest and wide-ranging. Do not be afraid to bring apparently insignificant things to God.

If you are not sure how to go about praying, take a look at the prayer below – you may be familiar with it. This is what Jesus taught his disciples when they asked him how to pray:

**Our Father in heaven,
may your name be kept holy.**

May your Kingdom come soon.

**May your will be done on earth,
as it is in heaven.**

**Give us today the food we need,
and forgive us our sins, as we have
forgiven those who sin against us.**

**And don't let us yield to temptation,
but rescue us from the evil one.**[11]

'Our Father in heaven, may your name be kept holy'

➡️ **The first phrase** of the prayer expresses how great God is, and reminds us that he is holy and the focus of true worship. It is good to begin our prayers by thanking God and remembering his goodness and grace.

'May your Kingdom come soon'

➡ **The second phrase** of the prayer reminds us of what should be our greatest priority: the rule of God over this world that he created. That takes precedence over our own needs, however urgent they may be.

'May your will be done on earth, as it is in heaven'

→ **The third phrase** is a reminder that for our relationship with God to be in any sort of healthy shape we need to do what he wants. There is an important element in prayer of seeking God's will for our lives, and also for the big-picture unfolding of world history.

'Give us today the food we need'

➡ With the fourth phrase, we ask God to provide for all our needs, whether they are for provision, peace or protection.

'and forgive us our sins as we have forgiven those who sin against us'

→ **In the fifth phrase** Jesus turns to forgiveness. There are always words, deeds and thoughts that we need to ask God's forgiveness for. It's helpful to regularly acknowledge where we have hurt God, someone else or ourselves. If we confess these things and seek God's forgiveness, the Bible assures us that we will receive forgiveness. As the Bible says in 1 John 1:9, 'if we confess our sins to him [God], he is faithful and just to forgive us our sins and to cleanse us from all wickedness.' Interestingly, the prayer makes the point that we must not simply be receivers of forgiveness. As we receive forgiveness from God, we must forgive others. The forgiven are to forgive, totally, or they will jeopardise their assurance of God's forgiveness themselves. Bitterness, resentment and unforgiveness are real soul-killers.[12]

'And don't let us yield to temptation, but rescue us from the evil one'

➡ The sixth phrase tells us to pray that we would not be tested or tempted beyond our endurance. The Bible makes it clear that this world is not neutral territory. There are temptations – and a tempter – that we need to resist. We need to have God's strength in order to live in ways that consistently honour him.

Try to spend time each day talking to God in prayer alone, and with others when possible. Some people prefer to pray silently, others have the privacy to pray audibly and others write their prayers down in a journal. Start by praying for just a few minutes and you'll soon find that you're inspired to spend longer in the presence of such a good, loving, gracious God. You will experience many amazing answers from him.

3. Having community with others

When you became a Christian you were adopted as one of God's children and are now part of the community of God. This has an interesting implication. We have not simply gained a loving heavenly Father, but also other brothers and sisters. The Christian life is meant to be communal, not solitary.

Joining a church community is vital. Through it you will meet with other people who know and love God, and you will find out more about him and grow in faith. The Bible says this: 'And let us not neglect our meeting together, as some people do, but encourage one another, especially now that the day of his return is drawing near'.[13] There is no such thing as solitary Christianity, for God wants true community.

In the church community, you will be able to worship God in a new way – to give expression along with others to the joy and thankfulness in your heart. You will receive teaching to inspire, challenge and encourage you. So get involved. Your church may run groups during the week where Christians meet for relationship, food, prayer, Bible study and social concern. You will find them invaluable.

It is important to remember that church is not a cruise liner on which we glide our way to heaven on permanent vacation. It is a battleship that requires all hands on deck as it fights its way to a glorious destination. Indeed, it is a vital principle of Christianity that although we are rescued by grace, you get out of the Christian life what you put in. The best way to be truly blessed is to work at being a blessing to others. You will, I'm sure, find that the church you get involved with will need helpers (I've never known one that didn't) and I urge you to volunteer your natural and spiritual gifts. Whether it's with a children's church, a youth group, serving those in need or just serving coffee, it's important that we serve. If we aren't faithful with little things, God rarely trusts us with bigger things.

> There is no such thing as solitary Christianity, for God wants true community.

4. Sharing the Good News of Jesus with others

We receive the Holy Spirit, not to stagnate like the Dead Sea without any outlet but to overflow to benefit others. We need to communicate our faith both visibly and verbally. Jesus said, 'You are the light of the world'.[14] The witness of a light in a dark place speaks for itself. So become intentional in praying, caring and sharing with those people with whom you naturally interact in your world.

6

God's on the line

Be near me, Lord Jesus,
I ask Thee to stay
Close by me forever
And love me I pray
('Away in a Manger', author unknown)

Perhaps this Christmas you have made a connection with God for the first time. If so, you may already feel different. If you have begun a relationship with God, very soon you will notice a change. God will start to work powerfully in your mind, heart and life, opening your eyes to new things and teaching you to live for him. You will experience his Holy Spirit illuminating your mind and heart.

I wish I could promise you a trouble-free life as a Christian. Christ did not, and I cannot. The Christian life is not easy. You will need to work at staying connected to God. There is a devil, the enemy, who will do all he can to break your connection with God. Your friends and family may not support your choice to become a Christian and at times it may feel as though the whole world is against you.

Yet God is always there for you and always listening. At times, it may seem as if God is a long way away and you may feel on your own but I assure you that God is present. When you go through tough times, God may seem closer than ever before. If this is not your experience, be assured that he is still and will always be present with you and there for you. Persevere through the hardships you face, because you now have eternal life to look forward to and with God our pain is never wasted. 'We can rejoice, too, when we run into problems and trials, for we know that they help us develop endurance. And endurance develops strength of character, and character strengthens

Nothing can break your connection with him whatever your circumstances

our confident hope of salvation. And this hope will not lead to disappointment. For we know how dearly God loves us, because he has given us the Holy Spirit to fill our hearts with his love'.[15]

Don't give up on reading the Bible, communicating with God through prayer, having fellowship with other Christians and sharing your faith with others. You will need these things to help sustain your faith in the years ahead. You are not on your own. Millions have gone before you and millions are with you.

Let me encourage you to be confident. Remember that if you have accepted Jesus and committed your life to him, you can have complete assurance that your relationship with God is restored. Nothing can break your connection with him whatever your circumstances, thoughts or feelings.

Remember:

God is with you.
God loves you.
God will never leave you.
God will be with you forever.

My prayer for you is that:

God would grant you the light of Christmas, which is faith;

The warmth of Christmas, which is love;

The radiance of Christmas, which is purity;

The righteousness of Christmas, which is justice;

The belief in Christmas, which is truth;

The all of Christmas, which is Christ.

End Notes

1   Romans 3:23

2   1 Corinthians 15:20

3   Romans 5:1

4   1 Peter 3:18

5   Colossians 2:13–14

6   John 3:16

7   Acts 2:38; Romans 5:5, 8:11; Galatians 4:6

8   John 1:12–13; John 3:3; 1 Peter 1:23

9   Romans 8:15–16; Galatians 4:4–5; 1 John 3:1

10 2 Timothy 3:16–17

11 Matthew 6:9–13

12 Matthew 6:14–15

13 Hebrews 10:25

14 Matthew 5:14

15 Romans 5:3–5

For additional resources from J.John visit:
www.philotrust.com

Twitter: Canonjjohn